Ivan Ruff was born in Northampt~~~~ ~~ ~~~~ London University he re~~~~~~~~~~~~~~~~~~~~~~~~~~~~, statistics, and relat~~~~~~~~~~~~~~~~~~~~~~~~~~~obs, in industry from ~~~~~~~~~~~~~~~~~~~~~~~~~~narket research and s~~~~~~~~~~~~~~~~~~~~~~~ultinational, all inter~~~~~~~~~~~~~~~~~~~~~~~some years he was c~~~~~~~~~~~~~~~~~~~~~~es of early journalis~~~~~~~~~~~~~~groups were published in *New So~~~~~ ~~~ the British Journal of Sociology*. He currently teaches mathematics, which is one of his recreations. He is married with one son, and lives in Dorset. He runs along the coast and still competes to half-marathon level. *Dead Reckoning* is his second published novel.

By the same author

The Dark Red Star

IVAN RUFF

Dead Reckoning

GRAFTON BOOKS

A Division of the Collins Publishing Group

LONDON GLASGOW
TORONTO SYDNEY AUCKLAND

Grafton Books
A Division of the Collins Publishing Group
8 Grafton Street, London W1X 3LA

Published by Grafton Books 1988

First published in Great Britain by
William Heinemann Ltd 1987

ISBN 0-586-07477-5

Printed and bound in Great Britain by
Collins, Glasgow

Set in Times

To
J

Senator H. T. Kuunas – House Sub-Committee on European Covert Operations

From W. J. Shealor

EYES ONLY

Appended herewith find two cassettes pertaining to Operative J. M. Goolan which I am informed your recently established Sub-Committee is empowered to request. Be apprised that Operative Goolan is as of now file deleted and all association of his activities with this Agency has been voided.

Tape 1

The guy they sent to meet me was no good. First I let him tail me from the airport, then I got a taxi driver to head into an Oxford Street snarl-up. En route I paid him handsomely for the few hundred yards, and snuck out of the cab while it was jammed in the traffic, keeping blind of the guy following me, and hunched my way through the stressed, impatient cars into the drifting mob on the sidewalk. I watched the tail go past. He looked agitated, maybe at the disappearance of the back of my head three vehicles in front. I didn't recognize him. I only wondered how the goddamn bejeesus he recognized me. I was so undercover my own mother wouldn't acknowledge me. They said.

The autumn sunlight was still a hazy pollen around the gigantic tourist postcard that was London's Parliament Square. Dwarfed by the statue of some dead politician, a woman was pointing something out to her kid, and I found myself hooked on the sight of them as I ate a lousy hamburger and tried to give myself a mental dry-rub. They both wore frayed jeans and broken-down sneakers, and the woman was crouched down, one arm round the little girl's shoulders, showing her, I guess, the Houses of Parliament. I wondered what she was saying, but maybe I was glad not to know. The language I had never heard spoken on its home ground, but the jangling nasality of Vietnamese was instantly clear against the London traffic and the dying waves of the season's tourists debouching at the feet of the mother of democracies.

I watched them until they became aware of me, and then I moved away, but they were taking no chances and moved on too. They crossed the square, small female figures with that very black hair, shabby clothes, erect bearing. A Boeing came over low, and the two Vietnamese froze and stared up, checking its progress through the sky above them. I remembered my brother Roy, missing in Vietnam ten years earlier. The connection between his bones lying in some jungle swamp over there, and these Vietnamese scuffing for a living over here, I couldn't form in any way that made sense to me.

An hour later I didn't have this problem when I stood across from a building in Bayswater and contemplated the prettified front of what had been home for me that year in London, a decade and an era ago. They had cleaned it up, cleaned up the whole row and coloured it a sage green pastel tricked out with white. It had residents' parking slots now, and automobiles that were modest by US standards but in terms of London town runabouts were flaunting quite a lot.

I tried to shrug it off, but somehow I couldn't quit the spot; my feet didn't have any place to go, and the power that fixated me to that stuccoed Edwardian pile had no off-switch. I watched myself go in through that doorway, seedier then, not painted to advertise itself as now. Each day I combed through the heaps of accumulated mail while the stereo bass from the African pad along the hall pulsed through the masonry. It was this doorway that gave Susie back to me, and that image condemned me.

Sure, I went looking for it – so what?

She'd be thirty-three now, maybe thirty-four. What a woman that would be.

So it's back to the machine. You, listening to this – well, OK, it's either this dies away unknown like a billion human fragments every second, or somebody is listening to it – you got your analysis sessions or maybe a friend to murmur to, nights, somewhere out there. For me it's this – the cassette turns gently, uncomplaining, remembers me the way I told it, no cheating.

Tape 2

I'd just started saying to myself, screw it, no more psychological duke-outs with myself till I was on that plane back to the US. But I hadn't even made it two goddamn days before I met Imogen and once again Susie Ellerman was stepping out of the shadows to . . .

When I think about it, it had to be Imogen. This is the dialogue, as near as I can get it.

'Susie,' Imogen said. 'She died, you remember?'

'Sure,' I said.

'Moresby came in for the seminar. Susie's dead. Just like that. You could tell he was an ex-naval officer.'

'They train them for those moments,' I said.

Outside the glass and plastic of the snack bar, the traffic swished non-stop out of Kingsway into the Aldwych. London seemed less human than ten years ago, but I guess it was me.

'He's still around,' I said.

'Moresby? He's retired.'

'I just saw him in the Strand. It was like a still from the past – *Guardian* under arm, strolling up from Charing Cross, into the tobacconist's for his tin of Royal Yacht. The same bow-tie and pigskin shoes.'

'Well, he's not teaching any more. I think they've let him keep his room on for a while.'

'You still keep in touch?' I said.

Imogen looked proud and said, 'He got divorced a few years ago. My firm handled his wife's side.'

'So you're a solicitor?' I said.

I thought back to the half-starved, chain-smoking, Oxfam-clothed *enragée* of a decade earlier, and looked again at the full-faced, business-suited woman across the table from me now, eyes bright with competence. With a name like Imogen I guess she had to come right in the end.

'They're having a party for him,' she said. 'You didn't get an invite?'

'No.'

'A reception in the Shaw Library. I'll give you the date. I understand anyone can go – students past and present, friends and colleagues, open house, typical Moresby stuff.'

'Could be I'll gatecrash that,' I said.

The first time I saw Patrick Moresby was one cold and gritty morning on the Victoria Embankment. It was a Sunday, must have been 1969. With a quarter of a million other people he was marching against the war in Vietnam. Every window in the Strand was planked over, and mounted police patrolled the route in force. Coloured pictures of Mao Tse-Tung bobbed above the marchers while thousands of voices chanted 'Ho-Ho-Ho-Chi-Minh.' I was one of them. At the time it seemed a good thing to chant.

Moresby was only a lecturer in those days. Later, people said he attended those things to pass on names of students to the authorities.

'I'd only just come up from the country then,' Imogen said. 'I bought a twin-set and patent leather court shoes because I thought London would be like *Country Life* set against the ten most famous views of the capital. It was so liberating to be scruffy.'

I looked at her, and she added quickly, 'Of course, it

13

wasn't really liberation. Anyway, those days are gone forever.'

'You mean the scruffy people now don't have any choice?' I said.

'I mean the mass demonstrations that shook the world. All that youth energy has gone somewhere else. All those revolutionaries are in computers now.'

'And Moresby cancelled the class that day, and I never did get to read my paper on the Soviet Marxists,' I said.

'They're in Afghanistan now,' Imogen said. 'Or hadn't you heard?'

We talked about other members of our group in post-grad school and what had happened to them. Susie was mentioned again – Susie, who was one of those girls all the men wanted to go to bed with but didn't dare try, and all the other women wanted to be like.

Imogen looked wistful and said, 'I wonder how many people remember her? Poor Susie. And Tessa – look, I'm due back at the Law Courts.' She gave me her card. 'If you fancy a drink later.'

'What about Tessa?' I asked.

'Come for a drink about 8.30 and you can see for yourself.'

The usual wind swept down Kingsway. Imogen kissed me on the cheek before hurrying away. For a moment the spot stayed warm on my wind-cooled skin. Never accept kisses from lawyers.

I doubled back along Portugal Street. In the London School of Economics I headed for Florrie's Bar. The bar was still there, although I guessed that by now Florrie wasn't.

Florrie's was the usual students' dive. Cigarette butts and discarded wrappers fought for table-space with flysheets announcing urgent meetings and ad hoc action committees. The posters on the wall all looked like their ancestors, except that now they also advertised courses on interview techniques and how to make yourself the right candidate for the job.

The students all looked the same too, except one. Jake Cromer had changed a lot, apart from sitting in the corner he'd always sat in. As I stared at him his name and image from the past were slowly dredged to the surface. He had the blank look of someone totally at home in the place, as though familiarity had blinded him.

His hair was thin and greying, and deep lines had appeared in his long hatchet face. I watched him roll a few strands of tobacco into a liquorice paper, light it and consume half of it in one deep inhalation. For the person he had been, he looked in a bad way.

He used to be the brilliant archetype, the Renaissance student, king of the seminars. He absorbed books by some sort of skin osmosis. He was going to get a First and a lectureship, and everybody better watch out. The rest of us kept in with him because we were scared of him.

Something about him still made me nervous. I was prepared to forget it and leave, but I saw that he had placed me and was coming over. Even before he sat down I could smell the mixture of sweat and booze in his clothes. His blue eyes looked furtive and unstable now, although they still had some of their power.

'I'm afraid I've forgotten the name.'

I told him. He asked if I came there often. I said no. He asked if I was there for Moresby's party.

'I might look in,' I said.

'And see all the creeps and arselickers showing off how successful they've been since they left here.'

'I see you're still part of the place,' I said.

'You might say that. At least I've outlasted Moresby.'

Cromer was bitter. I was living proof that ten years really had gone that fast. He certainly resented something about me, and maybe that was it.

I asked if he had ever got his First.

He kept a stiff face. He had been through this before.

'They gave me an Upper.'

Tough, I said.

'They accepted me for a PhD anyway.'

'So now you're Dr Cromer?'

He shook his head with a sublime indifference that was all phoney.

'They've rejected it twice. Seven years' bloody work. I only got a grant for three years. After that I scraped a living any way I could just to keep working on it. I mean, when you see some of the shit they let through – '

Right, I said.

He looked at me carefully. He was about to tell me – his thesis, his life, the works – then thought better of it.

'You weren't thinking of lunching at the pub?' he asked.

I told him I had already eaten.

I didn't ask how he kept himself alive. When I got up to leave he was already ignoring me. I was just another bastard who had crapped on him.

I traced my way instinctively through the complex of buildings up to Moresby's study. He always used to occupy a room high in the modern section which looked across acres of rooftops to the Old Bailey. On sunny days the golden statue of Justice used to wink across the sky at us. In one block they still had the perpetual elevators, a twin lift-shaft where open-fronted wooden chambers wheeled on a continuous cable, like upright coffins on an endless vertical circuit of the building. They were not slow, and you had to time the stepping in and out finely. But I found the floor I wanted had been taken over by economists. Politics had moved.

I chanced across Moresby's room in a poky corner behind the refectory. It was one of the old rooms, looking out onto a dreary wall of brickwork down which the thin daylight clawed at the grimy windows. Probably it had once been occupied by a Tawney or a Laski, while the penthouse offices were still first-generation.

The door stood open. Subdued lighting played onto decades of erudition stacking the shelves on three sides of the room. For a moment I stopped in the doorway. Patrick Moresby turned from the cluttered desk and met my eye.

He was the same Moresby, with the same mop of curly brown hair, the sensual ironic mouth with one corner always clenched on a pipe real or imagined, the muted bow-tie and the expensive suit worn day in, day out, till it acquired a patina of stylish comfort which no off-the-peg clothes could ever achieve. He wore glasses now, but they were gold half-moons which looked more like some strange anthropological jewellery than signs of failing eyesight.

He said 'Morning' with the same brisk geniality which I remembered clearly. I answered like an echo, then passed on. He didn't know me, and at that moment I didn't want to remind him. I didn't recognize myself at that divide, so why should he make the connection?

Via the usual collage of *photo-vérité* slides and concise chunks of random biography, I had been briefed on every aspect of Patrick Moresby I could ever want to know about, and then some. It didn't surprise me, for instance, to learn that he had been on the early marches against the Polaris subs when they hunched their way over the British horizon, but I did wonder why that fact hadn't hampered his subsequent meteoric career. I guessed that he had sold out – names, faces, it was going on even in those jazzed-out duffel-coat days. Maybe he had been a sell-out all along the line. His career certainly had some handy Kleen-wipes at all the crucial stages.

Ostensibly Moresby was a fifties liberal, and he stayed that way till liberalism got too popular. He was gung-ho on the domino theory, although that didn't stop him hanging out on all the Vietnam demos. By the time I spent a year under his aegis he was already a mysterious, threatening figure, glamorous and young for his forty-five years, a man of wide contacts, deep knowledge, charismatic with effortless, understated power.

He had made a lot of trips to the US, and done sterling service as a cold warrior. All the worse, then, that his hardnose was softening while still in his prime, and had begun to write and speak against the Kentucky Fried arms escalation that was the logical outcome of policies he had supported for two decades. In the briefing room at Langley his motivation was ascribed to some point on a spectrum from, at one extreme, the male menopause, a compulsion to recapture the high of youthful rebellion, to the inevitable suspicion that he had been seduced by the Red Bears.

They wanted me to drift back into his acquaintance and regain his confidence. Figuratively, I was to lock Moresby in a room with a loaded pistol and five minutes to make up his mind. They weren't specific about whether I was to be in that room with him. And on top, there was a question mark over that word 'figurative'.

* * *

18

That evening I kept my date at Imogen's. She had the ground floor of a converted house in a quiet street off Haverstock Hill, all Berber carpets and velvet-look covers and high-tech picture frames. I was expecting company, but we sipped our drinks alone.

'I said you'd be able to see Tessa,' Imogen reminded me.

She was enjoying something, and as I looked suitably aroused she tapped a button on a panel which flushed the TV set into life just as the news programme came on.

At first I didn't get it. The precise female voice-over, headlining the clips of news items to come, was to me just another of those *noblesse oblige* tones BBC newsreaders adopt to convey impartiality. Perhaps there are nuances that are lost on my Nebraskan ear.

But the face nearly put me on the floor. Time and the BBC make-up department had done wonderful things for Tessa Bateman.

'You see,' Imogen said. 'Class of '70, where are you now?'

You said it, Imogen. You sure did. Oh boy.

Senator H. T. Kuunas – EURCOOPS

From W. J. Shealor

EYES ONLY

The tranche of notes to which you refer is not known to me. You will by now be aware that Operative Goolan sustained certain practices not consistent with basic professional conduct as delineated in the procedures of this Agency. We have forwarded to you certain tranches of material recorded by Goolan during his mission in London, insofar as we deem this relevant to your enquiries within a framework consonant with the needs of our joint security. The situation has arisen of you receiving further material whose existence was not known to us. This understandably raises in your speculation the question whether this Agency may be withholding more of the same. We are at this stage not prepared to adumbrate further in this matter. Please be apprised that a failure to notify us of the source of these fresh papers, and to furnish us with full transcripts, will make an extension of this cooperation seriously problematic.

Tranche 1

At the door of the Shaw Library someone asked me for a ticket. People without tickets were allowed in if they paid, so I paid. It was the usual crush inside.

Academics mingled with students and pretended there was no difference. We're all students now – a typical Moresby remark. The long oak tables heaved with baguettes and tubs of butter, drink in large sizes, whole Red Windsor cheeses, bowls of pickles. People were grabbing paper plates and plastic cutlery and digging in. I gave a cursory look round and didn't know anybody. Gradually some of the academics' faces came into focus, but they were all ten years older, except the ones who were twenty years older. They wouldn't recall me. It didn't matter. I wasn't there to say, 'Hi, I'm John Goolan,' like somebody promoting the American Express card.

There was always Imogen. She was at the centre of a group she obviously knew very well. She had that look of relief on her face, and her eyes weren't travelling over the other people's shoulders; that said she was with people she knew very well. My eyes were travelling all the time. The past was like a waxworks slowly coming to life. As I tried to cut myself a slab of Philly while balancing a saucer of crackers I rubbed elbows and exchanged automatic apologies with someone I knew.

The last time I had seen this face it had been surrounded by wispy untrimmed beard and crowned by a centre-parted Jesus Christ hairstyle. Now it was neat, clean-shaven, and smooth Yuppie clothes had replaced the army-surplus parka and desert boots of earlier years.

'Never thought I'd see you again.' He had a northern British accent, with its self-conscious tone of shrewdness.

His name was Barry Hirst. In the old days he had been a dogmatic Marxist, with that ultra-reasonable manner whose reason stops at any suspicion that he may not be right. The only person he had respected was Cromer, and now Cromer was a wreck, while Hirst looked very cool and well-heeled. I told him I worked in business and was over here on a vacation. I asked about him, and he lit a small, fine cigar slowly, like it was part of his answer.

'I'm in the knowledge business.'

'Knowledge as opposed to intelligence?' I said.

He was still a humourless guy and said that he didn't go for those faggy distinctions any more. 'That was all a game,' he said.

'It seemed for real once,' I said.

'Listen,' Hirst said, 'by the time we were here they'd got it cracked. The riots were over; '68 had come and gone. You remember how the professors wouldn't go to the toilet without checking with the sociology students first? And everybody said, wow, this is participation, this is what we've been struggling for. And from that moment they stopped struggling. Then the Arabs hiked the oil price, and suddenly the market value of students disappeared down the toilet. And that was it – goodbye, Norma Jean.'

I admired his pith. Hirst was a small man, his hair was thinning and his waistline already starting to thicken. I trawled for any contact he might still have with other members of our group. He produced a personalized leather pocketbook and riffled through a battery of names. The only one that interested me was Moresby's wife, of all the people to have kept in touch with. The black and beautiful Delphine. He saw me notice the entry, but I didn't ask for the number, and he wasn't about to give it. Then he saw someone he had to speak to, and if he hadn't I would have.

I stood in an alcove between the glass-fronted bookcases, looking out into the night over Houghton Street. This was the exact spot I had stood in after I heard that Susie Ellerman had died. They said she had taken sleeping pills, vomited in her sleep, choked on the vomit, and died. There were a lot of deaths like that in those days. She had been alone at the time. I stood and looked at the rain falling on Houghton Street and thought of her, and now I thought of myself standing there looking out at the rain.

Moresby had been conspicuously absent, but the anticipation of his arrival kept things lively. The grand entrance he made in the end was the one nobody wants to make. A senior academic, very agitated, came into the library and hoarsely asked everybody for silence. The place went very still. He announced that Patrick Moresby had died, at work in his room, only minutes before.

Three hundred people discreetly putting down food and drink which they can no longer face is not a pretty sight. The Shaw Library began to empty. The dogleg corridor through the Anthropology Department echoed to a pack of uneasy footsteps that wanted to hurry but didn't know where to. The two elevators in total only held a dozen people. But a crowd assembled there and started punching the recall buttons, getting more staccato and anxious as the elevators took their time.

I waited in the library for the crowd to clear. But what I saw down in the street changed my plan. I slalomed through the heavy shamble of people as they drifted out. I hit the stairs. I guessed the connecting doors between buildings would be locked, so I went down the five flights to street level.

Several police cars as well as an ambulance were crammed into that narrow street which slices through the School. They had been clever, delaying the announcement until the police had done their work and the stretchermen had got the body clear. They were pulling out as I made the scene.

There was no point going to Moresby's room. The porters would have sealed it off. I gasped the fume-heavy night air. Then I got my first sight of Jake Cromer that evening. He was in one of the police cars that flashed their blue lights and shot away into the dense curve of traffic round the Aldwych.

At the same moment the television crew arrived, which gave me an idea. In the Aldwych I hooked a taxi. As it cut across London in the direction of Bayswater I wondered why they had wanted to kill Patrick Moresby. It bothered me that somebody else had got there first.

They had booked me into a small, anonymous hotel off Porchester Terrace. The bored Irishman at the desk, with bloodhound eyes and an insecure beard, looked up from his paperback and said there was a package for me. I took it upstairs, but for now all I was interested in was the television set in the room.

I didn't have long to wait. 'And now the Nine O'Clock News, with Tessa Bateman.' The phoney-dramatic music fed into the headline sequence and the image of Tessa's immaculate disembodied face. She had changed her hairstyle from the night before.

A professor being murdered, especially when they only

had an hour to prepare the item, didn't figure very high. It had to give precedence to the booming pound, the Russian threat, the Middle East, the drug menace. Halfway through they had some token shots of the LSE buildings with a stand-up commentator in Houghton Street giving a noncommittal account that said someone was helping the police with their enquiries.

I watched hungrily as Tessa introduced the item. I watched her eyes as she named Moresby. The performance was faultless, ice-cold and pretty and ready-to-melt, perfect as a snowflake. You couldn't guess that she had ever known this dead professor. I knew she had, and I could hardly believe it.

I scrubbed the rest of the programme. I was frustrated and uneasy about something. Shit, that's not true, it was a lot of things. Also the past was beginning to eat me, and I had just taken an object lesson in how the past should really be dealt with.

I tried to be charitable towards Tessa. But I felt like going to the Television Centre, wherever it was, and shaking her to see if those eyes, lips and teeth were for real, or had just been grafted onto one of those humanized robots, to give sex appeal to the news.

What did I want, tears? Did I really expect her to show a trace of emotion at announcing to fifty million people that someone she had known personally had been murdered that evening?

I bit it back as hard as I could. But goddamn it, in a way I did.

I refilled my lungs and my glass a few times and took a shower. Then I played the cassette which had been left for me at the desk. It was a counter-instruction which events had already made obsolete. It told me to now treat the target with extreme care. In no circumstances to terminate. To report back immediately on contact established so far. That was simple. If judged necessary, to become target's protector, with or without target's consent. That was less straightforward. Terminate meant kill. The target was Moresby. I recorded my answer. It would be picked up by the courier and tomorrow they would be playing it back home. I guessed they would recall me and blame me, but I was wrong about the recall.

Imogen had some tea ready. I had phoned, and she was expecting me with what appeared to be genuine pleasure. You can get out of the habit of these things. I like English tea, and this was the real brew – not some dust in a paper sachet – served in good china. There was a side to Imogen that would have chimed perfectly with some country house routine which I guess was her background anyway, but she had another aspect, comprising the floppy bows and the neat blonde hair and the shipboard manner, not exactly a Thatcher clone, but out of the same pork barrel. I was getting a dose of the first side, and I didn't complain. Imogen's family name was Selby-Hobbs, and in the old LSE days she had been embarrassed as hell about it; but this time round she had given me her card, and the full handle was engraved in a flourishing letterwork that didn't denote shyness. It was strange, but she regarded me as exotic, and that enabled her to relax and serve me tea and cake with pleasure. That happens with people who are made uptight by normal things.

We smiled and looked nostalgic and talked about as much of our communal past as we could raise from the dust. Then Imogen said, 'Flared trousers!'

I said, 'What?'

'I was trying to think of what captured those days and

set them apart from now, and that's it – as soon as I think of flared trousers, that whole time comes back. Think of flares – what picture do you get?'

I thought, and then said, 'Sunshine.'

'Right,' Imogen said. We catalogued our way through images of being young and resourceful and daring, although I could tell that Imogen was happier the way she was now. Me, I had no conclusion on that score. Still, she had a point. Fabric stretched tight over hips and fannies and flapping loose round nimble, insouciant ankles, in that lull between Vietnam and the Recession, said it all.

Then, inevitably, we got on to the subject of Moresby.

'Some way to go,' I said.

Imogen shook her head, lips pursed. She seemed kind of upset about it.

I asked, 'Did you know him personally?'

'No, we never met, after – But he was an impressive man, and I was always grateful for having studied under him. I feel it's a blank in my life now he's gone.'

She looked at me, and I was underreacting, and she said, 'Don't you?'

'Sure,' I said. 'I had plans to meet him again while I was over here. It was quite a blow.'

'What was your interest in him?' she asked.

'Nothing special,' I said. 'But I am kind of curious why someone should want to ice him.'

'Ice?'

'Sure, kill. Murder, assassinate, do in.'

Imogen clearly had a courtroom scene perpetually running in her head. She furrowed the space between her faultless eyebrows.

'I thought ice meant to put on ice, as in store, preserve,' she said.

'No,' I said, 'it means goodbye. The sort of ice that even TV dinners don't come back from.'

'So who do you think killed him?' she asked.

I shrugged. 'Assuming it wasn't a mistake – I really don't know. Not having lived here for ten years, I don't know what he was into. He must have crossed somebody.'

I drank my tea. I wanted Imogen to see that I was prepared to let the topic go. I didn't want to get her curious.

'He had a lot of Russian connections, of course,' she said, suddenly forthcoming. 'I suppose it was just academics, but you never know. He always seemed the ultimate pro-American. He certainly had a lot of top-level contacts in this country – politicians and the like, people in the media, maybe even the watchers.'

'The watchers?'

'Oh, you know, the cloak-and-dagger brigade.' (Sorry, Imogen, you really did say that.) 'I mean, that was how he always tried to appear, wasn't it – a laid-back pipe-smoker who had a finger in every pie and knew everything, but everything, that was going on – '

'A kind of political Hugh Hefner?' I said.

Imogen giggled. 'Now that you mention it,' she said. She liked the thought and laughed some more.

Our discussion of Moresby grew desultory. Imogen told me that he had retired because his books were selling well and he wanted to write more. He had a cottage in the Home Counties, she said, wherever they were, and he spent a lot of time fly-fishing. It was obvious that Imogen didn't know anything, and contrary to one popular belief, legal personnel do not have enquiring minds. What Imogen liked was gossip. This fact generated one interesting detail before I left.

'Did you see Tessa read the item about him being killed?' I asked.

Imogen had watched it. I said, 'She didn't even blink. Talk about professional.'

'Well,' Imogen said, 'I admire that kind of detachment. I mean, it can be necessary, we've all got jobs to do. Listen, if you promise – '

'What?'

'Don't ever tell anybody.'

'On my first edition of *Playboy*,' I said.

Imogen took a breath. 'Tessa slept with Moresby once.'

'You mean once, or once?' I asked.

Imogen giggled again and didn't treat it as a serious question. Maybe it was best that way. I had to leave, and we made a dinner appointment for a week later. I knew I would never keep it, but it was nice to toy with the idea. I thought I had gone there to discuss Moresby, but really I had wanted to talk about Susie, with a friend who had known us both. And we hadn't even mentioned her name. I just hadn't known how to do it.

One time Susie said, 'Do something for me.'

'Anything,' I said.

'Sleep with me.'

I said, 'Stop twisting my arm,' or some fool thing. But she meant exactly that, and Imogen's remark about Tessa and Moresby put me in mind of the terrible joke that ambiguity can sometimes confer. In the end it was two nights, Susie and me, and apart from a kiss we didn't touch. One of the nights there was a storm, and we held hands before falling asleep again. Later she told me that I was the only man who could have done that for her.

I felt used and frustrated, but flattered too. Susie said it made her feel better, but she seemed very scared about something. When I heard she had died I refused to believe that it was inevitable. I felt that I had unwittingly been part of the process that killed her.

I never knew why this certainty haunted me, but it got worse with the years. It got so that her image, naked and gorgeous on those two asexual nights, dominated my mind with every woman I made love with since. In the end it got so that I couldn't make it with anybody. The knowledge that Susie's ghost was waiting for me killed it from the start.

It was better that I hadn't told Imogen all this. She would have thought I was looking for sexual charity. And if I had told her, she would have been right.

The message says, leave the hotel. Cassette on Record, and wipe clean. I will be contacted in a week's time. A place and a time, but no name, and till then I don't exist. It sounds like a holiday, but it means that from here on things get complex. They have fixed several accounts for me in London, so I can get what I need by plugging a plastic card into the street wall of a bank. Apart from this I'm on my own.

The evening paper ran a profile of Moresby. The picture showed him with pipe and bow-tie and those dark, almost Mediterranean eyes. The story emphasized the side of him that totalled up to Wonderful Guy – champion of the student cause, defender of civil rights and free speech, an academic who actually quit the ivory tower and headed off into the barbed wire. They were looking to give his murder maximum puzzle value. The only suspect mention was also one of the touches of glamour, the fact that as an acknowledged expert on Soviet Russia (which curiously he had only visited once) he had for some years given a regular lecture course to 'members of the Home and Foreign Offices'. I hope the readership got the point on that one.

He had been shot. In the street I stuffed the paper into a bin which already contained a half-eaten Kentucky Fried chicken, and went back to the hotel. It was getting dark. This was the part I hated, the moment of losing touch with the original none-too-specific assignment, and of waiting for it to come to you.

I didn't need to go back to the hotel. I had several stashes around the city in various left-luggage places. The keys were locked onto my belt. Anybody who wanted them would have to walk through me. My papers were secure, and I had a moneycard in each trove. I wasn't carrying full time, but a Colt .45, silvering through the blue and with the legend United States Army and the serial number ground off, lay awaiting me.

I went back to the hotel calmly. I only had the one bag, so I could check out without it looking like I was checking out. The desk man had a message for me. There had been a call saying to expect another call at 10 P.M. In case the desk man was part of something, I told him I had to take some washing to the launderette but would be back inside the hour. I made a remark about London being as dirty as New York and patted the nylon shoulder bag as I strolled out.

Tailing somebody at night is hard. There are fewer people to blend in with, a smaller range of street activities to pretend to be engaged in, less opportunity to detect if the quarry's attention has been alerted. The guy who followed me on this occasion had trouble in all three areas. I took him around some unmemorable places, then made for the park. I made no attempt to lose him.

Along a path, deserted and poor in visibility, I stopped.

33

I turned, then slowly walked back towards him. He wore running shoes and jeans and some sort of sporting top, a kid. At least, to a thirty-five-year-old he was a kid.

I got nearer to him so that his eyeballs shone at me with a malign glare in the dispersed lamplight. I thought he was about to take off, but the movement led into a side-hand at my throat.

It was a panic shot, and I was ready. I moved with the blow, and this time he ran. I launched myself after him and we headed into the depths of the park. For a hundred yards I maintained the distance between us. Then I unhooked the nylon bag from my shoulder and swung it in the air. I timed the release well and the bolas hit his legs in mid-stride. His own speed took him over. He fell clumsily and wasn't about to scramble up again.

I pulled him to his feet and returned the slap to the head he had offered me. He put his hands up for quarter.

'Why the fuck are you following me?' I yelled at him.

'I wasn't following you.'

We were near some water. I dragged him towards it and told him I was going to push his head under. The fall had shot his wind and he was still gasping. He held his hands up again.

'Somebody's paying. I work for an agency. I follow people all the time.'

'What for?'

'I don't know.'

'What do they want you to tell them?'

'Where you go, who you see.'

'Who are *they*?'

'I don't know. I don't even know the people in the agency. I just get footwork jobs.'

'How did you know it was me?'

'They give very clear descriptions.'

34

'What are you going to tell them about me?'

'Nothing, I've only been with you since lunchtime.'

'You followed me south of the river?'

'Yeah, yeah.'

I had to screw the details of the agency out of him. But at that moment somebody came along in the shadows between the trees. A flashlight pivoted in an arc towards us. It had to be police, looking for muggers or gays or whatever the London police look for in parks at nightfall. He had caught our voices bouncing off the surface of the water and was coming our way.

The kid scrabbled himself up from the mud and shouted for help. As he got himself upright I planted my foot in his belly. He windmilled the air on his way into the shallows. The splash drew the notice of the man with the light. I ran for my bag and got the hell away.

The sign on Waterloo station still read 'Gentlemen and Barbers'. I knew I would never understand it, but I also knew that down there I could take a crap and run a razor over my face. As I went down I saw somebody heaving a puddle of yellow puke onto the public area. When I came to ground level again a catatonic Asian cleaner was swabbing it away. People were stepping round it with a precision that didn't seem to involve their eyesight. Time was, I thought, when a Britisher would have jumped under a train rather than throw up in public.

When I first came to Waterloo, on a childhood visit, it was still the home of great iron monsters pumping out smoke, like Monet's painting of the Gare St Lazare. Now it was all plastic and canned music, neat surfaces that made a lot of the human traffic look out of place. The computerized route schedules flipped over for trains few people wanted to catch. The vagrants were gathering

35

uneasily for the night, for a few hours of piped warmth before they moved on.

The Bakerloo Line took me to within a short walk of Imogen's apartment. I didn't phone ahead. If she was out, I would wait.

The ground floor situation made it easy to hear that something was going on in the apartment. A dinner party would break up about midnight, leaving time for the dishwasher to be stacked and interesting personal encounters to be followed through. So I sat in a pub till closing time, then a late-night (by British standards) fast-food joint near Swiss Cottage. My breath would smell of beer and onions, but by midnight everybody's breath had to smell of something.

When I went back it was quiet, and the light was still on in the apartment. I pressed the lowest of the three bells. More than one voice came from inside. The house door was a bondage fantasy of bolts and chains, from behind which Imogen peered out at me. It had rained a little, and I knew that my armpits needed freshening up, but Imogen's reaction was something else. 'Hello' from the English usually sounds clipped and unwelcoming, and I was some days early for our date, but she contrived to make the word a soufflé of warm air, sweet and light as a Hostess Twinkie.

I stepped from the hall into her flat. In the cosily half-lit interior a male guest, tall and bald and imperious, in a good three-piece suit with his tie loosened, looked coolly at me from the marzipan Chesterfield.

'This is John,' Imogen crooned, then introduced him. His name was Tony, or maybe Steve, some contraction that he obviously didn't use with everybody. As if on cue, and being very gentlemanly about it, he cleared his throat and got up. 'I really must be going,' he said.

They exchanged a few words about a super evening, and out in the street his car made the disgruntled noises that he had been too polite to make.

Imogen came back in and said, 'Surprise, surprise.'

'Bad timing,' I said. 'Sorry.'

'On the contrary,' Imogen said. 'He was sure you'd been set up – I could see it in his face.'

'Why?' I asked.

'He wasn't going to leave until I let him fuck me.'

'Didn't you want him to fuck you?' I asked.

'Not really.'

She waited for the initiative to come from me. I didn't take it any further, although I appreciated that she had used the word as a come-on.

'What can I do for you?' she said.

I couldn't tell her I just wanted somewhere to sack out. I claimed loneliness and disorientation in the big city had driven me to where I was sure of a friendly face.

We made small talk for a while, then I said, 'I may need an alibi for when Moresby was killed. You saw me at the party.'

Imogen looked suddenly nervous and legalistic. 'I only saw you momentarily,' she said. 'I couldn't swear to a time.'

'A joke,' I said.

'Moresby was shot – did you read about it? A pistol with a silencer. You know they arrested Jake Cromer?'

'Yes,' I said, 'but he didn't do it.'

She poured us both some brandy and asked how I knew.

'I met him the other day. Forget the possible motives – he couldn't put a bullet in the Hilton Hotel at ten yards.'

'He could have been involved.'

'Cromer's washed up. Take it from me. He wasn't about to participate in a killing.'

'Swear to me that you're nothing to do with it.' Imogen looked at me intently. For a moment her solicitor's desk stood between us.

'I swear,' I said. I let her eyes search mine. She seemed happy with what she found.

Then her eyelids drooped and she was plainly tired. She was in court the next morning. When I judged that she was going to ease me out I asked, 'Should I do anything about a robbery?'

'What do you mean?'

'My hotel room was turned over and all my money taken. I can ring the States for some more tomorrow – '

'Surely the hotel will accept that?' she said.

'I paid them off with what I had on me,' I said. 'It was a doubtful place. I think it might have been somebody there who did the room.'

'You want to spend the night here, right?' Imogen said.

'It was the best idea I had.'

'Well, I can put you up gladly,' she said. She was efficient, Imogen. 'But you'll have to help me stack the dishwasher.'

'My pleasure,' I said.

The evening had worn her out. She slept with her bedroom door closed. I stayed awake for an hour, then went to the bathroom. Her address book was on the small shelf near the phone. I took it back to the spare room.

Out in the expanse of Nebraska you always knew where people were – there was no point writing it down. Whereas people living crowded within a few square miles lose track of each other so fast they keep address books as talismans against that feeling of total aloneness which every city street hands out for free.

It was a good move. She had Tessa Bateman there, one address crossed out and another inserted. I noted it and returned the book. I could just have asked you, Imogen, but why let people know things?

It was a mews street in the shadow of the Brompton Oratory. The houses were dinky and white or pastel-coloured with flower-boxes, hanging baskets, Mediterranean shrubs planted in half-barrels. The road was cobbled and the whole place suggested neat back gardens with fig trees and vines growing against protected whitewashed walls.

I figured that someone working on the late night news would not be up much before ten. So I did my first innocent walk along the street at that time, to check out the house. I wanted Tessa to be up, but not too far up.

There was no doorbell, only an ancient iron lionhead knocker rescued from some act of demolition. The street level was a garage, with a side door to a flat above. I knocked very gently. There was no sound for a while. I tapped the lion's head again, no louder than a cough. I kept near the door, so as not to be seen from above. There was no fisheye that I could see, but I had to assume I would be looked over before the door opened. The armful of cellophane-wrapped flowers would help.

The door opened on a chain. I said, 'Special delivery,' and held out the bouquet. It was Tessa all right, only neither the Tessa I remembered nor the talking face from the TV screen. But it was a beautiful mutation. She had her hair in a towel, no make-up, her face pale from sleep. She didn't seem too surprised at the flowers. She took them, not looking twice at me. She only looked up when she read the card. It said, 'I was just passing, love, John Goolan.' She stared at me, and it registered.

'Good lord!' she said, very English.

'It's true,' I said. 'I just came to say hello and thanks for the crosswords.'

In addition to Moresby's politics class, we had shared many hours in adjacent armchairs of the Shaw Library while Tessa elucidated the *Times* crossword for me. She had got me very skilful at cryptics. It struck the right note.

'Can I offer you some coffee?' she said.

I maintained my air of someone with little time to spare, but gratefully followed her up. It was a greasy way to behave, but it beat kicking the door down. The living room was like one of those pictures in decor books, where everything is integrated with everything else. I had cleaned myself up before leaving Imogen's place, so I didn't feel too bad about sitting down. We had the coffee and the elusive chat of people who don't have the time to go in too deep.

'It must have been strange for you,' I said, 'reading that flash about Moresby.'

'It was strange afterwards, but at the time it was just another piece of news.'

'I was watching your face very carefully,' I said.

It was the wrong thing to say, but in a way I meant it to be. Tessa seemed threatened at the thought of all those people studying her face, and nothing she could do about it. She shook her hair loose out of the towel. It was freshly washed, several tones of highlit blonde, and made the room smell like a field of herbs.

'Don't you ever react?' I asked.

'We relax and smile towards the end of the programme,' she said, but she was tensing up towards me by the second.

'Do you have any idea why he was killed?'

40

'I've really no idea.'

She was too cool, and it irritated me. I said, 'You just read the news.'

'That's right.'

The flowers looked good in the vase. I felt she was about to hand them back to me. I took more coffee. While I still had my eyes on the cup I asked if she still remembered Susie Ellerman.

'It's all a long time ago,' Tessa said.

'Was her death an accident?'

Tessa's mouth went slack, the way I had seen it slacken as her eyes turned sideways to the monitor after she had introduced a video clip. The gesture seemed to act as a mental cut-out.

'I've got an appointment soon,' she said.

'Weren't you sharing a flat with her when she died?'

'Do we really have to go through this? Is this why you came?'

'Did she kill herself?'

'It was an accident, she choked – '

'Listen, don't fob me off. I'm not the great television-viewing public. I know more than you do. I just want some help.'

Tessa appraised me coldly, with the self-possession of someone who made her living from her talent for detachment. She probably figured I might be trouble, although that was wrong. But I was happy for it to look that way.

She folded one leg under her and said, 'I don't want to see you again after this.'

I said, deal.

'Susie was very disturbed before she died. You've got to understand, I don't know anything for sure, this is only suspicion, and I don't recall things accurately.'

'I won't quote you,' I said.

'She was involved with someone, and the feeling I got was that he was infiltrating left-wing groups in the university and reporting back to the authorities. It was all rather paranoid after '68. They had information on a lot of people, and the material in those dossiers came from inside. I think Susie had found out.'

'And was going to blow it?'

'I don't know.'

'Who was the guy?'

Tessa shrugged.

'Was he one of us?'

'No. Oh God, he's just a shadow now. I think I met him, but I've lost the name.'

'Do you think Susie was killed?'

'I'd like to think it was an accident. I loved her.'

'We all loved her,' I said.

'I've really got to get ready,' she said. 'My life doesn't have an off-switch.'

'If I wanted to trace this guy?' I said.

She shook her head.

'Look,' I said, 'you can't lie to me. I'm in the business. You're holding something back. The only way you can make sure I don't come back is to level with me.'

Her lips pursed slightly. She didn't like being shoved around.

'He was a friend of – Do you remember Jacob Cromer? A friend of his.'

'Which one was Cromer?' I asked.

Tessa gave me a few details, and I went through the motions of summoning up Cromer's hazy portrait. Tessa stood up. She was angry, but too well-bred and just too damned efficient to show it.

'Thanks for the flowers,' she said.

'When you look at the camera,' I said, 'think of me out there.'

'Twenty head cases a week want to make love to me,' she said. 'I'll class you with them. Goodbye.'

It was raining on the cobbles and the flower-boxes. I looked over my shoulder. 'They're not head cases,' I said.

It took me two days to find Cromer again. Since he was no longer a student at the school there was no point trying the Registry. I couldn't count on him searching the pigeon-holes for mail. I checked out the underground bar beneath Clare Market. Cromer used to be at his savage, arrogant best there, and it was still his sort of place.

When I picked him up it was on the street. He was a shell, skulking around the only place where he had felt the warm grasp of glory. I followed him into the book-shop. I don't know where he hid the paperback he stole, but ten minutes after secreting it in his clothing he walked out, without any bulge or unnatural position, as if it had just been digested by his armpit. He was physically, in terms of build and savouriness, not the kind of person you would want to frisk.

I went after him down into the bar. While he waited for his half of bitter to be pulled he got the book out, flicked its pages, then put it inside the ratty briefcase he always carried. The case was full of papers. I joined him at his table. He was rolling one of those emaciated cigarettes. He didn't look too friendly.

I told him I had seen him swipe the book.

He stared back at me and said, 'So what?'

'Your blow against a corrupt society,' I said.

'What do you want?' he said.

I was wearing broad-welted leather-soled shoes. They were not great for hours on London pavements, but they would damage a shin-bone now and then. I jack-knifed my leg under the table, and Cromer winced, cursed, grabbed his leg, and knocked his beer over, all in one movement. I got hold of his briefcase and walked out of the bar. I figured he wouldn't lose sight of it. I was right.

The porter was half asleep in his glass box. I got out to the street before I let Cromer hobble up to me. He was cracking a little, but he managed to shout, 'Give me that case, you bastard.'

I said, 'We're taking a walk, Jake.'

He tried to seize the case back, but I said 'Uh-huh' and jabbed the edge of my hand gently against his neck. He was physically larger than me, but he didn't have the muscle or the speed or the moustache that I had.

'What's in here, Jake?' I asked. 'The lifetime's work? What would it do to you to lose it?'

I led him into a public garden on the edge of Lincoln's Inn. The acrid smell from inside his baggy overcoat, stirred up by fear, was getting worse. I tapped his case to remind him of the stakes he was playing for.

'You remember Susie Ellerman?' I asked.

'Who?'

'She was in our group. Think back ten years. Moresby's seminar. She died of an o.d. or suicide, nobody ever knew.'

'Oh yeah, vaguely,' Cromer said. 'Why?'

'She was involved with a guy. I want to know who he was.'

'Why ask me?'

'Because you know the answer, you prick.'

'I can't help you.'

'Meet me in the bar at twelve tomorrow,' I said, 'and let me have the name and where I can find him now. Otherwise I deep-six this lot.'

'I'll go to the police.'

I laughed.

'How about I tell you now?' he said.

The change of tack didn't convince me. Panic and servility made a cruddy mixture. He'd tell me anything to get his years of work back – all that paper, all those words. He needed a night without it.

'What you'll do,' I said, 'is think it over, and then you'll take me there. No face, no masterpiece. And whoever he is, don't warn him.'

Cromer looked at me. His sharp, once sensitive features were pinched and bitter.

'You fucker,' he said. 'What's your game?'

'Hang in there, Jake,' I told him.

New apartment. This place, near Ladbroke Grove. Taken it on a month's hire, instant cash, no questions, beaming Cypriot landlord. For a time nobody knows I'm here.

Senator H. T. Kuunas – EURCOOPS

From W. J. Shealor

EYES ONLY

The tape which you have submitted to us, and whose provenance we would be more than interested to know, so far from embarrassing our case, only succeeds in underpinning the nexus of fundamental errors perpetrated by Goolan during this mission, to wit a breach of operational normalcy and the eccentric habit of recording sectors of his daily program such as to gravely prejudice his field security.

To answer your questions on specifics, our responses are as stated subsequently.

(i) Until this mission Goolan had no record of unstable conduct or attitudinal pathogenicity.

(ii) Goolan was not regarded as a top-echelon man, rather a sound middle-grade operative whose pride lay in his competence to do a job well and then disappear.

(iii) He was not gregarious, had no definable caucus of friends, was predominantly a 'lone gunfighter' figure, and as such in line with the profile norm of many similar operatives and thus not egregious in this area.

(iv) Voice analysis of the tape cited reveals no abnormal stress, either alcohol-induced or resultant from any other identifiable pressure.

It is a matter of perplexity to us as to the reason for Goolan manifesting the need to record such a piece of material. We perceive no germane relevance of this tape to the core of your enquiry, except insofar as to lend enhanced credit to our already postulated view that Operative Goolan was in *the grip of a prima facie breakdown during the course of this mission. The intended recipient of this tape was Mrs Delphine Moresby. Routine investigation has evidenced that we have no further interest in this person.*

Tape 3

I know you didn't believe it, Delphine, but Hirst really did pass me in the street and suggest that if I had nothing to do we could drive around, and I had nothing to do . . .

We talked about Pat. Hirst had ten different theories about why he was killed, and he wanted to try them out on me, and I smiled and shrugged with all the confidence of someone who really didn't know. Then you were mentioned, and Hirst said he still saw you sometimes and knew where you lived. And maybe at this I did show some reaction, or maybe he wanted to impress or upstage me – but whichever, he said let's go there. I said OK, and I got that feeling at the pit of my stomach that told me both that this was a mistake and that there was no way I could resist it.

He was eager for me to go – I realized it when we arrived – because it gave him a reason to call. I was his ticket to a meeting with you which he got very excited over and you didn't seem to care for. It was a tacky scene, and I'm sorry I had to appear abrupt and produce a phoney prior appointment that meant I had to leave. But I figured it would be easier for you to ged rid of Hirst without me there as his safepass.

It didn't make it easier when I came back, because although you had got rid of Hirst, the joke that was on him was on us too. I don't know if you wanted me to return, but I know that once I was there you didn't want me to go away. This tape is all I can give you. I have to lay it down now, because this moment is going to pass, and fast, and there won't be another space for me to focus on these things. Then maybe I'll mail this to you, some time later, and who knows?

The party was settling down for a late session under the stars, one of those midsummer nights that seem to lead into a different kind of eternity from the one we normally inhabit. People were spread out on the lawn, chatting in groups on the terrace, wandering in and out of the house. It was in Harrow, wasn't it, somewhere like that. Listen, I'm chronically uptight about not being a racist or a sexist, but I've got to say that your black skin that night made your eyes and teeth stand out, along with that shimmery light-as-air robe you wore, in a way that was totally unreal, like spectral and enchanting, and you moved around through the guests at that party not only not like a hostess but like somebody from a different . . . from a different somewhere. I was devastated, Delphine. I got tears in my eyes just thinking about it – Crummy bullshit, sure. But you can't say some of these things without getting into the crummy bullshit.

You went inside, and I followed you. There was food in there, or I could be going to the john, but in truth I was coming after you. I don't think it was your intention that I did this, or anybody else in particular, but you were like some sorceress knowing that one of the mortals would be drawn into the deadly magic. We'd only been briefly introduced, you knew I was one of your husband's students, but apart from that it didn't matter, we were in a bedroom with one veiled lamp in the corner and a light music of guitar and conversation coming from the garden outside. You smiled and said 'Hi,' and stepped past me, I swear without touching the floor, and turned the key in the lock. I can still see the way you inclined forward slightly to release your breasts from the pink bra that held them, and the flex of your shoulders that went with it, and all that conveyed . . .

You were the first black woman I had made love with, and the contrast of black and pink flesh and the feel of your skin and the lashing sensuality of your tongue were things I wasn't prepared for and didn't have the necessary time to absorb into my mind. It was the most efficient screw of my life, Delphine, and I realized how a lot of women feel when men use them for a five-minute ball, then get back to the real business of their lives . . . I couldn't help noticing that the room was somebody's bedroom, and since as far as I knew you and Moresby didn't have kids I assumed that one or both of you slept in there. So although I was as eager and helpless as you, I also was very clear about what you were doing in there. I wondered how many other Moresby students you picked for similar work-outs, and what kind of bitterness really lay behind it. As we lay in a moment's sticky embrace I got cold and dissatisfied, and I wasn't smooth enough to gloss it over and hide how I felt, so you made out it had been fantastic. Then we had to get dressed and return to the party. Soon after that I left, and walked the streets for a while, and eventually found a hooker who did anything I wanted once she saw my wallet. When you and I had finished, just as we were about to get off the bed, it was funny, you kissed me lightly on the end of my nose, and it felt like total mockery, and I knew you wouldn't even remember who I was, but when you got into bed with Moresby that night you'd have this deep vindictive satisfaction because you'd fucked one of his students behind his back. I had to put something between me and that knowledge. This whore couldn't have been more compliant. She was just happy that I didn't want to beat up on her or abuse her. It was OK. All I wanted was

51

time. I didn't even climax with her. Even that didn't seem to surprise her . . .

Then – I don't know how at this distance – we met a number more times and even became friendly, you and I, but that night was never referred to or repeated. You were a terrific woman in those days, Delphine, and I could see that Moresby must have been drunk on you when you were first together. I could also see how liberal he would have felt, having a black wife, and for that matter how strange a black person you were, a ruling caste Ivory Coaster with your French accent and your flowing clothes and your combination of black pride and colonial arrogance and perfectionist sexuality . . . As I got to know Moresby better I could also see the problems he must have had with all these things. I later heard that the two of you hadn't shared a bed since the fifth year of your marriage, I don't know if that was true, but it certainly fitted in with things . . .

And now I've met you again, ten years on, divorced from Moresby, the house at Harrow only a memory, alone in a small flat in Maida Vale, surrounded by a lot of possessions you've hung onto that don't look right crowded together. You're thinner, your skin has got grey and lined, your hair has started to whiten, you look somehow shrunken. I wondered what we would talk about when I came back after Hirst had gone, and there wasn't anything. You see the detail in which I recall that brief spell we had on a bed together. As soon as I saw you I knew that for you it was totally eliminated, a memory that didn't belong to you. Which is the worse torture, Delphine, to remember everything or to forget everything? We found things to chat about, you gave me some yoghurt-coated peanuts to eat, which seemed modest and exotic at the same time. You chain-smoked Silver Thins, elongating your fingers with the cigarette the way you always did, and each time you inhaled, your eyes seemed to turn inward with the breath, and I tried not to see the emptiness . . .

I had at least two motives for being there. One was the strange relationship we had, and the other was to talk about your ex-husband. I really think I hoped to see the same gorgeous woman of ten years ago. It saddened me to find you so depressed, and when I thought that we were maybe going to discover something personal to say to each other, you told me that you'd had a breast removed and that the cancer might still be present . . . And I knew that to summon back the past would be obscene because, fuck it, we still didn't have time . . .

You hardly seemed to have heard that Pat had been killed. That was how it came across, and I knew that you weren't pretending. When you hate somebody for a long time and then it isn't relevant to hate them any more, life has closed down the game, but the habit of your feelings won't quit, the easiest way is not to hear the news. I couldn't use you for information, Delphine, although all along on the car ride to your place I'd been rehearsing exactly how I was going to do that. You didn't know, you didn't care, he hadn't been part of you for years. When I asked you direct why you thought anybody should have wanted to kill him, you said you had no idea, and you were overtly bored by the question, but then you added, 'He was a shit' . . .

I know now that there's no way I can give you this tape, I wouldn't want you to hear it. But I'm not going to erase it – not yet, anyway. Please believe that it's an act of love, not to do that. We owe each other one act of love.

H. T. Kuunas – EURCOOPS

From W. J. Shealor

EYES ONLY

It is clear that at this stage of his mission Operative Goolan had taken refuge in an obsession with private emotional parameters, and the notebook which is here appended is simply a further delineation of the psychologically tenuous schema which we have heretofore targeted. No comment by this Agency would appear to be in point.

Tranche 2

The note in the pigeon-hole had spelt my name wrong, and the typist curtly informed me that my weekly tutorial had been postponed because of Professor Moresby's other commitments. He was notorious for axeing student appointments, but you were supposed to accept it as a badge of conspicuous importance, your own self-esteem enhanced by contact with such a sought-after teacher.

When I arrived on the landing I found that I had been telescoped in with Cromer, who hadn't been told and immediately said, 'We need the whole of the next hour to go through my paper on Marcuse.'

'Fine,' I said, or something equally striking. The truth was, I was already more interested in seeing those two together than in anything I might say myself.

The elevator door opened, and Moresby stepped out onto what was virtually his own private landing. Along with the relaxed academic style he had that quarterdeck manner, the pipe clenched and the eyes ready for business and checking over every detail of your appearance. He led us into his room. Outside the plateglass of that new section of the LSE a dense river-mist submerged all but the tops of buildings right over to the City. The room itself was functional, but shelf on shelf of hardback books did a lot to soften the harshness.

Moresby stretched back in his executive-style chair. 'Marcuse,' he said. 'Interesting animal.'

I knew Moresby's background: he was an Oxford man, and when he said words like 'interesting', he meant something else. Cromer's face was blank – not even aloof, just blank, as if Moresby had to prove something to him.

'The problem,' Moresby said, lighting his pipe – and already I knew he was not going to say what Jake wanted – 'is the gulf between theory and the real world.'

'Indeed,' Cromer said. That was a recurrent Cromerism from that year, and he wanted to show that he wouldn't let Moresby patronize him.

Sweetly, through a cloud of smoke that nestled against the window and tried to make it with the mist outside, Moresby said, 'I felt you hadn't quite succeeded.'

He rocked in his tycoon chair. Cromer had spotted his essay on the desk and was trying to read upside down some comment or grade. He wasn't best pleased.

'What did you think of the section on Althusser?' he asked.

Moresby said, 'Passable, but I didn't think you integrated it clearly enough with the mainstream of your argument. I mean, in the end are you saying anything that Kolakowski hasn't already said better?'

'Kolakowski?' Cromer bordered on indignation. 'Which bit of Kolakowski?'

Moresby reached the wodge of paper across the desk. 'I've made notes where relevant, and suggested some further reading.'

Jake took his papers and prepared to leave. We had been in there all of five minutes, and I was surprised till I looked at his face and realized that pride wouldn't let him stay longer. Moresby wasn't put out either. It seemed normal for both of them. They didn't bother with anything as trivial as goodbyes.

Moresby looked out at the thinning mist, through which the rooftops were starting to surface.

'A brilliant young man,' he said. 'I'm sometimes rather

58

hard on him, but I fear I'm his main connection with the real world, and I see it as my duty – intellectual if nothing else – to bruise him occasionally. He always comes back for more, so the treatment seems to be working.'

Before he could place who I was and why I was there, the phone rang. This was routine in a Moresby tutorial, and sometimes most of the session would be taken up with listening to a string of phone conversations. Moresby had that gift of being totally uninhibited by someone else's presence, yet completely allusive in what he said, giving nothing away to even the most careful listener. I sat back and read the spines of his books. I knew them all pretty well by now.

He always spun his chair round and conducted the conversation with his back to the room. When he finally swivelled back to me we had both lost interest in why I was there.

'Yes, the real world,' he said. 'It's very tempting, Mr Goolan, to sit up here and look out on all that, and think that by manipulating words and ideas one's exercising control over the real mucky world. One of the prize delusions of the academic mind.'

'How do you solve that without ceasing to be an academic?' I said.

'Quite,' he answered. His dark eyes sparkled momentarily. He thought he was really hot shit, and he loved to tease.

'What's your involvement in the real world?' I asked.

For a moment Moresby didn't know whether to be coy and hint at something just to impress me, or withdraw into his Trappist mystery-man persona and impress himself.

'Most people are pawns,' he said. 'The real fulfilment in life is to be an influence – out there.'

He gestured at the now visible roofline. No way was he going to let me interrogate him.

'How do you propose to leave your mark?' he asked.

I don't remember my answer. I said, 'Good question,' or something equally evasive. We weren't about to trade biographies.

'I think my secretary's got your essay,' he said, and switched the intercom.

I don't know why I recall this tutorial now, except that it was the only time I was ever alone with Moresby and Cromer. As I went away I had the strange idea that in reality Jake was Moresby's illegitimate son. I still do.

Before I checked Cromer's briefcase in at the desk in the LSE basement I extracted a wad of important-looking papers and secreted them in my new apartment. They looked important because they contained a lot of fair-copy handwriting and had many references to extensive background reading. When I met Cromer he asked for the case back first. I told him he was kidding.

'What do I have to do to get it back?' he said. He was indignant, already prepared for a rip-off.

'I want to meet the man,' I said.

'You never said anything about meeting him.'

'What did you think – ' I said, 'you were going to show me somebody's front door then kiss me goodbye?'

'How do I arrange a meeting?'

'You knock on his door – hi, I was just passing, this is an old friend from the States. I'll let you know when it's decent to leave.'

Cromer didn't like it, but there wasn't much he could do. He deferred the trip till evening. From a meeting-place on Denmark Hill he led me to a complex of apartment blocks, sizeable by London standards. They were sturdy, pre-World War II, and judging from the wide entrance halls, double doors and elevators, they had once been luxurious. Every flat had a token balcony, narrow damp-traps where nobody would ever want to sit. Now these exclusive apartments were overpriced dumps where some of the original occupants still hung on, slowly decaying behind their dirty lace curtains, and the rest of the blocks were taken over by floating tenants who would all rather be living somewhere else. Every city had these places.

'It's up here,' Cromer said, leading me through an art deco door.

'Nobody's expecting us, right?' I said.

He nodded. I had never seen Cromer drink, but he always exuded this essence of booze filtered through his body with the sweat and the other glandular discharges, coming off him like a stale cologne.

'If you blow me – '

He shook his head, miserable with sincerity. 'I'll play it like you said.'

We went up two flights of stairs and along a wide corridor where the carpet was worn through, the linoleum cracked, and dim lights burned at intervals along the walls. The trellis door of the elevator gaped open at us, but it didn't have a working-order look about it. The greying cream paint was flaking from the ceiling, and the walls exhaled the food smells of several decades. Cromer was furtive and shabby and looked quite at home in this sort of place. He approached a door without checking any numbers on the way. The door had one of those old sprung bells which explode into a shrill groan once the button is touched. Cromer pulled his hand away as if the door had taken a bite at him.

61

A girl's head appeared between the door and jamb. A waft of joss drifted past her.

'Simon in?' Cromer said.

For a moment I thought he had it wrong. He didn't seem to know the girl. She shut the door. Then it was opened again and Cromer said, 'Hello, Simon.'

The bearded face inside grunted something that could have been 'Jake' and opened up. Cromer stepped in and said, 'Just passing,' a pair of words I keep bumping into this trip. There was the girl and another woman, a redhead, in a living room of moulting furniture and walls dingy except for a bold mosaic of posters, letters, souvenirs. A photograph of the British Prime Minister was stuck over a dartboard, riddled with punctures. We were offered some instant coffee.

'This is John,' Cromer mumbled. 'He's an old friend from LSE days. Back in London for a stay.'

It was all very tense. Simon nodded. He was a pale-faced, gaunt man, with a high-domed forehead and long hair, coarse and straight down to the collar of his heavy wool jacket. He had big teeth that showed when he spoke, discoloured but with a lot of bite to them. He gruntingly introduced the women, but not so I could remember their names afterwards.

'What do you do in the Great Imperialist Satan of the West?' he said.

'I'm sorry?' I said. But I said it a shade too politely and he thought I was being clever, and just looked at me with dark expressionless eyes. We sipped at our tasteless coffee.

'You were at LSE with Jake?' Simon then asked.

'Right,' I said. I gave a simple-minded smile. When you have neat hair and a suit it's easy enough to look unthreatening.

62

'Funny we never met.'

'I'm sure we would remember,' I said.

'Yeah,' he said. He seemed to lose interest. He picked a few of his big teeth with a fingernail.

'Simon was at UC,' Cromer told me. I nodded.

'All boppers and ravers in my time,' Simon said. 'A real pisshole.'

'Did you hear about Moresby?' Cromer asked him.

'I heard. Which one was he? They all sound the same, these academics.'

Cromer muttered a few incoherent things which nobody listened to, designed to convey the regard in which he had held the late Professor Patrick Moresby.

'You're still in touch, then, Jake?' Simon said with a genial derisiveness. 'Scribble, scribble, scribble, Mr Gibbon? All those university arseholes who sold you out? Time you got your feet in the shit and started fighting the real enemy.'

'All wars are fought because of conceptual misunderstandings,' Cromer said. It had the smooth, hollow sound of something well-worn. Before anybody could go for him he said, 'We have to leave.' His eyes checked with mine to see that this was OK. It was OK. Cromer wasn't the argument cruncher he used to be. He papered it over with enough feeble remarks to make it sound like we really had only looked in for five minutes, and we got out. Simon looked hungry for more time in which to insult Cromer. The two women reclined in worn-out armchairs and held their contemptuous silence to the end.

The elevator was working after all. As we passed the first floor it came up, rising to the second or third. The occupant stared out through the bars of the door. Cromer, who usually refused to waste his gaze on other people, looked hard at this guy for some reason. Out on the street

I gave him the numbered LSE key and told him he could reclaim his case. He grabbed it and took off into the night. He surely didn't want to spend any more time with me. He had a surprise coming.

I bit the night air, clammy but burnt-tasting as it was, and took an aimless walk to let certain thoughts start eating me. Whatever I had expected, it wasn't this. I felt a sudden revulsion from any idea of getting back to Susie, especially if it demanded revealing myself to some other guy who had been involved with her. It was a bad scene of classic dimensions, and I was just about grateful for the hostility we had met there. It sure made it easy to leave, and I was glad to be out of there. The streetlamps were friendly by comparison – as friendly as I could deal with.

Imogen, that hauntress of public spaces, entered the restaurant as I was paying the check. She had company, but said she had something to tell me, and asked me to call later. She said, 'Stop by,' so there was no ambiguity. She said ten. I was there at a minute before.

She had tried me at my former number and been unable to trace me.

'I was afraid I might not see you again.'

Her bushy hair had the spun-sugar look of blondes just starting to silver. Her eyes were very twinkly. I told her there was no way she was not going to see me again. She was relaxed and warm.

'You seem ill at ease,' she said.

'I'm all right,' I said.

'Is there something on your mind?'

That note of concern made me nervous. I said, 'No. You had something to tell me.'

'Yes,' she said. 'I came across a piece of information the other day – '

In British English 'the other day' means anything up to five years ago. 'Came across' means went looking for. I waited.

'You were talking about Susie. Apparently Moresby gave evidence at the inquest. He was very much against a suicide verdict.'

'Interesting,' I said.

'I thought it might add to your dossier.'

She brought me a refill and sat on the arm of the chair I was sitting in.

'Do you remember when we said goodbye?' she asked.

Why did so many things she said sound like the titles of songs? It couldn't be because she was a lawyer. I said I remembered.

'I was really sorry to see you go.'

That had to be another song. I pictured us on the main steps of the LSE, outside the glass doors that always figure on TV whenever students demonstrate or a professor is murdered. We embraced for the first and last time. It was a nice moment, mainly because it *was* a moment.

Imogen looked down at me and smiled. Her eyes were the kind that never, themselves, smiled, but the skin beside her eyes softened into warm creases. She leaned her head down and kissed me. I could taste her lipstick and feel her lips in the same foreign external way as my foot felt my shoe. I knew that the snippet about Moresby was a strangely businesslike way of saying she wanted me.

'You can stay,' she murmured.

From that moment it had to turn bad. 'I can't,' I said.

Imogen was not about to haggle over how long a period counted as a stay. 'As long as it takes,' she said.

She was wearing a dress that buttoned down the front. She moved her hand slowly and undid the lowest two

65

buttons, exposing her legs in stockings and letting me see that her thighs and crotch were accessible to my hand. But one of my hands rested woodenly on her hip and the other clung to my glass.

'What is it?' she asked. I didn't speak, and she could see from my face that I was going to make light of it. 'Come to bed,' she whispered. 'It'll be OK.'

But it would be like a set of physical tests, and I knew I would fail. Imogen would think it was her. It wouldn't help to know about all the others. If I had to humiliate her, it was better that it happened while we both still had our clothes on.'

'Are you gay?' she asked.

I said not as far as I knew.

'Perhaps you're gay and don't know it,' she said, and an edge of hurt vindictiveness had distorted her voice.

'You're a really nice lady, Imogen,' I said.

'Oh Christ, don't.'

She got up, foolish and wounded. She left the room, and when she came back minutes later it was with her clothes straightened and her face pale and rigid.

'I took too much for granted,' she said. 'Sorry.'

'You don't have to apologize,' I said.

'It wasn't an apology.'

We sat there for a minute because the script of normal behaviour had run out.

'Maybe we could talk,' I said.

She gave a brittle laugh that suggested layers of confusion and pain beneath the professional carapace. Maybe you're as screwed up as me, Imogen. We just couldn't rescue each other at the same time.

'Or maybe I'll leave,' I said.

'Yes,' she said. 'Just leave.'

* * *

What could I tell you, Imogen? I had been through this so many times that I was deprogrammed, I couldn't describe what I felt any more. How could I outline to a rejected woman the deep well of depression that sex forced me into, a depression bound up with the fact that I had loved Susie Ellerman and she had killed herself and I hadn't understood why or been able to do anything about it?

And I had slept with Susie but never made love to her, and every woman I tried to make love to now mocked my failure to reach back to that sweet, lovely ghost.

Impotence is in the mind, right? And the well became a sea, and like the sea its chill got to the testicles long before it gripped the heart.

Cromer would hunt through his papers and pretty soon discover the chunk that I had kept hold of. He might even have a feel for it, some sort of nervous apprehension, before he even opened the bag. At any rate I expected him to phone. It was morning and I was shaving and wondering whether to change my routine of no breakfast when the phone zinged itself awake. Over the line Cromer sounded the way he looked. The midnight cowboy shabbiness crawled out of the wire. He didn't confirm who I was. He just started right in.

'You bastard, you lied to me. Where are my papers?'

'This is no way to start the day,' I said.

'You better let me have them, or I'll go straight back to Simon Blakeway and blow you.'

'Listen, cream bun,' I said, 'me guarding these papers is the surest way of keeping your mouth shut I can think of.'

He reflected, and realized he hadn't thought it through far enough. I could reach out and squeeze the seedy despair oozing from that phone box somewhere in London.

'There's something else,' he said. I didn't talk. He went on, 'I want to talk to you. I'm scared.'

I told him, 'The one time you don't want to talk to me is when you're scared.'

The pips went. He pumped in another coin. I decided to take him seriously. He was too proud and narrow to play street games.'

'What's eating you?'

'Somebody I saw. I've got to talk to you.' This time the fact that I didn't talk must have communicated my interest, and the bummer in him took over. 'It's tasty and it'll cost you,' he said.

'I can afford you,' I said. 'Fix a place.'

So I found myself, still undecided about breakfast, riding the subway east. Cromer had designated Temple station. When I saw him he was walking up and down, looking around all the time, a wrinkled stub of hand-rolled cigarette moving with his lower lip. It was a mild day, but he wore the same baggy dark overcoat I had never seen him take off – a sign of deficient body heat. He made me follow him to the gardens by the round church. I didn't regard this as significant. People with an unfulfilled sense of their own grandeur always pick locations like that.

Cromer was raw-boned and shifty. A golden stubble shone on his pink cheeks. His wispy hair needed combing, and traces of what had once been food stuck to the skin near his mouth. I still remembered how he had put everybody down in those seminars. When I looked at him now I felt sorry for him. It didn't show, and I knew it never would. Or I couldn't afford to feel it.

He started off with the high-horse bit. His voice

68

retained an intellectual aloofness which must have made a lot of situations tough for him.

'Where are my papers?'

'They're safe.'

'You have no right to steal them.'

'Sure. Now, why are we here?'

'Just what are you involved in?'

'You don't need to worry about it.'

'I want to know what you're using me for.'

Fall was colouring the trees. People looked mellow, now the stress of a city summer was over. A yellow crane swung above the skyline. I kept missing the police sirens.

'Listen,' I said, 'I don't want any more shit about your papers. We both know they're just a way of making out you haven't wasted your life. You said you had something to tell me. It's worth twenty, but don't take all morning.'

Cromer sat on a bench. I sat at the other end. He rolled one of those cigarettes that looked as if they had died of cancer themselves. An old woman came and sat between us and began scattering scraps of dried sliced bread for a bunch of sparrows that she addressed by name. Cromer and I got up and walked about again.

'When we went to Simon's – ' I shot him a bleak glance. 'As we were leaving, somebody went past us in the lift.'

'And?'

'I'd seen him before.'

'You said you were scared. Why?'

'I think he recognized me.'

'That was bad?'

'It was the night Moresby was killed. The police picked me up in the building.'

'I've always meant to ask,' I said. 'What were you doing in there?'

Cromer got defensive. 'I often walk about in there.'

'Looking for things to lift?'

His eyes were blue but bloodshot. He didn't reply.

'So you saw this guy?'

'We passed in the corridor. I know he registered me.'

'Had you heard a shot?'

'No.'

'Even with a silencer a pistol still spits.'

'I wasn't near enough.'

'Did he have a gun visible?'

'No. But I knew he had done it. He killed Moresby.'

'And that was him in the elevator last night?'

'Yes. Oh Christ, I know he saw me.'

'Why didn't you tell the police about him?'

Cromer was starting to sweat visibly. 'I did tell them, for Christ's sake. I told them anything I could to get the heat off me. I'd never seen this guy before, and I couldn't give them a description. I'm not interested in how people look.'

'What makes you think he recognized you last night?'

'I saw his eyes through the lift bars. He knew me all right.'

Cromer stopped and faced me. His red-knuckled hands were mangling each other.

'What am I going to do?' he asked.

'I ought to advise you to go to the police again.'

A hunted look swept across his features.

'Or get out of town. Get the fuck out, before this shithead comes and finds you.'

I peeled off a note from a bundle in my pocket.

'I'll make it fifty. Get it changed as fast as you can. And keep it tight, or some old wino's going to bury a bottle in your head and get happy at your expense.'

'Where can I go?' Cromer wailed.

70

I asked if he didn't have a family. He said stiffly that he didn't see his family.

'So go see someone else's. But phone. And no post-cards – I hate them.'

H. T. Kuunas – EURCOOPS

From W. J. Shealor

EYES ONLY

In the matter of the suspicion accruing to J. M. Goolan, the subsequent tape is regarded by this Agency as critical in postulating the belief that Goolan's motivation in transcribing many aspects of the daily events of his mission was in effect to instigate a 'smoke-screen' mode, namely to compile a record not of the actual truth but a series of semifictional factoids which he might in the long term use to his own advantage. The specific substance of this advantage remains to date material for speculation, and we do not wish for your committee to be burdened with any extraneous view in reaching its own conclusions. However, be apprised that the interpretation here is unambivalently one prejudicial to the account of this event as circumscribed by Goolan.

The addressee of this tape is Miss Geraldine Rettiger, an employee of this Agency, whose personal and operational security have been deeply jeopardized by Goolan's actions.

Tape 4

The Garland of Roses was a small Victorian pub, little more than a street bar, off the top end of Kensington High Street. It might have been a flower shop once, but the rest of the connotation had worn thin. They had told me nine o'clock. I got a half of lager and squeezed onto the end of a bench seat. The bar was already full. It was a district of ornate but crumbling red-brick mansion flats, mausoleums for the affluent elderly, the wizened little ladies with glassy eyes and poodles, the white-haired air commodores, retired, with booming voices and Labradors. People like this filled the bar with desperate geniality.

I guess I stuck out, but for you I had to stick out. Apart from being the only one not to call the barman Jock and ask for the usual, I was following instructions and reading the regulation text. Why do they go through these farces? It was the 1961 Pelican edition of Wedgwood's *The Thirty Years' War*, with page 237 torn out, and I guess you had that page somewhere on your person. Who does Uncle Sam pay to dream these things up? I mean, Christ, the only other reading matter in that place was a *Daily Telegraph* on which a caricature colonel in leather elbow-patches was struggling for his third clue in the crossword, and the beer mats.

Your hair was the most memorable thing about you, but don't get the idea I hadn't noticed anything else. It was a distinctive red, not carrot-red or copper-wire-red, but that deep oxblood sort of colour that seems to have originated somewhere in eastern Europe. Later I would discover that your accent was American. I happened to be watching the door, so I had a moment's lead over you. I saw you look round, glance at me as part of your visual sweep of the bar, and I realized that you had not recognized me. The person you were looking for seemed not to be there.

You kept your hand on the door, then went out again. I also made no sign of recognition. Training beats reflexes every time, sure. The fact was, I didn't want to bump into anybody now. Chance meetings usually spell screw-up. I was relieved you had gone out again. I was also reflecting that this was no coincidence, you had to be my twin, when you came back into the bar again.

The gap was ten minutes. What did you do – walk up and down, making a running decision how to handle this one? Or did you have a phone convenient enough for that ten minutes to permit a check to be made with someone higher? Could be, honey. And what did they tell you, I wonder? Play him along, don't let on who you are, find out what Goolan's real game is? Because I knew that from this moment nothing was ever going to be simple again.

I absorbed myself in a few paragraphs about Gustavus Adolphus. Without raising my eyes I could see that you had gone to the bar. I heard you order vodka. It was a transatlantic voice, transatlantic from the Garland of Roses, Kensington. I didn't know what to make of you, but I knew I would have to make something of you.

You stood at the bar next to the guy with the Labrador, who was declaiming to the bar staff about oil being great in the North Sea, lifeblood of the nation and all that, but bad news on the south coast of England, destroying our heritage and ruining the environment. A few sentences later he was talking about his yacht, which I guess he didn't keep moored on the North Sea. By this time you were getting sucked into his monologue, and at a moment when you were looking round for escape I caught your eye. You hesitated briefly, then your face lit up in recognition. I smiled, and you came over and sat down.

'I know we've met,' you said, 'but I can't place it.'

'A flat on Denmark Hill,' I said. 'The night before last. We didn't exactly meet.'

'Right,' you said. 'You came in with someone, then went away again.'

'That's it,' I said.

'Are you a friend of Simon's?'

'No,' I said. 'That was the other guy. I was just tagging along.'

Then we went through a protracted conversational dance-routine, remember? It was already 9.30 and I knew everything I was going to know.

I asked if you were waiting for someone, because you seemed to be looking for someone when you came in. You said you occasionally met a friend in there, but it was only casual – sometimes he was there and sometimes not, it didn't matter.

Your name is Geraldine, and you like to be called Gerry. I didn't remind you that you had entered the bar and left, then returned a short time after. I didn't tell you that I was waiting for my contact either.

Your surname is Rettiger, at least that's what you've told me. Your cover story is that you work for a market research company off Piccadilly, and I'm sure that would check out like a charm. I told you I'm on an extended vacation between jobs, and we both came on like Yuppies. One thing Yuppies always do is take each other's fronts on trust. I wanted to get rid of you, but it was like jumping off a burning boat; I would never get back on again, and I would never know what had started the fire.

I sank the dregs of my beer. Your eyes flickered about at the prospect of me leaving. You finished your vodka quicker than you wanted to. I smiled and said I wanted an early night, and you replied something about having to leave too. Out on the street we went through a polite and fatuous goodbye. And that was it. I was surprised, because I'd expected you to do anything to stay with me. That had to mean you'd pinned a tail to me – I couldn't take it any other way. It was one of those classic moments of fear, when I realized that you were not as dumb as I wanted you to be.

I said a formal goodbye, which you echoed gracefully if indifferently, and we went opposite ways along Hive Street. Once out of sight I stopped, and I guess you did the same. But boy-scout antics in big-city streets are not my strong point, so in the High Street I took a taxi. At Piccadilly Circus I jumped the taxi, had coins ready for the slot and ran down the escalator, and got in the car just as the doors slid together . . . Anyway, Gerry, nice meeting you.

H. T. Kuunas – EURCOOPS

From W. J. Shealor

EYES ONLY

Reference the appended tranche of notes, our paramount response at this juncture is as itemized below.

(i)   Goolan continued to manifest low-level judgment in demarcating the zone between his personal obsessions and the demands of his mission.

(ii) When he interfaced with other activities and/or personnel of a security nature, his behaviour pattern as delineated by himself displays all the signs of a man suicidally courting danger, and conflicts in every particular with the procedural norms instilled in such field operatives and hitherto practised by Goolan himself.

(iii) This operational eccentricity must be accorded maximum weight in concluding that Goolan's account of events, significantly in later episodes, is not the whole story and should not be granted the status of evidence.

Tranche 3

'Why are you still in town?' I said. Cromer sounded as if
he had swallowed a lot of the money I had given him, the
fast way. He said he couldn't decide where to go, so he
had stayed. I asked why he was calling.

'You said keep in touch.'

'Look, you son of a bitch, if I'm lonely I can ring Dial-
a-Prayer. What do you want?'

The bleeps went. He stuffed more coins in.

'I thought I was useful to you.'

'Not while you're pissing in your pants.'

'I think I'm being followed.'

'Who the fuck would want to follow you, Jake?'

'Listen, I mean it, I saw somebody.'

I grunted internally. I had enough problems now. I
took a deep breath and said, 'Tell me your address. I'm
coming right there.'

I hoped this would scare him to admit he was snowing
me, but no chance. So I wrote down his address. It was
obvious that Cromer never told anybody where he lived.
It required a moment's uneasy thought, and it came over
as a confession which weakened him in the telling. I could
see why when the taxi dropped me there. Gleet Road,
Dalston, meant nothing to me or the cab driver, who
needed his map once we had passed Islington. Gleet Road
was a seedy, rotting street in a district of the same. I left
the cab and walked along, looking for Cromer's number.
On a shattered end wall of a house nobody could bother
to finish demolishing, someone had printed in big precise

letters, NIGGER SCUM OUT. Underneath it said, MILLWALL FC, and another graffitist had added a U and a K to the football club initials. I tried to picture Cromer walking along this street with his briefcase full of abstruse notes, as his life went by.

The houses in Gleet Road were the kind you always see the backs of from trains pulling out of London. As if to confirm the thought, at that moment a train rumbled grudgingly through a cutting the other side of a row of jaundiced villas. Now I was seeing them from the front. These places had fallen arches and bad breath, and they couldn't hold their heads up any more.

Cromer was looking out for me, and was in the front doorway before I could decide which of the cracked, decrepit bells to press. He had his overcoat off, and a furtive, defensive look on his face. He could have made a terrific intelligence man, Cromer, except that he would have wanted everybody to know how good he was. Over a shirt that looked like it had grown on him he was wearing at least two layers of moth-eaten wool. He looked more scared than I had ever seen him.

'Let's get one thing straight,' I said. 'I didn't fuck your life up by coming into it. It was fucked up already. I don't normally charm my way into places, but for you I'm making an exception.'

Cromer turned and lumbered up the gloomy stairs, treating my words with resentful contempt. I followed him up. It was the kind of place where even the daylight is metered. His room was an armpit. The window was shuttered by a yellowed lace curtain which at various spots was shredding into holes. The sink area in the corner held dirty crockery, but a surprisingly small amount. I guessed Cromer only ever used one cup, one plate, and probably regarded it as beneath him to possess more. He hadn't made the bed, and it had a sort of body-shell shape to it which looked like it would defy making. The table and old fake-marble mantelshelf and every other space were stacked with books and papers. A box with 'Kellogg's Cornflakes' on the side was crammed with empty bottles.

Among the books I spotted a hardback of Moresby's *Normal Society*, the book that had made his reputation. It was an instant classic, although fifteen years later I guess it was already dated and unreadable. On the flyleaf it said 'To Jake Cromer, Patrick Moresby – the world changes itself, only philosophers can interpret it.' The date was Summer 1973.

'I never realized you were so close,' I said.

'Moresby liked flattery,' Cromer said. 'Like all academics, he was just tripping out on narcissism. It suited me to flatter him in those days.'

'Maybe he thought it was a good idea to keep on your good side too,' I said.

Cromer answered sourly, 'Well, if he did, it didn't last long. What's the date in there?'

'Seventy-three.'

'It's not even history, it's necrophilia. Who remembers 1973?'

'Me for starters,' I said. 'Mick Jagger was singing "Angie" all over town, the Marxist government in Chile had been overthrown, and people were still wearing flared trousers.'

'Allende had been murdered by the CIA,' Cromer said.

'What kind of Marxist are you,' I asked, 'proto, crypto, or neo?'

'The only thing I admire about Marx,' Cromer said, 'is the purity of his lifestyle.'

I replaced Moresby's book. In that room the ceiling

was brown, and every shred of fabric stank of dead tobacco fumes. Some of them had died slowly. Cromer tipped the ash of his roll-up into an unwashed jam-jar which was already half full of discarded butts. I guess at the end he would just put the cap on the jar and junk it. I'll say one thing for Cromer, if he was creepy, it was with the total lack of self-consciousness of the chronically alone. It almost amounted to a style.

He didn't offer me refreshment, and it saved me refusing. He had a nervous tic around the mouth, a fastidious pouting action, which I had noticed he did a lot of when life's tough moments came his way. He was doing it frequently right now.

'So what's it about?' I said.

'What?'

'Your call.'

Cromer was fighting agitation. 'Look, I noticed somebody. I'd seen twice before, the last two days. He was hanging around. When I called you he was there, and when I came out of the box he moved off. I went a long way round and doubled back and sure enough I passed him.'

'And then?'

'He went into a shop. He didn't even look at me. But I knew he was watching me.'

'So where is he now?'

I tried to think of people I had seen on the street as I came here. But between the taxi and Cromer's place I could only recall two teenage boys in studded leather jackets shouting obscenities and pretending to puke in the cratered roadway.

'That was the last I saw of him,' Cromer said.

'That guy you saw at Denmark Hill,' I said. 'You ever see him again?'

Cromer shook his head. He didn't like the thought.

His room looked onto the back. I stared out through the ragged net curtain at an overgrown remnant of a garden. Thick uncut grass and sprawling bushes fought each other for every inch of soil and ray of light. A busted pram lay upside down in front of an asbestos shed with its window pane stove in. A few gardens away people were heaving old roofslates into a skip, syncopating the music from a tinny radio.

'Is there a back way out of here?' I asked.

Cromer frowned as if it were an insult to ask him this. 'Not as far as I know.'

'Whose are the kids?'

Two children had appeared. They sat gouging holes in the lawn with shards of asbestos. In one corner an evil-looking ginger cat squatted, then walked away without even pretending to scratch the earth.

'The landlord's. He's Greek. They live in the basement.'

It would be dusk within the hour. I asked Cromer if he had a street plan. He went straight to one of the heaps of dust-coated books. With impressive accuracy he lifted out an *A to Z* which looked like it had been dropped in a pot of tea and then dried out by a one-bar electric fire. I got paper and pencil and asked Cromer to clear a small space on his table. He was fussy and reluctant, but he did it.

'I'll give you a route,' I said, 'and the key to my flat. I want you to move in there for a day or two. Keep to the route exactly. If anybody's coming after you, I'll pick up on them.'

'What are you going to do about him?' Cromer asked. I could see 'accessory to murder' burning its way into his brain.

'Leave that to me. There's food in the apartment. Stay there till you hear from me.'

I drew another copy of the plan and went through the details while Cromer condescended to pay attention. I knew he wanted to tell me to piss off. But he knew I was the only protection he had. We waited for the daylight to fade.

When I saw Cromer in the mouth of Essex Road station, he was carrying a newspaper. That told me he had doubled back and caught sight of his tracker. He was holding it under his right arm, and that told me which side of the entrance the tracker would be coming from. Cromer learned fast.

I was already off the street, inside the subway station. My itinerary had been shorter than his. A sudden wave of passengers emerging to street level signified the arrival of a train. At this time of day the traffic was mostly people returning home from work in West End service industries.

Cromer looked down and saw that I was there. I already had his ticket. As he passed I swapped him it for the newspaper. Hiding behind this I watched for somebody pursuing Cromer into the subway.

The tail didn't take too much spotting. There was a ticket machine, but it was out of order, and he had to go to the window. Cromer was already through and out of sight. The tail wasn't happy. What happened next was beyond my range of vision. I could only assume that Cromer was doing what I told him.

Another train came in, and the ghostly rumble below ground was followed by another delivery of harassed commuters. As soon as I heard somebody running up from the guts of the subway station I took up position to the left side of the entrance. We had staked everything on

Cromer's ability to run a few score yards, including some uphill. It wasn't a gamble on which to stake anything you cared about, but fear had done a great job on Cromer. He hit the street and hared away as planned.

Some seconds later his tail rounded the corner. There were still people coming and going. They had taken enough jostling for one day, and it showed. Their presence concealed the fact that it was me who hooked the legs from under the chaser. I kicked him away fairly decisively, and he didn't even stumble, he cut the air efficiently like someone diving into a mirage and found himself winded and outraged on the garbage-littered sidewalk, entangled with a shrieking old woman and the contents of a Safeway carrier bag.

That was the schedule. Cromer was away. I strolled quickly off in the opposite direction as the crowd cleared. The tail brushed himself down and concluded that he had lost his prey. There was no evidence that he had company. My next bet said that he would return to Cromer's place. But he just vanished down into the subway.

It was a grim, simple station, with just an up and a down line. There is no problem in tailing somebody who has no suspicion they are being followed, especially in the aftermath of an episode that promotes introspection. I felt this guy was not going to be any trouble. Whether he would lead me to anything was another matter. He looked like some sort of private dick as I studied him along the platform. I noticed he was dragging one leg. I had levitated him so neatly he was probably convinced it was his own clumsiness.

He changed trains and rode west on the Central Line. On the underground the evening rush had given way to a ghostly, drained emptiness that sighed up the escalators and along the tunnels. We both got out at Marble Arch.

From there I dogged him at an easy distance down Park Lane. The streets here were generous and laid out on a grid system, and he would need to be working hard to disappear in the time it took for me to blink the street dust from my eyes.

He turned down Aldford Street. For a moment I had the idea he might be headed for a particular building in Curzon Street, or some other branch of Fuck-Ups Anonymous in the vicinity. The red-brick streets were mellow and stylish and quiet. Around here the evening people did not go about on foot. My guy walked with a sudden businesslike air up to a pair of red phone boxes at the junction of Aldford and Park Streets. I stopped and looked into a window that displayed some stunning Bokhara carpets with nothing so vulgar as a price tag on them. Out of the side of my eye I couldn't see much, but it was clear he was not telephoning anybody. After a minute he came out, conspicuously not glancing back up the street, and continued the way he had been going.

In South Audley Street there was a small church with a symmetrical Dutch-type façade. He went in there. That gave me long enough to get to the phone box before his customer did. I didn't run, because this was Mayfair after all, but I was more than fast enough.

He seemed a worthy sort of guy. Treading in somebody's footsteps for a few miles across a big city makes you form an impression of that person, whether you do or don't wish to. When I thought 'worthy', I guess I meant 'no good', although there are a lot of people in this business whose whole career strength is their ordinariness. But this guy had an air of specially decent mediocrity that suggested either he was working his way up a long ladder real slow, or he was about to land a solid but terminal position in a filing basement somewhere.

Whoever they were, they had given him a soft target. But apart from knowing me, I couldn't see why Cromer was being watched. It had to be because of that visit to Denmark Hill, and probably they had tailed him direct from there. So after that, what? I opined that this podgy innocent I was now trailing through Mayfair was just a leg-man checking out that Cromer was no more wicked than he seemed. They had set a loser to tag a loser, like it was some sort of competition, and I was tramping the streets after both of them. I frowned and got a pain in my duodenum every time I thought about it.

The church was the Grosvenor Chapel, South Audley Street. A plaque on the wall said it had been the US Forces' church during the war. The interior was discreetly lit, mostly white with reliefs picked out in gold, a restful place in whose depths my guy knelt in an attitude of prayer. From a quick view of the microfiche which he had taped to the underside of the phone-box shelf, I inferred that by now his mind was a total blank, but also that he was grateful for an interlude of peace while the back of his shirt dried out. The fiche now lay in my pocket, and a lot of the mark's repose depended on not knowing that.

I went in and knelt at the rear of the church. As he got up I continued to meditate behind my clenched hands. I only rose as he approached me. He was one of those moon-faced people who from infancy must have looked middle-aged, and now at about thirty he was starting to resemble an overgrown schoolboy. He had a long thin nose that did not match his round face, and hair neatly parted and greased down. He looked surprised that someone else was there, but showed no sign of having seen me before.

We whispered 'Good evening' to each other. I followed him out.

'A beautiful place,' I said. My accent seemed to reassure him. American equals tourist equals safe. I didn't want to say 'Do you come here often?' But then I didn't need to.

'One of London's nicest churches,' he said. 'Are you American?'

'Yes,' I said. 'I always come to this chapel when I'm on a visit. My dad was over here in the war.'

His schoolboy face lit up. I knew it was only politeness, but that good old British gift for small talk was working for me.

'Oh really?' he said. 'What was he in?'

'Screaming Eagles – 101st Airborne.'

'Oh,' he said, pleased at being able to reveal expertise. 'Normandy or Arnhem?'

'Normandy. He was badly wounded at Caen and shipped back.'

'Still alive, I hope?'

'No, he died a few years ago. He ran a small timber company. He was a nice guy.'

'Yes. I'm so sorry.'

I remembered my father, and wished I hadn't lied about visiting that chapel. The guy's sympathy was restrained and therefore felt genuine. I had an impulse to apologize for what I had done to his leg.

'I'm at a completely loose end this evening,' I said. 'I don't guess you'd care for a drink?'

He beamed and flapped a little and said, 'Delighted.' I suggested, 'Why not make it dinner? I'd be honoured if

90

you'd be my guest. I'm not too well up on the eating places around here.'

He gave a fluttering, overwhelmed acceptance. He had some knowledge of local eateries, which I would hazard was more from window-gazing than actually troughing down in them. His liquid-to-solid intake was highly biased towards the former. We were both well pleased with the way things were shaping out.

His name was Philip Devoil, and some hours later I was unloading him from a taxi in a section of Redcliffe Square where the houses had scaffolding up and their windows boarded over. I jockeyed him up the front steps and struggled for the key in his pocket. These were looming Edwardian townhouses, with marble-pillared porches and five floors. When they were built they needed a small army of servants to run them. Now a property company was emptying the whole row as the leases ran out, and in this particular one only Philip Devoil was still holding out against Paradise Developments plc.

He lived in the top flat but one. The stair light was on a timer and coughed out when we were halfway up. Devoil's flat was where maybe the cook and head maid had roomed together, with the skivvies in the roof above. I dragged him inside and let him collapse on a threadbare sofa. He made a drunken attempt to remove his tie but failed. Before I could survey the place he started to heave about. A hoarse groan that sounded like 'Bathroom!' belched from his mouth. I got him there just in time to vomit into the bath. Then he passed out on the rotted carpet. I swilled out the bath and left him there.

I went through the flat – living room, bedroom and bathroom, and a small kitchen down some steps, tacked on the back of the house like an afterthought. There was no real comfort in the place, with dirty laundry scattered about, greasy plates, grey scum on half-finished mugs of coffee. It was a different kind of squalor from Cromer's, but I didn't have time to contemplate the finer points. There were empty bottles of cheap wine everywhere. It was a good place to crack up in.

On the bathroom floor Devoil had curled himself up in a cosy foetal sleep, his head nestled against the toilet bowl. I hoisted him along to the bedroom, and then stripped him to his underwear and socks and shoved him between the yellowed sheets. As I rolled his head onto the grease-stained pillow he gave out a profound snore with the release of someone who never wanted to wake again.

In the confined entrance hall there was a chest of drawers. It contained clothing. The bottom drawer was full of female underwear, all carefully folded, well-worn bras and suspender belts and nylon stockings. If Devoil was a transvestite he had very boring tastes. More likely it was a leftover from some previous resident, which for reasons of his own Devoil had chosen to live with. The other drawers all held his own clothing and personal junk, thrown there in chaos and yielding nothing.

Slowly, methodically, I turned the flat over. It was already past midnight, and I would have to sleep sometime. The supermarket coffee in Devoil's kitchen tasted like creosote, and the only milk in the place had been left out and had rancid lumps floating in it. I took two cups, black. The drinking I had needed to do to get Devoil drunk was catching up on me. I kept looking. At about two I settled down to sleep.

The curtains were drab olive velvet, ancient and starting to decompose. I drew them back, to reveal two windows that stared out into a churchyard full of lime trees whose leaves were going a deep, melancholy yellow. It was just after seven, and there was already a buzz of traffic up towards Earls Court. I replaced the seat cushions. In the bedroom Devoil had kicked the bedclothes off. His humped body was pathetic in its stained underwear. He showed little sign of breathing. One arm reached out, as if to seek another person or a soft toy.

It was tempting to go out for some decent coffee. I made myself stay and get by on the creosote-flavoured stuff in Devoil's kitchenette. When I came back up the cramped stair Devoil had surfaced. I had the next move clearly designed. I went into the bedroom and put a friendly hand on his shoulder.

'Here you go, pal. I've made you a coffee.'

Devoil was startled. He twitched and turned over, while his round boyish eyes roved about nervously.

'Who are you?'

'I brought you back last night. We had quite an evening. You forgotten? Here, drink this.'

Devoil dragged himself upright and sucked at the coffee.

'You don't mind me staying?' I said. 'But you tossed your cookies all over the bathroom and I had to clean you up and get you to bed. Thought I'd stay and see you right.'

Devoil was embarrassed. 'Yes – I see – thanks – I'm sorry.'

'You get yourself together,' I said. 'I'll fix you breakfast.'

There were some eggs, but I couldn't face the uncleaned frying pan. I came back with bread, a tub of margarine and a jar of rubbery jello. Devoil had made a trip to the bathroom and got into some clothes. He was unshaven and disoriented. I noticed the periodic tremor of his plump white hands. His dark trousers needed a dry

93

clean, and his black shoes were dulled with London dust. I tried not to look too shrewd.

'A pity about this place,' I said. 'Having to leave and all.'

'You're telling me,' Devoil said.

'Listen,' I said, 'I work in property. Mainly for US clients, but I get a lot of useful access. You need to make contact before a property hits the marketplace. How about I look a few things out for you?'

Devoil's face lit up. 'Would you really? I don't think I can face another estate agent.'

'No sweat,' I said. 'I could drop by in a few days' time with any likely places, if you give me a financial limit to work in.'

Devoil said that was fantastic. He must have wondered about me, but it didn't show. I took notes while he told me about his money affairs and the parts of London he didn't want to live in.

'I'll be in touch,' I said. 'Your phone still connected?'

'Yes, I'll give you the number.'

'Fine,' I said, although I already had it.

After I had gone he would search the flat. He would find nothing missing and no sign of anything discovered. That would set him up nicely for the next time.

The Metropolitan Line breezed out into the daylight and rattled through a wasteland of shoe-box apartment blocks. Ladbroke Grove was a windblown stop on a route to nowhere, a frontier station where you couldn't guess what was on the other side of the frontier. I felt like the garbage that blew along the streets was blowing through me. I needed a shave and a mouthwash, and something hard had been in my lower intestine for too long.

I had given Cromer the key to my flat. I tried the door

before ringing, and found it open. I recalled the care I had taken in going through Devoil's rat hole, and a wave of resentment hit me when I saw that somebody had not done me the same honour. I was ready to paste the shit out of Cromer until I saw him stretched out on the bed. Everything in the flat that could be moved had been thrown around the place. As for Cromer, it was difficult to say whether he was dead or asleep or in some state of relative consciousness. That question mark would still hang over him when his last moment came. I looked for blood but didn't see any. I nudged him awake, but he didn't take to the delicacy, so I pushed him over and gave his face a brisk slap or two.

He was an ugly sight. He had been a handsome man once, and a swollen lip and maturing bruises on his cheek and forehead made him look bad. Even after he recognized me he looked scared for a minute. I rolled one of his cigarettes and put it in his mouth and held a light to it for him. He seemed to recover quickly. The life of survival-level squalor, petty thieving and pariah values, had trained Cromer well for this moment. He wasn't delirious about the experience, but he wasn't a gibbering wreck either.

I asked what had happened. 'Somebody jumped me,' Cromer said. When he spoke his lips moved like one of those sorbo-rubber finger puppets, not quite fitting the words.

'When you got here or later?'

'When I came in. The lights were off, I remember switching one on, but it stayed dark. Then somebody hit me.'

'What with?'

'I think it was fists. Maybe with gloves.'

His face stared at me, lugubrious and distorted, like a clown's.

'You bastard, you knew all the time.'

'Not true,' I said, but I didn't expect to convince him.

'Why did you want me to come here? Somebody's out to get you.'

'You and me both.'

Suddenly Cromer got pathetic. 'Why should anybody want me? I haven't done anything.'

'You saw somebody, remember,' I said. 'And anyway, you steal from bookstores. The Retailers' Association have probably got out a contract on you.'

'I need a doctor,' Cromer said.

'Ten years too late,' I said. 'What you need is a wash. Get cleaned up while I tidy this lot.'

They had tipped everything out that could be tipped, scattered everything that wasn't screwed down. Maybe they had done it in daylight and waited for me to come back after dark. Or maybe Cromer had interrupted them. I wondered what they were looking for, or if it was just to make me sleep badly nights. All the information about me I carried in a body belt. The belt made me sweat at times, but everybody had some facts about themselves that had to make them sweat. Anything else of value I either put in a bank deposit box or a temporary stash on railway stations and such places.

I went to the window and stared out. One part of the panorama was taken up with a slice of the Westway dipping over the rooftops and apparently chuting its load of traffic into a line of distant bedrooms. I had feared it all along – I didn't have the time for a long game with Devoil. I shouldn't have played him so delicately. If I had wanted to know why he was tailing Cromer I could have

96

squeezed it from him easily enough. I had thought I could get more by playing him. I had been conned by my own smartness, and now something in me was going chicken-shit. Before I could get anything out of him he might loop up my arrival in his life with the disappearance of the microfiche from the telephone box. He sure as hell knew about that by now.

I turned to see Cromer standing in the doorway. It was the first time I had seen him stripped down as far as a shirt. Without the habitual overcoat and pullovers he looked gaunt and vulnerable. An incongruous beer-gut sagged over his buckled waistband.

'You better come and see this.'

I followed him to the bathroom. Across the mirror, in red board-marker, was scrawled 'Go Home Yankee.' I took the remark as humorous. The felt pen wasn't mine and didn't go with the apartment, so they had come prepared. I got Cromer out of there. The bundle of clothing he took with him smelt like it had started life wrapping cheese. I shut the door. I needed half an hour under some very hot water.

First I told Cromer, 'Go back to your house, and let me know if there are any more faces.'

I thought he might mention the return of his papers, but that didn't seem to trouble him any more.

'What are you going to do?' he asked. He put the question man to man, like he thought I might tell him.

'Go see some estate agents,' I said. In spite of his rubber lip he made a good stab at sneering to show he didn't believe me.

We passed through the array of scaffolding and went up to the porch. Even with open sides that porch was more of a house than most of the world's population had ever dreamt of. Although we had been to several watering-holes, Devoil didn't need my help this time. I kept my eye on his key drill. He had a ring with several Yales on it, along with a few smaller ones. Once inside the flat he tossed the ring onto the sideboard that crowded out the entrance hall.

I had given him enough moonshine about apartments, gleaned from the agents' handouts and the property section of *The Times*, to maintain my front. Devoil was a grateful and receptive audience. Either he believed every word or he was stringing me along with panache. When he went to the bathroom I got up and pocketed the key ring. It was quick that way. To remove one key was time-wasting, and one missing key would evidence a theft, where an entire set could just have been mislaid.

When he returned I asked him, 'Do you get laid much?'

Devoil's round white face shone with a nervous sweat. I persisted. 'You get to screw a girl occasionally?'

When I went through his things I had not found a trace of pornography, male or female. For a young man living alone it seemed unusual. But I wasn't interested in what turned him on, only in making him feel uncomfortable.

'Not much,' he said. It was a miserable subject, and I looked at him coldly while he avoided it. Then I said I had to go. Devoil expressed regret, but his facial muscles slackened visibly with relief.

I said I would call again. He thanked me for the property stuff and offered to see me out. But I insisted on finding my own way down the once grandiose but now dank, oppressive stairway. It was four flights of stairs to the ground. I opened the street door and loudly closed it. The thud echoed through the cavern of the empty building.

I waited a few minutes. The pavement along the front of the house was unsighted, especially with the scaffolding down the façade. So even if Devoil was watching for me, he would have to assume I had left. Keeping the light off, I went back up, silent on polyurethane soles. I passed Devoil's door and continued up to the tiny landing of the studio flat in the roof, where I settled down on the floor. Either he came out or I went in, it didn't matter which.

When I pressed the light button on my watch it was midnight. I moved slowly down to the next landing. I could see no light through the frosted panel in Devoil's door. I had studied the lock as he opened it. There was no stiffness. I gripped the handle and eased the door towards me as I finessed the key in the slot. The door sighed ajar, and I moved in.

From the bedroom the snores were quiet but drawn out, signifying a sleep of brainless depth. I slipped off my shoes. Using the thin beam of a pencil flashlight I went down to the kitchenette. I checked out the wall unit. It hung from two hooks crudely rawlplugged into the plaster. I checked for crockery I might knock over. I needed a free space to set the unit down. I set the flashlight so that I would lift the unit down its elongated beam, and went to work. First I emptied the unit of its contents and put them aside piece by piece. Then it took me three minutes and a lot of muscular coordination to raise the wall unit and get it silently to the floor.

Behind the wall unit an air-brick had been removed. The hole sheltered a cardboard box which was full of documents and chunks of microfilm. I had left it as it was, unexamined, rather than alert Devoil. I suppose it was a mood thing really, but suddenly I wanted the contents of the box more than Devoil's belief in my friendship. I reached up to the cavity.

I took half a step back. I hadn't expected it to be empty. Frustration locked my teeth together. Then I was hit between the shoulder blades by a blow that kicked the breath from my body. I sprawled into the blackness of the kitchenette.

The empty bottle had missed my skull by a millimetre. Whatever outfit Devoil worked for, the training that had got him this far failed him now. He swung the heavy spirit bottle as he plunged into the confined dark space which still reverberated with the noise of shattering crockery. I had no shoes on, but my left foot made a perfectly judged strike against Devoil's balls. He bellowed with pain and roared for breath, and with that it was all over.

Devoil huddled on his sofa and buried his face in his hands. He was wearing only his off-white underwear. I got him an armful of clothes. I wanted our conversation to be serious. It didn't take the wince of anguish off his face, but it calmed him down a little.

'Just tell me where the box is,' I said.

'How did you know it was there?'

'Where is it now?'

'What if I don't tell you?'

I took a few deep breaths while he contemplated the thrill of defiance. Then I got up and went across to him. I cuffed him round the side of the head and grabbed one of his ears. While twisting it half off I dragged him to his feet and led him at a rapid pace to the bathroom. I bent his head under the bath tap, started the water running, and plugged the bath. He was like a big schoolboy being ragged on his first day. He had obviously done this before somewhere. I had wasted a lot of time, and I felt mean, Devoil soon started yelling for a truce. I gave in only after he had been in the jet of water long enough to get it in his windpipe and down his nose a few times.

We went back to the living room. Devoil nursed a red ear and a wet shirt.

'You,' I said, resuming where we had left off, 'are going to tell me.'

'Only if you tell me who you are.'

I took out the roll of microfiche and held it up between thumb and forefinger like a phial of poison he had to swallow.

'Don't bargain with me.'

Devoil's face was puffy and sad.

'I've got to know who you are. I'm under instructions –'

'Who from?'

He shook his head against the temptation to talk.

'I'm under orders too,' I said. 'One of my orders is to beat the living shit out of you unless you answer my questions. Now, you're either a low-grade British intelligence officer, or you work for a security firm, possibly one which subcontracts for the intelligence service. Or you're a spy, but pardon me if I smile on that one.'

'I'm not a spy,' Devoil said. A very patriotic nerve had quivered somewhere. 'Please believe that.'

I paused. Devoil looked at me pleadingly but admiringly. It was a good example of the masochist impressed by the efficiency of the sadist.

'You're watching somebody called Jacob Cromer. I want to know why.'

'It's a job.'

'Who gave you it?'

'I don't know.'

'What are you reporting on?'

'Where he goes. Anybody he makes contact with.'

'Since when?'

'Two days.'

'Had you reported on me?'

'No, no.'

'When you met me at the church, had you – '

'The first time I'd seen you, I swear.'

'Why did you remove that box?'

'How did you know it was there?' Devoil asked.

He frowned to let me know how really puzzled he was. His bewilderment was intense and sincere. I was beginning not to believe him.

'Why did you move it?'

'Something made me nervous. I thought I'd better – '

'What did?'

'You've got the reason in your hand.'

'The collector called to let you know it wasn't in position?'

'Yes. So I moved the box.'

Too many questions were conflicting in my mind and beating each other out of the way before my mouth could get to them.

'Who was the collector?'

'I don't know. I'm just a middleman.'

'You prick, you must know somebody.'

'I have a contact, I don't know who he is. He passes me the stuff and gives me the drops.'

'Who's it for?'

'I don't know.'

'You're lying. Are you Intelligence, or some prick of a gumshoe, or just a newspaper boy who branched out?'

'I'm sort of Intelligence.' Devoil said it as if admitting to a grand felony.

'Then you sort of fucking know what this information is sort of about, don't you?'

I shouted. Devoil must have had his strong points, but listening to me shout wasn't one of them. Both his ears were glowing now. At the same time, he wasn't doing enough. He was playing the idiot to stall me. Under the squirming he was too calm by a mile. He had also tried to lodge a triangular Glenfiddich Straight Malt bottle in my upper vertebrae. He had not been asleep when I came into the flat, he had been acting. The bastard was too well prepared all along the line.

'They're some sort of military plans,' he said innocently.

'Where are they now?'

'I had to get rid of them – '

'They're here somewhere. I'll give you one minute to take me to them.'

Devoil used a lot of body language to persuade me that he couldn't help. He had looked at his watch twice since we had been sitting there. I took it as a hint. I don't like hints.

I said, 'OK,' and went for him. By the time I pulled him to his feet he was already agreeing.

'They're in a flat downstairs. The door was left unlocked. I found a place under the floorboards.'

We were already on our way down. The power was off. I used my pen light, keeping Devoil in front and letting him do the work. A section of floorboard had been sawn up and replaced loose by an electrician. Devoil reached inside and drew out his box. I knew he was thinking about knocking my torch away and improvising it from there, but he also knew what I was thinking.

I trained the light on the contents of the box. I told him to explain some of the microprints to me. At the same moment I heard a hollow, quiet thud, distant in the building. It had to be the street door.

My guess was that while I was in the kitchenette, before coming at me with the scotch bottle, Devoil had signalled somebody. A flashlight from the window, silent and effective, a prearranged code. All they wanted was for

103

me to have my dukes in the till. I still didn't know who the outfit was, but it was deep shit whichever way you looked at it.

There was a fan of spectral light from the lamps in the square. The dark space we were in must once have been a bedroom. It had a built-in wardrobe, with a latch on the outside. I took the box from Devoil and put it down. Then I slammed him into the wardrobe and wedged the latch. While he beat on the inside of the door I rammed my pockets with a sample of the fiches.

The catch on the sash window undid with no trouble, and I let myself out onto the scaffolding. It was the third floor, and the buzz of the traffic was a long way down. I climbed carefully along to the nearest walkway of planking. The metal tubing of the scaffolding was dry and cool, and I tried to keep my palms from sweating. As I tacked my way down toward the brighter lamplight, the ornate balconies on the front of the building gave me a minimal feeling of security. I told myself that they would break my fall, but I knew that they would break my back first. I went carefully, and by the time Devoil came out of the closet, I was blocks away.

H. T. Kuunas – EURCOOPS

From W. J. Shealor

EYES ONLY

In the appended section, this Agency holds, Goolan demonstrates beyond any doubt or interpretation that by this stage his paranoia had become such as to severely pervert his grip on the necessary realities, in especial as respects his accountability to those whose trust he still possessed.

Tranche 4

In an inspired moment I had looked Moresby up in the phone directory, and sure enough he was there. Of the two P. J. Moresbys listed I guessed he was the Kentish Town one rather than the Catford address. I tried the number a few times and got no answer, then a female voice interrupted the ringing of the phone in what my mind saw as a deserted house.

'Could I speak to Professor Moresby, please?'

The voice that answered was youthful. Its silence threatened me. Once again I hoped that being audibly American gave me an upfront innocence that I could capitalize on.

'I'm an old pupil of Pat's,' I continued, 'just in town for a couple of days. I usually look him up when I'm passing through. Can I leave a message?'

'You haven't heard?' the girl asked.

'Like I said, I've just arrived in England.'

'He was murdered last week.'

The words had a numb resonance. She had said them enough times to do it without thinking.

I simulated a shocked silence. 'Murdered? I don't believe it.'

After a long pause she said, 'It's true.'

'Listen,' I said, 'I'm truly sorry to have troubled you. Are you his – ?'

'I'm his research assistant. As least, I was.'

'It must be terrible for you. I'm really sorry. But thanks for telling me. Goodbye.'

The dead voice at the other end said, 'Goodbye.'

All this was before I paid my second visit to Devoil. I slept as well as you can the night after somebody has wrecked your apartment and beaten up the person they thought was you. I wanted to find out more about that voice on Moresby's phone and what went with it.

I came up from the airless quiet of the tube station to a district where the houses were rapidly rising upmarket, freshly whitened and rejuvenated, discreetly comfortable and indifferent to the cracked sidewalks, the dog crap and the garbage in the gutters. Moresby's place was a small, solid property in a cul-de-sac, with black iron railings and pale cream paint on the stucco, the sort of house that carried a blue plaque saying that a totally forgotten Royal Academician had died there. I rang the bell and waited.

The young woman who opened the heavy, dark green door had a familiarity which initially I accounted for by our previous phone conversation. She was in her early twenties, and seemed used to opening that door. I apologized for disturbing her, and referred to our earlier dialogue. 'I had to call again to find out more. Professor Moresby was very important in my life. I was devastated by what you told me.'

She hesitated, and I added, 'I won't take more than a minute of your time. I would very much appreciate it.'

She led me in, and we went to a cool room at the back, overlooking a small enclosed lawn with a sundial. She said she was trying to sort out all his papers, and as she said it, moved her hands sideways, like a swimmer tiring.

'Why should anyone want to kill him?' I asked.

She shook her head, and dark hair fell across her forehead.

'I don't know.'

108

'Have the police caught anybody?'

'I don't think so.'

'You don't mind me asking?'

'No.'

She lit a cigarette and smoked nervously. I thought she was treading a fine wire between breakdown and acceptance and trying not to look to either side.

'Do you have any idea who might have done it? Did he have enemies?'

'He was an idealist. Idealists always have enemies.'

'What particular ideals?'

'I thought you knew him,' she said.

'I just meant a particular issue where he might have upset somebody.'

'Not that I know of.' She stubbed out the cigarette halfway through.

'Had you worked for him long?'

'Two years. Since I came down from Oxford. Why do you want to know all this?'

I couldn't play the old friend card too strongly if she had been with Moresby for two years. Her eyes had started to look alive again. I changed direction. 'Listen,' I said, 'I haven't been straight with you. After you told me he'd been killed I made a few enquiries. I think I have an idea who it was – if we put our ideas together we might get somewhere.' It sounded feeble. 'But if you prefer not to, I understand.'

She considered it. I expected her to ask why she should trust me, and I had no satisfactory answer to that one. But then the doorbell rang. She stiffened and went out of the room. In a moment she came back and said, 'It's the police. Do you want to be here?'

I said no. She opened the french doors into the garden.

Along a wall of reddening creeper she indicated a way out.

'I'll call you,' I said. 'Thanks, Miss – '

'Ellerman,' she said.

Maybe it was the shock of the name, but I put Ms Ellerman to the back of my mind for what was likely to be a long time. Something else bothered me even more right now, and that was the intrusions on my privacy since I hit England. I had been tailed from the airport, somebody had turned my apartment over, although not overtly searching for anything. I didn't buy that for a minute, and professional vanity wouldn't let me accept that they were just trying to scare me. Plus, Devoil was dogging the cruddy path of Jake Cromer, and that had to be because of Cromer's association with me.

I hunched that all these visitations were linked, but for the moment I didn't want to think what freakshow was co-ordinating them. Random flak it wasn't. The salient factor had to be that call at Blakeway's flat. There was no other time I had been careless. I had gone in search of my personal life, and I had gotten a disease, and there it was.

The other problem was Gerry Rettiger – not who she was, because I knew everything I needed to know about that, but what she was about to do next. And again, the junction was that seedy apartment off Denmark Hill. I wondered what they would make of me there the next time, and once I had that thought I just had to find out.

By the late afternoon I caught Simon Blakeway in. I said he probably didn't remember me, but he said 'Yes,' curtly and with no obligation to appear amicable. His eyes looked at me just a second too long.

I reminded him anyway. 'I was here with Jake Cromer.'

'Right.'

'Can I ask you a few questions about him?'

'I don't see much of Jake any more. I doubt if I could help you.'

'Can I ask anyway?'

He said OK, and left me to shut the door on my way in.

It was a gloomy flat, with large spaces which the iron radiator under the window would never reach. A big table, covered with papers and books, typewriter and phone, all the badges of somebody running something, dominated the room. The furniture was the kind of outmoded junk that landlords shunt from one furnished let to another, and tenants try to ignore.

Having handed me a taste of his indifference, Blakeway came on a little more friendly. He offered me tea, and made it in a large stone pot that matched with his fisherman's sweater and the Greenpeace posters on the wall. I stared at the map which damp had drawn on the ceiling, and reminded myself that this was where I had first met Gerry Rettiger. I couldn't be sure what she knew about me, but whatever it was I had to assume that Simon Blakeway had access to it. He might also know about my place being shaken down. He might even be wondering where the bruises on my face had gone.

'Your name slipped my mind,' he said, handing me tea in a clumsy clay mug.

'John Goolan.'

'Blakeway, Simon,' he said.

Our eyes met again. I could handle it, but it was not a pastime I wanted to develop.

'You wanted to know something about Jake?'

'Yeah. Is he a thief, as far as you know?'

'Why?'

'I had some stuff disappear, and I think he took it. I need some confirmation.'

'What you mean is, has he stolen anything from me?'

'For instance.'

'All Jake's ripped off from me is ideas. Jake's what happens to intellectuals who don't get to be academics but can't face wearing a stripy tie every day.'

'OK,' I said. 'Did you know Patrick Moresby?'

'No. I knew of him. I didn't like him.'

'How did you feel about his murder?'

'Fine.'

'Why didn't you like him?'

'He wrote a lot of stuff against the peace movement. He was a NATO propagandist, one of those people who survey the human scene from another planet and can't be touched by it. Somebody else does the arithmetic and the hardware, and the killing, and people like Moresby wrap it up in words.'

'Is that why somebody killed him?'

Blakeway shrugged. 'It was probably personal.'

'Why?'

'He seems a bit tame as a political target. And these people have a lot of enemies. Rival egos, people they've ripped off. Maybe he screwed one student too many. The reasons for murder are usually trivial.'

I remember the passenger in the elevator as Cromer and I left that building, and the fear that Cromer gave off afterwards.

'Did you know any of the LSE crowd apart from Jake?' I asked.

'Maybe a few. It's a long time. More tea?'

I accepted. This time he also passed me a tin of biscuits. I took a digestive biscuit and dipped it in the tea. Blakeway watched and said, 'You have to drown this type.' He submerged a biscuit, and bubbles speckled the brown surface. As soon as the air stopped popping, he pulled it out and his strong teeth closed over it. 'You have to get them quick, or they disintegrate.'

I held mine under till it stopped breathing. Blakeway watched with sardonic approval. He was getting relaxed and genial. It meant he felt he had my measure.

I mentioned other names from the past – Imogen, Barry Hirst, Tessa Bateman. Simon made a noise of recognition for some and not others. Then I asked, 'Susie Ellerman?'

He wasn't thrown, and said, with a hint of distance, 'Did you know her?'

'I was just a friend,' I said.

'Susie,' he said. He said it like I hadn't heard him say anything else. It was warm and it glowed, but also it was hollow and it ached, and he wasn't the only one.

The phone rang. Blakeway excused himself, and after a minute's listening launched into telling someone why a demonstration they were planning would be a failure. He was monosyllabic and brusque, and he didn't try to fill in the gaps that followed what he said. I didn't attend too closely, because I was looking at a photograph of Susie Ellerman which he had passed me a moment before taking the call.

As soon as he hung up I gave it back to him. It made me so sad my feelings verged on sickness. 'It brings a lot back,' I said.

Blakeway was guarded, but something out of his control was going on inside him too. 'I still miss her,' he said. 'As if it was yesterday.'

I asked, 'Were you very close?'

'Oh yeah.' He almost sighed the words. He wasn't afraid to appear vulnerable. That alone gave him an authority that I tried not to be too impressed by.

'I don't want to rake something up,' I said.

'It's OK,' he said. 'I haven't talked about Susie for years. Maybe I need to.'

He gazed at the snapshot again. It showed her in a park, in the middle of a laugh, back arched and hair falling forward. It was like a still from an interrupted movie. I knew that in his mind he was trying to get the film running again. Take an infinite number of frames like that, and you still don't have a life. I had no picture of Susie, and now for the first time in ten years I was glad I didn't.

'People talk about suicide,' I said. 'I never knew the truth about that.'

'The coroner said accident.'

'Were you surprised?'

'What do you mean?'

'Sometimes people telegraph their accidents.'

'It was totally unexpected.'

'Were you living together?'

'Not when she died. I think she was sharing with this chick who reads the TV news now.'

I asked, 'Did you give evidence at the inquest?'

'I wasn't called.'

'Moresby did.'

Blakeway said, 'You seem to know a lot about it.'

'Susie was one of those people. A lot of things came together around her.'

'Yeah.' He reflected. 'Did you ever sleep with her?'

I said no, but I wasn't answering the question he was asking.

'You know she was a singer?' he asked.

I said I didn't. But immediately another thread

114

unlooped itself and I remembered something about her singing in a jazz club.

'When I met her,' Blakeway said, 'she was living with some guy – fat, greasy, middle-aged and powerful – who wanted her in show business. He fixed her up with occasional gigs, but what he really wanted was to spread himself out on her once a day. When she moved in with me he offered me a few hundred quid to hand her back. It was like that.'

'What was she like as a singer?' I asked.

'All right. She used to smoke to make her voice husky.'

I remembered the hoarse reaches of her voice, and the trace of East London in her otherwise classy accent.

Blakeway got up. 'I never play this now, haven't played it for years,' he said. He fished around in a box of cassettes and slotted one into a tape deck that fed a stereo system. As it rewound he went on, 'I recorded this myself. It was in some club, Susie doing a few numbers. The band was crap and it's all interference, but it catches something.'

His amplifier gave out a crackle, which soon got lost under the scratchy tape and the background talk and the noise of glasses. Then a hesitant piano and clarinet started up. People went on talking several bars into the piece, but settled down by the time Susie's voice cut through the tape hiss that was like the audio equivalent of smoke and darkness. I don't know if I would have identified her unprompted. But knowing that it was her, I felt a line of cool sweat begin to soak its way down the centre of my shirt-back.

The atmosphere was everything. It didn't matter how good her voice was. I didn't know the song, and her style wavered unsurely between a sentimental, Piafian gutsiness, and something more detached and elegant. When the song was over the brief applause gave way to extraneous noise again, and through the aural fug I made out Susie, in indecipherable words, announcing the next number. I was rigid with unease as I listened again. She had style as a singer. She must have been all of twenty at the time, and although they were workmanlike, the band were not in the same grade. There were spaces where somebody had to catch up, and the audience and the tape cleared their throats a lot. But on this flimsy, raucous tape of a now dead evening when London was still young, something electric sparked and threatened to flare.

I hadn't known Susie; the idea was throttling me from inside when the tape stopped. It ran out in the middle of that second song, just cut away into silence. I felt as if I was in a dark tunnel with an invisible train coming at me.

'Bloody thing,' Blakeway said. 'I forgot to replace it. It's all I've got. Want to listen again?'

'No,' I said.

'I don't react to it any more,' he said. 'Bit like a museum piece. It used to carve me up, but not now. You all right?'

'Sure,' I said, 'fine.'

We stayed silent for some minutes. I found that I resented Blakeway's possession of bits of Susie's life. He had possessed her body, and maybe more than that. There was a picture and a tape, more of a legacy than many people ever left, and Blakeway had them both. I realized how jealous mourning can get you. I looked into myself and saw my own feelings as if someone else was inspecting them. For the first time in ten years I felt active dislike for them. It was time to leave.

The buzzer on the door squawked into life. It took the decision away from me, and I didn't mind. Blakeway let in the girl I had met there before, the one who with Rettiger had treated Cromer and me to a wave of chilly silence. He introduced her as Fran. She said an abrupt hello and removed a woollen hat, shaking her hair loose, but it was short and didn't have a lot of shake in it.

'I thought Gerry might be here already,' she said.

My skin prickled, but I kept it to the skin inside my clothes. Blakeway said nothing.

Fran had an aggressive speech style that seemed not to require answers. She sat down and asked me, 'What do you do, then?'

I said, 'I'm over here on vacation. In the States I work in business.'

To an American, 'business' explains itself, but to the British it seems to convey nothing. She asked, 'What business?'

'Securities,' I said.

'Is that the same as security?'

'I guess it recognizes that there's a lot of ways to be secure.'

'Tell that to your government,' she said.

'I don't have a direct line.'

'Well, we do.'

Blakeway intervened. 'Leave him alone, Fran, he's a guest. We have some friends in common from the old days.'

'OK, I'll lay off,' Fran said to me. 'It's just that you look like a missile salesman.'

'I failed the interview,' I said.

Her face registered enough unamusement for the put-down to be clear. I wasn't too concerned. She turned to Blakeway and said, 'Shall I get a bottle of something?'

'Yeah, why not?'

Fran seemed relieved. She jammed her hat back on and shut the door crisply behind her.

'Fran can be heavy,' Blakeway said. 'It's not personal.'

I ignored the consolation and asked, 'What do you do here? What's your life about?'

He gave a deprecating shrug. He oscillated between the friendly, at moments intimate, and the remote, with great assurance. 'I work in pressure groups. Running campaigns, things like that.'

'You make a living that way?'

'There are sources of funding, if you know how to tap them. I coordinate information. I've got a microcomputer in the spare room.'

'What sort of information?'

'I couldn't begin to tell you.' He smiled. 'It's surprising what you can hack into if you're clever.'

He didn't mind me knowing he was clever. I asked where he got it.

'A lot of it's published. We don't have a Freedom of Information Act here, but a heap of stuff is made public, except that the public don't know it, don't know where to find it or how to interpret it. Somebody has to do these things. Then you have people leaking. They need somebody to leak to.'

'What kind of people leak?' I asked.

Blakeway gazed at me with a balanced cynicism. 'People who are being forced to do things they don't like. People with ideals. People with grudges.'

'How about people with power fantasies?' I said.

'Sure, why not? That doesn't make them any worse than the people who govern us. What are governments but a bunch of people with a collective power fantasy, monopolists of power? I don't mind having some dirt on my hands. It's not a clean game.'

'Specifically?' I asked.

'What?'

'What are you working on now?'

He shrugged, to signify that it was unclassified. 'This country is becoming one enormous US missile base. The Americans are making us their forward target, and to secure that they have to take over civil governments. The entire British population has to submit to the control of American bases that are so secret they don't even put them on maps.'

'That's the price you pay for 1944,' I said.

'Come on,' Blakeway said, 'the Russians soaked up the German war machine long before 1944. If they hadn't, the Normandy invasion would never have got off the beaches. And I mean the British beaches.'

'Sure,' I said, 'and the Russians would have left the West to rot away. Once they had their ring of satellites, they'd have made another compact with the Germans. In London you'd still be saluting Nazi flags and starving your life away as a slave labourer. The British ripped off the world for centuries. At least the Americans earned the right to be here.'

Simon Blakeway was not an easy man to get to personally. I hadn't told him anything he didn't know, and he was about to chew it up and spit it back at me when the phone rang. He gave me a moment's aggressive stare which said, it'll keep, and reached out for the receiver. He didn't address Gerry Rettiger by name, but I could sense her at the other end of the line. My skin got that sensation again.

He told her I was there, mentioning my name and recapitulating who I was. It seemed to get a favourable reaction. I bet, I thought. He was saying things like 'Good idea' and 'Why not?' Fran returned with a bottle in a

119

plastic carrier bag. Blakeway hung up and said that Gerry would be meeting us later. Then he asked me if I wanted to go to a party.

The place was a red-brick Hampstead house whose back faced west so the sunsets ripened its walls to a faded dusky vermilion. It was still warm, and when we got there we found a party already in action, two or three dozen people sipping drinks and chewing on each other. I had no idea what the occasion was, and I didn't ask. I was open-minded to the probability that the party was more interested in me than the other way round. It was not a dress gathering, although some people there were very well dressed from habit. The house was in a road off the West Heath, an area of which I had memories, mainly of an endless summer evening through which Susie and I had walked from the Spaniards up to Jack Straw's Castle. After talking to Blakeway I was learning to share those memories, and it freed my mind for other things.

Gerry Rettiger was already there. Her hair was almost the colour of the brickwork, as the late sunlight glowed through it. Her eyes had small wrinkles at the sides, but I felt they had got there over her dead body. Everything else about her was pastel-shade, cool and incisive. She took me up as soon as we arrived on the terrace.

'Hi, I didn't know when we'd meet again.'

'I knew it would be sometime,' I said.

She laughed. It was a nice laugh, a musical exhalation which made me uneasy because it didn't fit the challenge which my presence confronted her with. We made some small talk about our respective parts of America – she was from Philadelphia – and it was too bland, too god-damn facile altogether.

'What's this bash about?' I asked.

She guided me with her eyes. 'You see that man over there, the one with white hair and a louder than normal voice?'

I had seen and heard him since we got there. He dominated the party like a statue come to life, addressing people in a sing-song, rolling-stentorian manner that proclaimed either that he owned the place or was the one they had all come to see.

'He lives here,' Gerry said. 'His name's Rupertson, he's wealthy, and among his other activities he supports various fringe groups. Simon's very close to him.'

'And are you very close to Simon?' I said.

She raised her eyebrows.

'I'm sorry,' I said. 'I'm not interested in your private life. I just wondered how you fit into all this.'

'I do some work with the peace groups,' she said. 'At the point where it ties in with the women's movement.' I smiled knowingly, and she changed the subject. 'The dips look good. Shall we get some?'

We went to the long white-clothed table. The human background gave off the usual gamut of conversation from the conspiratorial whisper to the shrill gabble that you would hear on any Hampstead terrace on an average afternoon. From within the open french doors a hi-fi system breathed muted Vivaldi past the rustling curtains. I waited for the moment when everybody else would turn and point at me.

Somebody cooed hello to Gerry and called her away. 'I'll just introduce you,' she said, and began looking round. 'Yes, come and meet Susie.'

It's strange how you can avoid even a common name for ten years. My blood chilled, a curious tingling cold that accentuated my heartbeat. I would have suspected Gerry Rettiger of planning this, but I suspected her of too many things already. I went over. This Susie was a large blonde woman, mid-thirties, with a blank stare and a big floppy bow inside her striped suit. Almost all the women there were back in pointed-toed shoes with thin high heels, which was great for the ones who had the right legs for it. It made others look uncomfortable and somehow predatory, and this Susie was one of them. She knew I was being dumped on her, and a profound lack of appetite showed through the veneer of social arousal.

I asked what she did and she said, 'I'm working on a history of the world, written from the point of view of women.'

'It needed doing,' I said.

Irony was not a large part of this Susie's life. She smiled in a way that suggested the receiving of compliments was routine for her. She made a similar enquiry about me.

'I used to be head of the CIA,' I said, 'but I couldn't stand the anonymity. Now I write badges.'

'Badges?'

'Sure,' I said, 'badges.' I pointed to her lapel, where she was sporting a badge that read 'Peace Is a Niece, War is a Whore.' The lettering was small, so the message was only for intimates. I said, 'Somebody spent a day on that. There's a whole career in those things. It's modern man's window on the soul.'

The smile on this Susie's face had become a rictus, and she said, 'Interesting,' and looked over my shoulder somewhere. From inside, the music had changed. The sneaky opening of 'Brown Sugar' pulsed from the stereo, bounced off the walls and collided with itself somewhere in the middle of the room. It was time to explore. I asked this Susie if she wanted to dance, but she didn't think so. I excused myself and went in.

It was a long room, with a Turkish carpet in exact

proportion to the floor, smouldering inside a highly polished border of golden woodblock. The furniture had been moved back, and a few people were jigging around. They looked middle-aged and had no rhythm. I also looked less than youthful, but I had been good at this once, so I got rid of my jacket. First I shifted all the important things to my trouser pockets. I knew every salacious beat of these songs, and I danced from an era when it had still been sexual and self-expressive and not a set of disco aerobics computer-programmed to flatten your tummy and tone up your cardiovascular system. The only thing I didn't have was flared trousers, but it was the world didn't have flared trousers now.

People drifted in, and a little knot of serious dancers got going. A girl who was good at it danced opposite me. I didn't want to chance a pick-up, but the body language was fluent and cried for more. They played 'Gimme Shelter', and I had a special hip movement for that which came back so easily that I started to laugh as I pranced around. The girl laughed too. I was aware of a split in the party, of a disapproving group who thought the occasion was losing its gravity in this dervish direction. While I whirled around, I reflected some more about why I was there, and why Blakeway and Rettiger had given me such an agreeable ride.

I was there to be seen. Maybe they had plans for me later, but first they wanted somebody to look me over. I worked hard to appear not to realize this.

The man in the safari suit edged his way round the room and disappeared further into the house. I broke off dancing and grabbed my jacket and went after him. The camera was no longer in his hand but I assumed he still had it. The last time I had seen it, it was pointing at me. It was a space-age piece, and it made the most delicate whirring noise. I had glimpsed it at several different times and positions. Maybe it was normal to photograph guests at these functions, but it wasn't normal for me to be there, and some of these pictures had me in them. That may not have been the sole reason for their existence, but I gave myself the benefit on that one.

The photographer wore photochromic glasses which were still brown from the outside light as he turned to see who was following him up the broad oak staircase. He seemed to know his way round.

'Could you steer me to the bathroom?' I asked.

He smiled and said, 'Was it actually a bath you wanted, or something else?'

I tried not to look baleful, and he added in a semi-camp way, 'They're different rooms, you see.'

'I'd like to empty my tank,' I said. 'Preferably not on this staircase. Could you show me where?'

The photographer had scored his point and seemed happy. 'Yes, it's along here.'

I went with him down a stretch of landing. 'Sorry to be a nuisance,' I said.

'It's all right,' he said, 'as long as you don't do it in the wrong place.' It was obviously his sense of humour, but he condescended one degree too far. He made the mistake of opening the door for me. Before he could take his hand away I slammed him inside.

He made some outraged noises. I turned the key in the lock. It was a dandy little cubicle with a bidet and a heated towel rail and other items of basic survival. I smacked him against the wall. I looked mean. He no longer had the face-lift of superiority.

'The camera,' I said.

He spluttered. 'I don't know – '

I held his collar with one hand and, with the other

clenched, probed the soft wall of his stomach. 'Don't act dumb, I want that fucking camera.'

I shucked his skull against the wall mirror. At any moment somebody could be outside rattling the door handle. I had no other way out.

He saw that I was about to take him apart. He began to gasp. 'In my pocket –'

I slapped around his coat. The camera was a compact model which he had snapped back into its leather case. I told him to open it. I didn't ask why he was taking the pictures. I didn't want to give him anything useful to report. The film disc hadn't been removed. I put the camera in my pocket while my other hand searched him for more discs. He was clean. I hooked my fist up under his ribs. It didn't hurt me, but it left him on the floor retching for breath. I locked the door from the outside and took the key. I headed back down the staircase and let myself out the front door.

I walked to the corner, then ran, in the direction of the main road. A taxi came along on the opposite side and I flagged him in. He did a U-turn and coasted alongside me.

I got in and said, 'Kentish Town.'

The guy in front said, 'Any particular bit, guv?'

I had forgotten the address. 'The tube station,' I said.

The driver pulled out in front of an oncoming bus and said, 'We do a house-to-house service, sir.'

But my mind was already there, and he didn't press the point.

It was getting dark, and I waited till it was dark before I approached Moresby's house. There was a light on somewhere inside. A faint reflected glow painted the front window. The girl whose name was Ellerman opened the

125

front door. I said 'Hi' and smiled as disarmingly as I could. She looked lonely and I assumed that the police visit had left her depressed. Perhaps that disposed her to let me in. She let me in, and we found ourselves standing in the same room from which I had escaped that morning.

'Sit down,' she said. I sat on the least comfortable-looking chair in the room. She waited for me to say why I was there.

'Would you have a friend who develops photographs?' I asked.

She thought a moment and then said neutrally, 'Yes.'

'I have some film I have to get printed. In a hurry.'

'I don't even know your name,' she said.

I sidestepped. 'I've forgotten yours too.'

'Judy Ellerman.'

I asked, 'Did you have a sister?'

Her oval face moved and became sharper in the lamplight. 'How do you know?'

'It was a hunch. You're Susie Ellerman's sister?'

'Half-sister. Did you know her?'

'Yes, I did.'

'Is that why you came here?'

I shook my head. 'I never knew you existed till today.'

She lit a cigarette. 'I still don't know your name.'

'What did the police want?'

'Only some papers I'd sorted for them. They're looking for clues among Pat's files. They didn't know you'd been here, if that's what you mean.'

'My name's John Goolan,' I said.

I thought this would seal the first stage of our friendship. But Judy's face tightened up in a kind of sick fear. Something sucked the colour from her skin.

'I'll change it if you don't like it,' I said.

She looked down. 'Just go away.'

126

'Why, so suddenly?'

'Just go.'

'You've heard my name before?'

The cigarette shook in her fingers. I went on, 'You've got to tell me where you've seen my name.'

'It was the last entry in Pat's diary.'

I exploded. 'He kept a diary? With my name in it?'

'I only found it after he was killed,' Judy said.

I realized she was answering questions out of fear of me. I asked, 'Have the police got it?'

'No.'

'Do they know about it?'

'No.'

'Why haven't you told them?'

'Just because you're dead, it doesn't mean people can wipe their feet all over you.'

I reassessed momentarily. There was more to Judy Ellerman than I had thought. I asked what Moresby had written about me.

'He was worried about things. One day he was cleaning out his room at the School and you passed by, looked at him, and went away again. He recognized you and took it as a sign of something. The next day he was dead.'

'Why did seeing me worry him?'

'He wrote that you were an American agent.'

'Those words exactly?'

'He said CIA.'

'I had no contact with him for ten years,' I said. 'I don't get it. I thought he'd forgotten me, but all right, he remembered. But how could he think I was CIA?'

'Are you?' Judy asked.

'Let's say I work for the government. Or did. I'm not sure if I work for anybody now.'

'Why did you come here?'

'I'll level with you,' I said. 'My task was to investigate Moresby. As an ex-student of his, they thought I could get close to him. I'm as interested to know who killed him as you are.'

There was a long silence. It was a gentle silence, not menacing, but I couldn't read all the messages that room contained. Then Judy said, 'How do I know it wasn't you?'

'I had an alibi. I was at his farewell party when he was shot. You probably were too. But it's a good question.'

'He was expecting something,' Judy said. 'He was definitely afraid – or, not afraid, but resigned, he knew that a moment had come – you know – '

'He was expecting somebody, and when I showed up he thought it was me.'

'Perhaps it was you. Perhaps you've been set up.'

'Maybe,' I said. But I still had Geraldine Rettiger eating at the back of my mind, and I didn't think it was like that. I switched the subject. 'This diary – apart from naming me, does it give any leads?'

'I'm not prepared to talk about the diary,' she said.

I asked why.

'I think Pat has the right to privacy even if he is dead.'

'Was it written for you?' I asked.

'What do you mean?'

'People writing diaries usually have a recipient in mind.'

She shook her head. 'He started it before he met me. I don't think I was ever supposed to see it.'

'Somebody was,' I said.

Judy said, 'Sometimes it's to stop people cracking up, or to get at the truth about themselves.'

'OK,' I said. 'I don't want to fight you. How would you like to be the one person in London I'm not fighting?'

'I think you're probably insane,' Judy said. 'What was that about a film?'

I took the camera from my pocket and disengaged the disc.

'Can we talk about Susie sometime?' I said.

'I was fourteen when she died. I don't have much to say.'

'Can we anyway?'

She didn't answer, which was an answer. She reached for the phone, and within a minute she had fixed for someone to develop and print the film. She told them the pictures were for her.

'Eleven o'clock?' she said.

I asked if it was OK to go there.

'I'm staying here for the moment, getting things in order for the executors. So it's OK. You're not going to be trouble, are you?'

'No trouble,' I said. 'But thanks.'

This time I left by the front door, and I felt like a criminal. It gets you that way.

EYES ONLY

The tape subsequent to this memorandum was directed at the Judy Ellerman aforementioned in Goolan's text, and it is our contention that at this time Goolan was infiltrating himself into Ellerman's confidence, namely to gain her credulity by personifying himself in an accurate light incident-wise where Ellerman had her own faculty for verification, in order to then exploit this situation in a future pay-off. In this tape also Goolan manifests symptoms of severe sexual malaise of a kind not regarded with favour by this Agency, as tending to destabilize in advance an operative's field efficacy. This tape above all lends substance to the view that suspicions adhering to Goolan at this time were well grounded. In response to your question respecting Ellerman's precise role in these events, we prefer not to speculate.

Tape 5

When I look back on it I always remember first the tracks which your bra had made in your skin, the fine ripples of red against the faded tan, and the small mole at one vertex of your pubic triangle. I summon up these details with a nostalgia bordering on love, because they humanize that moment of sexual bonding. . . You might wonder, why does it need humanizing, and the answer is that it was so cataclysmic in my life that I was in danger of labelling it the far side of paradise, and I don't want to put it beyond reach . . .

I was still watching the house when you returned, and I saw your neat Renault pull into the cul-de-sac. I watched you let yourself into the house. I gave it ten minutes, and when nothing else happened I crossed the street. I sniffed the air as you let me in.

'It's just Chinese takeaway,' you said. You looked shrewdly at me. Candour was always a large part of your body speech. 'I didn't really think you were going for a meal.'

'What do you think I've done for the last ninety minutes?' I asked.

'I don't know, but not eat. I'm starving. Do you want some?'

Suddenly I was very hungry, as in seconds my mind caught up on hours of repressed appetite. You took the foil packages off the electric hotplate and we spread it all out and started eating without too much ceremony.

'I was watching the house,' I said. I wanted you to know.

I began to look seriously at you. You had an oval face and almond eyes. Your hair was medium long and looked good without the attentions of a stylist. You will look fabulous in middle age. I don't know why, but I remember thinking this as we shared that first awkward meal. We drank some wine, a bottle taken from a rack in a cool corner of the kitchen. Presumably Moresby had stocked it originally. This didn't bother me, and for once that fact didn't bother me either. It was a nice kitchen to be eating and drinking in, and I felt a devious gratitude to Moresby for it. For the first time in a week I was drawing slow easy breaths.

You asked, 'Why watch the house?'

'Neurotic habit,' I said.

'Because you didn't trust me?'

'No, I trust you. I'm like a cat that keeps catching sight of its own tail and every so often has to pounce on it to make sure it really isn't being followed.'

'So what did you see, apart from your own tail?'

'Nobody called. It wasn't exciting, but I was happy about it.'

'This is a very dull street,' you said.

I said, let's hope it stayed that way. I asked if it got to you, this being Moresby's house.

'I'd rather be here than have it stand empty. It seems a better way to remember him.'

'How long have you got to sort his papers?'

'A long time. I think there are complications about the will. The papers are the easy bit.'

'Where are they going?'

'To the University.'

'And you?'

134

'I'll edit the book we were working on. It's almost finished anyway.'

We went on eating. Your eyes looked at me steadily. Their whites were very white, and the irises deep brown, like the eyes in an Egyptian wall-painting.

'No, I won't tell you,' you said.

I laughed and said, 'I wasn't going to ask.'

You laughed and said, 'You were too.'

I shared a cigarette with you. I didn't like the smoke, only the act of passing the cigarette from hand to hand.

'You haven't asked about the photographs,' you said.

'I'm avoiding it.'

'I'm afraid I peeped at them.'

'My treat. The least I could offer you.'

'Somebody was very interested in you.'

'I hope I came out well,' I said. 'Did you recognize anybody else?'

'I didn't have time to look.'

'Maybe we can go through them later.'

'How late is later?'

'I'm in no hurry.'

You leaned across and kissed me. Your lips were neither thin nor wide, and moved on mine in a way that said everything was for giving and taking. I knew I was being used, but I was happy to be used. The problem lay elsewhere. I sat on the bath while you cleaned your teeth. I said there was something I had to tell you. You're one of those people who cup the water from faucet to mouth in the hand. You lapped it and spat it out again and looked sideways at me, quizzically.

'I can't be too graphic about this,' I said. 'I come from Nebraska, from Calvinist, American-Gothic people, good and God-fearing, who probably don't think about sex, much less talk about it. The thing of it is, for several years now – and not because I'm gay, it's not that simple – when I've tried to make love with a woman, I haven't been able to get past – I have this fear of coming inside a woman's body – '

Judy, I don't know how I ever said that to anybody. You looked back at me. You were an Egyptian fresco again, but a later, more Coptic image, with a third dimension that included compassion. Traces of toothpaste foam whitened the sides of your mouth. I envied and longed for that physical nonchalance of yours.

With a simplicity I had never been able to extend to myself, you said, 'How about outside?'

I was definitely a chronic case, as witness the fact that I could discuss all this without too much overt pain, like an old operation whose scar tissue was now a curiosity and not even part of me.

'It doesn't normally even get that far,' I answered.

Your shirt was open, halfway down, and what I could see of your tits tormented me like a mirage. They were not large, and they were unarguably tits and not breasts, to me at that moment. My throat was dry with desire for them.

'Did you ever make love with Susie?' you asked.

'No,' I said. 'I slept with her, but just sharing the bed, nothing physical. Over the years, that's come to seem how it should be. A ghost took hold of me from then on.'

You asked, 'Do you know what I was going to do tonight?'

I was a down-home boy to the end, gauche and respectful. I said, 'Whatever it was, I'm sorry to have interrupted it.'

You wiped the toothpaste bubbles away. 'Kill myself.'

You put an arm on my shoulder. 'So let's go to bed. That's something. The details don't matter.'

136

You were sufficiently like Susie, and sufficiently unlike, for it to unlock all those things. I kept a tight rein on myself to avoid saying stupid things about feeling grateful, but that was what I felt.

Eventually we passed out, in a haze of sensuality, and when we awoke again there were traffic noises outside in the daylit street.

We turned over and kissed, and even with stale furry mouths it was one of the great, indelible kisses of my life. Then I went down to get the photographs. We lay in bed and looked through them like somebody reading the early papers for a review. They were monochrome, and the definition was good. Your friend had blown them up to about eight inches by ten.

'You're sure you don't know any of them?' I said.

You shrugged your bare shoulders. 'Only this guy. I wouldn't invite him to a party.' You pointed at one of the shots of me. I nipped your thigh so that you shrieked and flinched away from me. I went with you and made love to you from behind, my face lost in the aroma of your hair. Our legs scattered the bedclothes and the pictures on the floor. When I finally retrieved them I asked if you could drive me somewhere, a few miles. We showered first, and I offered to buy you breakfast after we made our call.

As the Renault weaved its way to Dalston I listed some of the things that were troubling me. Like most lists, it made no sense without a hidden factor which the list itself did not contain. So far all I was doing was adding items to it.

I directed you from a street atlas. You let me out a few doors before Cromer's and waited in the car. Cromer's room looked over the back, but there was a front landing window, and I stood so as to be visible from there. I rang as hard and as long as it took. If he was there he would still be in bed, and I was prepared to annoy him out of it. There were some unwashed empty milk bottles on the fractured step, and when Cromer appeared in the doorway he stood staring down at them as if trying to work out why it was me waiting there and not the milkman. A warm fetid smell reached out from inside the house, and Cromer's overcoat added its own subtone of body odour and last week's beer. His face was still swollen. Instead of settling back into his face, the bruise lay there, a disgruntled purple rejected by the off-white flesh beneath. Accretions of sleep wax lay in the corners of his red-veined eyes, and even from where I stood I could tell how bad the inside of his mouth felt.

'Sorry about the croissants,' I said. 'I just didn't have time to pick them up.'

The old Cromer still lurked somewhere inside this mess. In a voice of nausea and disdain he said, 'What do you want?'

I said, 'I've got some pictures, Jake. You mind if I come in?'

He looked through me and scratched some irresistible spot on the side of his head. Then he went upstairs and I followed him.

'I've been doing a lot of work,' he said. It was an explanation, a boast, and a reproach, all at the same time.

The room was littered with books and sheets of manuscript. Cromer had the minute, fussy handwriting of someone who set greater value on his words than he knew anyone else ever would. He was back into his fantasy in a big way.

I spread the photographs out on top of the scholarly disorder which covered his table. I avoided the jar full of cigarette butts and the unfinished passion-fruit yoghurt. I said, 'Just tell me if you know anybody.'

The way Cromer scanned the pictures, I thought he was going to refuse even to recognize me. I was the star model, there was no doubt of that. The purpose of the shots had been to get an ID on me. Why, I was leaving on the back burner for the moment. But incidentally the guy had snapped everybody else on that terrace too. One of these faces jerked Cromer out of his pose of Olympian gloom. His finger was shaking as he indicated the face. The subject of his anxiety was bald, moustached, and had square-trimmed sideburns that ended level with the top of his ear-lobes. The ears themselves were distinctive, pointed at the top and, as ears go, fearsome.

'Is that the guy?' I asked.

Cromer whispered, 'Yes.'

'The guy you saw near Moresby's room and that time in the elevator?'

His voice drained away, and he just nodded. I cleared the pictures and left a couple of five pound notes on the table. The way Cromer stared at them, the Duke of Wellington could have been an accomplice.

I told you about that place in Kensington where they did a very good toasted sandwich for the time of day, but I wanted you to do a little more to earn it. While we ate I explained the next move. We left the car, and from a call box near Earls Court station I rang Philip Devoil's number. He was in.

'Hi,' I said, 'this is John Goolan. I see your friends let you out of the clothes closet.'

The voice at the other end was more prissy and uptight than ever.

'What do you want?'

139

'I want to meet.'

'What for?'

'About these documents I lifted from you.'

'When?'

'Will you be in for the next hour?'

'I don't know. I'm not sure.'

'You appreciate the importance of this, Philip? Either I see you, or I'm going to some other people.'

'It'll have to be later.'

'I'm coming over to your flat right now.'

'No, don't – I have to go out.'

'When will you be back?'

'I don't know – '

'When can I ring again, Philip? And don't snow me. No little bits of bullshit this time, or I'll bite your putz off.'

'Yes – say two – can you give me two hours – that's – shall we say eleven o'clock?'

I said nothing, and all Devoil heard was an abrupt buzzing. He would hear it for a long time after he hung up.

There was no way he would stay in his apartment after this. He would run for mother, whoever his version of mother happened to be. I quit the box and ran along to Redcliffe Square and found you at the entrance to the churchyard. From the shelter of the trees we saw Devoil appear in the marble-columned porch and step through the scaffolding down to street level. He craned his neck both ways, like a child practising crossing the road. As he took off along the square I faded, and you went with him.

I went back to my flat to pack some things. This time nobody had hammered the shit out of the place while I was gone. It was a good place to take a bath, but that apart, I couldn't get to like being there. I stared from the window at the gap in the buildings opposite, through which the Westway still pumped automobiles into distant bedroom windows. The unlived-in tidiness of the flat was a desolation. I perused a London street atlas as a gesture towards escape.

Habit, really, the habit of training, had lodged Delphine Moresby's address in my mind, and I took the map book and walked the mile or so across to the street off Maida Vale where she was living. The other time I had been there I noticed an almost empty bottle of Chartreuse on the sideboard, and equipped with a new, full one, and an extravagant armful of flowers, I rang her bell. It was early, but I knew that at least one of my gifts would take precedence over the hour.

Delphine let me in. A thin cigarette smouldered in her fingers, and her eyes looked heavy. She was about fifty, would not live to a great age, and had decided not to care.

'You want something,' she said. Her voice always had that same black-French effect of lethargic contempt.

'Yeah,' I said. 'Is that bad?'

She saw my presents. 'No,' she said, 'that's not bad.'

She led me up. We shared a jug of coffee. At some moments I thought she didn't even remember who I was, at others it felt almost unbearably intimate. She spread the bouquet around some African-style vases.

'Flowers for the dying,' she said, 'and drink for the living.'

'I guess we're all both,' I answered.

A slight twitch of her features swept the subject away. 'What do you want?' she said.

'To ask you a few questions about Pat.'

'I don't want to talk about him again.'

141

'Just one more time,' I said.

'I didn't see him for maybe eight years. What should I know?'

'I wanted to ask you about when he was young.'

'He was never young. He was middle-aged all his life, until forty, then he became adolescent. All those young girls. Then he detested anything that reminded him of his actual age. It's a certain kind of man who is like that.'

'I know you hated him,' I said.

'He also hated me,' Delphine said with finality.

'Can I ask you about something else?'

Delphine shrugged. 'Ask.'

'How involved were you with his work?'

'Nothing,' she said, shaking her head. 'Maybe I didn't want to be, but he never – he was one of those broken-up men who live their lives in sections which don't connect. I was the great ornament in his life, but he didn't give me an entreé into the other parts.'

'I suspect you didn't mind,' I said.

Delphine lit another cigarette. Asperity was never far below the surface of her elegance.

'You want me to tell you something,' she said.

'Perhaps.'

'Something that would harm him – his memory, his reputation.'

I said, 'Not necessarily.'

'Why else would you be here?' She was a pitiless realist, Delphine.

I answered, 'Sure, I want to find something out, but just to explain why he was killed.'

A film seemed to pass across Delphine's eyes, and her black skin momentarily looked ashen. I didn't know if the pain was physical or emotional, but I realized that she wasn't going to thank me for putting her through this.

'At one time he was going to write a book about the Intelligence Services – not only the British, he had a lot of foreign contacts. All I know is that he was doing years of research into this, and then it vanished – all stopped, as if it had never been. This didn't seem to worry him. About that time he seemed to become much more powerful, he got his professorship, there were all the young girls – He seemed a very happy man.'

'You think they bought him?'

'Why not? You can always buy a man like that. Maybe at the end he decided to try and wipe out his corrupt life, and they had to get rid of him. Why not?'

'Sure,' I said.

'He used to tell me little details about the girls – just to let me know how many there were, and how exciting he found them, what a connoisseur he was. There was one – I really hated her, although I never met her, just from the way he talked about her – green ice, he used to say, she has these eyes like green ice. I tried to laugh at him because of it, but he would get hurt, and when he was hurt he got very unpleasant.'

A surge of cold blood went through me, and I thought Susie, and after that I thought, Susie and Moresby. Then something in me said, come on, leave that room unopened, you already know what you'll find in there, keep the hell away from all that. I refocused on Delphine. She was becoming voluble as her bitterness increased.

'You know what he wanted me to be? Pleased. He was like an infant showing off his toys. I've always remembered that bit about green ice – the expression of a complete fraud. He was so naïve, and he was corrupt, in the way that all naïve people are corrupted in the end.'

I had nowhere to go after this. Even if she knew anything useful to me, Delphine could never get past the

143

vengefulness. I didn't feel proud having tried to make her. After a decent silence I stood up and said, 'I'll call again while I'm in London, if I may.'

She said nothing. She led me out of the flat, that flat with its musty smell and ethnic objects undusted and cramped together, and on the stairs she said, 'Don't bring me your fucking charity.'

I didn't reply. How could I, to someone who could smell the rats at a hundred paces? But Delphine had cool, and she had style too. Even having said that, she saw me down to the street door as if we had just enjoyed a sweet causerie.

'I'll drink your health in the green liqueur,' she said.

I looked at her impenetrable face, which had once kissed me so passionately. I remembered the cancer, and I knew she would die bravely and well, but somehow in a way that made you feel sorry for the nurses. I smiled gently and said 'Thanks,' and tried to observe the formal skin of the occasion, but as I walked away I shuddered.

It took me an hour to shake this off. I killed the rest of the day reviewing the questions that had piled up around me, but whether I arranged them in order of time, urgency or threat, I made no advance in clarity. If I had spent that day with you, I might have shelved some of them forever. I still didn't know why they had killed Moresby. The diary might tell me, but I was not about to use you to get to the diary, and I didn't want it to look that way. I didn't see how I could get to the diary without it looking that way.

When Moresby saw me pass his door at LSE and we exchanged an impersonal greeting, he had identified me, but he had in a sense been expecting me, to the extent that he thought it worth writing in his diary. He surely didn't know the truth about me, but the point was, he shouldn't have known anything. And then Devoil, who had been watching Cromer, had also been planting microfilm of USAF bases in Britain at drops in public places. Somebody was filtering stuff through him, and although it wasn't my business, I'd gone in too far to lose interest now.

Further, my contact for this London mission had blown. She had refused, and I guessed been instructed to refuse, to acknowledge this. She was playing me, but I couldn't see what for. I wished I had stayed at the party long enough to find out why I was there, because I figured that by now a lot of people would be wanting their photographs back, and I don't just mean the character I left choking into the bidet.

And also my employers must be getting at least as touchy about me as I was about them.

When I met you as arranged back at Moresby's house in the late afternoon, you told me, 'It was easy to keep up with Devoil. He took the tube to Green Park, then crossed Piccadilly and walked to an address in Shepherd Market, one of those smooth, sinister places that seem as if nothing ever goes on in them. There were several plates by the front entrance. One of them said JX Security Consultants, and the rest sounded vaguely financial.

You kept on the same side of the street, so nobody would spot you with a few random glances from the window. You thought I'd like that bit, and you were right. Devoil was in there half an hour. When he came out he was with another man, a large man with ginger hair and a birthmark on his left temple. They split up almost immediately. The tall man had a slight limp.

'And a check jacket?' I said.

145

You were surprised and said, 'That's right. You know him?'

'He always wears check jackets,' I said, and asked you to continue. You didn't follow Devoil, because you were afraid of overdoing it. When you came back here you thought of ringing that Mayfair address and asking to speak to Mr Devoil, just to test the water, but you waited to check with me. I laughed, and you smiled self-deprecatingly. I asked if they were phone-listed, and you already had the number. I was impressed and offered you a new role.

You dialled the number and asked to speak to Mr Fernley, with a relaxed intonation that implied you already knew him. I could only hear the briskness of the receptionist's voice but not the exact words.

Without identifying yourself, you said, 'I understand Mr Fernley wanted a companion for the weekend.'

A confused, restive gabble came down the wire.

'No, I'm sorry, I can only discuss terms with Mr Fernley in person. Is he there, please?'

The receptionist was off guard and couldn't get back on it. You pressured on. 'I hope you're not saying I've been misinformed. I was told that Mr Fernley was most interested in our services. Will you give him my number and ask him to get right back to me when he comes in? Thank you.'

You gave the number of another security firm, which we had taken from the yellow directory. When Fernley got to figuring all this out he might just dismiss it as a practical joke. Meanwhile his receptionist had confirmed what I wanted to know.

I gave you a big hug. Oh, baby. It was nice to get close to another body without fearing what it was about to do to me.

* * *

I admired your competence, but in my business you can't be impressed for long without suspicion stirring in the foliage somewhere – why should she be that good, why is she so willing? You said you wanted to go to your flat that evening, and I didn't react except favourably. It gave me the chance to break out too, although I quickly strangled the thought of following you. I wondered if you had handed me a dare to do just that.

The truth was, I didn't have many friends left in London. I didn't think Tessa Bateman would ever be a friend, but she might be useful, and I had her number, plus that compulsion to go on casting in a different part of the stream. After you had quit Moresby's house I dialled Tessa. It was an idle gesture, really, and if I had expected her to be in I guess that I might have put in more time on exactly why I was calling. But I didn't, and I hadn't, and she was. I had no flowers to offer this time, so I tendered an elaborate apology for my behaviour the previous time, and said I was due to return stateside the next day. Maybe the comfort of hearing this helped her accept my offer of a drink.

Later, I figured by now Moresby's house was probably being tapped, and even if it wasn't, Tessa's line, in view of what she told me, almost certainly was. For an idle gesture, it was a real stupid call to have made, but that thought didn't trouble me as I rode the subway to within walking distance of Chelsea and the secluded, rustic-type pub to which Tessa had assigned me.

She was wearing her hair up in a silk scarf, which made her look very different from the TV image. No doubt she knew this and traded on it. I got us both a scotch and a bottle of spring water to share, and joined Tessa in a corner.

'I'm sorry about the other time,' I repeated. 'It was real boorish, and I've been wanting to apologize.'

'Forget it,' she said. She seemed to be looking at me with a kind of tolerance, as if remembering the days when we were postgrad students together, united by an obsession with the *Times* crossword.

'I thought you might be working tonight,' I said, 'but I just took a chance.'

'No, I'm off tonight.' Her eyes kept wandering, then came back to me. 'You haven't heard?'

I shook my head – no I hadn't. I then discovered why she'd thought I called her, and probably why she'd agreed to see me.

'I'm being chopped.'

I asked why.

'You're never told,' Tessa said. 'Ratings, a new look, it's presented as a reshuffle. They've offered me a general brief to work on some news programmes, which themselves could soon be axed – it's just to save my public face.'

'Tough,' I said.

She shrugged, and watered her scotch a little.

'I'm not exactly worried,' she said. 'A New York agency has been head-hunting me for a while, and this might be the time to go with that. It could be a big favour they've done me.'

'I and your other fans will miss you terribly,' I said.

Tessa smiled, and said sweetly, 'Bullshit.'

'But why?' I asked. 'You surely don't think it was political?'

'It often is, one way or another. Not necessarily my politics, of course, but somebody's.'

'Maybe the company you keep?' I asked, and I wasn't thinking of me.

'I think I'm discreet enough in my choice of friends,' she said, and there was perhaps a sharp edge inside the velvet of her clear, deliberate diction.'

'I guess,' I said.

Tessa asked what I guessed.

'You must have been positively vetted,' I said.

'You think so?' she asked.

'Come on,' I said. 'MI5 has its own man inside the BBC; the screening never stops.'

Tessa asked how I knew, cautious but curious at the same time.

'I read it in the papers,' I said.

'Then you surely don't believe it,' she answered.

'Raincheck,' I said, and added, 'You don't think it was Moresby?'

I tried not to look too hard at her. I had delayed bringing in the Professor's name, because I didn't want to panic the whole occasion. Tessa was unflapped, but she started to clear her glass, and it was plain there wouldn't be another.

'In what way?' she said.

'Just a hunch,' I said. 'I wondered if you'd been associated with him at all.'

Telling herself that I might already know the answer, Tessa admitted, 'We sometimes met when he came to the TV Centre. He used to be called in for spot commentaries – '

'What sort of subjects?' I asked.

'Oh, I don't know – NATO, Russian defectors, that sort of thing. He was very telegenic.'

'He also said the right things.'

'Like what?' Tessa asked. By now she was glancing at her watch.

'Do you hear any rumours why he was killed?' I asked.

All the conversational niceties had to short-circuit, but I still knew Tessa wouldn't give. She was getting shrewd now, amicable but cute.

'What are you doing in London?' she said. Her body was poised to stand, and the question and the pose together put it on the line: I had one shot at an answer, to persuade her to stay, maybe to trade, and only the one shot.

I decided it wasn't worth it. Never trust the media. 'Pure nostalgia trip,' I said. 'Just like I told you.'

'I have to go,' she said, smiling.

For someone who had been fired she looked in great shape. She wished me a good flight back.

'Sure,' I said. 'I'll see you on CBS.'

'I'll always remember you're out there somewhere,' Tessa said.

'Right,' I said.

The streets smelled of wet tarmac and fresh gasolene, and we didn't know how to say goodbye. Our hands twitched but didn't connect. In the end I kissed her on the cheek, and my lips were surprised how much powder they found there. We parted, and I told myself that although this interlude didn't add much, it seemed to leave the slate cleaner for other things.

James Xavier Fernley liked to be called JF, but even better he liked to be called X – at least he did in Washington, five years ago. I reckoned that not much about the man would be different now. After forty the personality doesn't change much any more. Fernley was a comic-strip English figure. I got on with him well enough to call him X. He had a hell of a brain, and being a comic-strip character he was well suited to the secret world.

Now he seemed to have gone private. Maybe the secret world couldn't live up.

The next morning I walked into the office in Shepherd Market. I gave my name and said I would wait. A chick with purple lipstick disappeared into a maze of pearly glass partitions. When she came back she made it to her swivel chair just in time to avoid being trampled by Fernley himself. He strode at me, proffering one of those big meaty hands, held out rigid and weapon-like, covered with thick tawny hair.

'Johnny!' he roared, and in an atrocious American accent, 'Baby!'

'Hello, X,' I said.

'Hey, that takes me back.' There was the faintest trace of Irish in his voice, as from some distant ancestor.

I said, 'I didn't know if you'd remember me.' He looked mock-hurt, and I added, 'Sorry.' He gave me a playful thump on the upper arm, which nearly left me without one.

We went through to his office. From the cylindrical leg of a walnut occasional table he got a bottle of Jameson's whiskey, and we sat in black leatherette chairs to sip it. The empty chair, the one behind the desk with the elaborate intercom, looked a touch more leathery than the others. The modest wealth-concealing façade of a Mayfair street basked in a shot of late sunshine outside the window.

'This is a nice surprise, Johnny.'

'I had to look you up, X,' I said. 'Is X still OK?'

Fernley's eyebrows and shoulders shrugged in disarming unison. They said, be my guest. But that was sort of what I had come about.

'How did you find me? Bit of a backwater, this.'

'I got the word you'd privatized. It's still a small world.'

'And getting smaller, Johnny.'

You bet, I thought. Since I got to London I'd felt all the expansiveness of someone locked in a padded cell. 'You're doing well,' I said.

'Everybody's doing it, Johnny. Clocking up their time, getting the pension right, then quitting for the private sector. Face it, a lot of governments prefer us. We have the knowledge, the contacts, and we're not accountable to a bunch of fart-arse elected representatives. We run a smoother operation, we get better results, and we're cost-effective. Plus we don't fill out forms in triplicate. Then there's the other sort, of course – piss off somewhere beyond the jurisdiction of the Act and write their memoirs or plant things in the press about spooks and moles. I know a guy drives a new Merc every two years on the strength of that.'

He mused, watching me, his eyes always about to light up then tantalizingly dulling over. The plum-coloured birthmark on his temple glowed.

'I need your help, X,' I said.

'Are you still a good guy, Johnny? Not gone under the wire or anything silly?'

'I wouldn't be here if I had.'

'You'd be amazed,' Fernley said. He was bluff and genial and as cheering as the ocean around a drowning man.

I told him, 'I was sent here to make a contact, and it fucked up. I know who the contact was. What I need to know is why it crapped out. I can only give you a name.'

'We often get by on much less than a name,' Fernley said. He reached for a pad. I told him the name Geraldine Rettiger, a few details of physical appearance, and the address of Simon Blakeway. I said I thought Rettiger was the one who had gone under the wire, and as I spoke I watched Fernley for a reaction, but it got no rise out of him.

'Where can we get in touch, Johnny?'

I gave him the Ladbroke Grove number. He could easily find the address if he wanted, assuming he didn't know it already. Everything I valued was at Moresby's house now, and meanwhile anybody who wanted could take their temper out on the other place. 'I need a quick answer,' I said.

Fernley's hand closed on mine like a shredder.

'If it's not quick, it's not an answer,' he said. He saw me down to the dusty sunlight of the street and benignly watched me along to the corner. He was still there the only time I looked back, and he waved.

To a background of something by Mozart on the stereo, you were sorting through another section of Moresby's archives. You didn't look happy. I had sensed that, since my arrival in your life, the task of combing Moresby's documents into some kind of order had become less pleasurable. I didn't have a theory as to why, it was just a feeling. The music was too lively for the way I felt, so I ignored it. I guessed you were ignoring it too, but I didn't like to say.

You wanted to know more about Fernley, which wasn't surprising. I told you he had worked for the British in Washington, and now he worked in London, probably for anybody. You asked what he was likely to do as a result of my visit, and I said we'd find out. You were in a withdrawn mood, which I didn't want to disturb but couldn't avoid.

'Anything unusual happen?' I asked.

'Like what?'

'Anything?'

153

'I haven't lived in this house long. I don't know what's usual around here.'

'You'd know if you saw it,' I said, but it wasn't reassuring. I went upstairs at regular intervals to check the street. There was nothing to note out there, just cars and the occasional human being going about their business. But the siege was inside the house, in here with us. It had entered with me the first time I stepped into this elegant, deadly place.

We had lunch, but it was a strain, as if we were both waiting for something we didn't want to put a name to. You asked if we could go out that afternoon. I said, 'Where do you want to go?' but it came out defensive, like I was defying you to think of a single place. You said, 'Just away from here.' Because you sounded depressed, and although I didn't want to, I tried to make a discussion of it, until the doorbell rang. I got up instantly, with an air of readiness that probably surprised you, and began gathering my plate, cutlery and glass from the kitchen table.

'What are you doing?' you asked. You were irritated, but a reflex kept your voice low. Ultimately you knew we were both playing the same game.

I didn't answer, because I didn't need to. There was nothing on the ground floor of the house that testified to my being there, except the lunch things and me, and I soon got them upstairs. From the front bedroom window I assessed the street while you answered the caller. I couldn't see any sign of back-up out there. I knew one thing – I hadn't been tracked back here from Fernley's office. It had cost me two hours, but I would saw my legs off if I had been followed from there.

Downstairs, a male voice which I didn't know said, 'Is John Goolan staying here?'

We had rehearsed for this. You said, 'I'm afraid I don't know the name.'

'I was given this address.'

'I've never heard of him,' you repeated.

'They told me I could leave a message for him here.'

'You can leave a message, but he won't get it, because I don't know him.'

'This is very tricky,' the guy said, and there was a pause, as of him checking the address. 'Look, can I just come in for a minute?'

You asked why. The answer he gave was high on action and low on verbal reasoning. The door slammed behind him as he came in and you staggered back into the house.

'Now you'll tell me, you fucking bitch.'

He sounded cool and in control of what he was there to do. The first blow was just a slap, the second less loud but primed with the obscene solidity of expert technique, of someone who knows how to make his bone tell against helpless tissue. We had only anticipated verbal questions. We didn't want to think about any other kind. It was already too much, to hide upstairs while you got pounded by a sadistic gorilla who wouldn't believe your lies and was about to use you in ways that had nothing to do with obtaining information.

He was dragging you from room to room, slapping you and shouting and looking for signs of my being there. This gave me a chance to get down the staircase unseen. On the hall table there was a vase of dried flowers, a big Victorian object, blowsy and overdone but light for its size. I lofted it into the kitchen doorway, aimed to land behind the attacker. He was in fact a smallish, trim man, the way the real psychos always are. As six pounds of porcelain shattered on the floor I wished I had gone for his head.

It had the desired effect, it loosened his grip on you. As he spun round, his teeth bared slightly like he had waited a long time to meet me. His hand went inside his jacket, and while I was trying to decide if I had seen him before, I realized he was about to make sure I would never see him again. On reflection, I doubt that he was there specifically to kill me, but the way things worked out I prefer to think the worst of him.

The grimace on his face bared wider in a snarl that surprise alone couldn't explain. From the table you had seized a knife. It was originally a breadsaw with a pointed end, which minutes earlier we had been using to slice a Brie. Now its cheesy edge slid through its first and last rib-cage. The pointed tip must have penetrated his heart. He froze, in a moment of recognition that was too late for pain, a pain that came too late for remedy. A deep guttural groan inside him yielded to a bubbling of blood in his throat as he went down on his knees.

The knife was still in him. It was a decent knife, Swiss with fine serrations and the word Rostfrei along one side. The shards of coloured porcelain and the dried flowers crackled as he rolled over among them. I stepped past him to get to you. You hadn't known what you had been doing, and that's why it had been so effective. I gripped your arms. You couldn't speak.

As gently as I could I told you, 'He would have killed us. Don't worry, the deaths of people like that never make the papers.'

I steered you across the kitchen to the sink. I said, 'You did bloody well,' and repeated 'Bloody well' as I swung the mixer tap aside so you could get your face close to the stainless steel.

* * *

156

The leather tab on the dead man's car keys carried the Chrysler insignia, and his suit came from Marks & Spencer. That apart, he was anonymous, and it was best to keep him that way. You were swilling your mouth and washing your face under the kitchen tap, and as you towelled it I said, 'Go out on the street, walk around and look if there's anybody hanging out in a car. And watch' – I held up the key tab – 'for this make. Any problem, get the hell back in here.'

You looked sick. You stepped over the body without lowering your eyes to it, but you went. I removed the knife and put it on the floor amid the rubble. The speed with which the guy had drawn the gun, whatever his intentions, made me less than fastidious. I was already planning a discreet inner-city funeral for him. The pistol was a Walther. I wiped it clean and put it in his jacket. It would make him a less attractive corpse. When you returned I had poured two glasses of cognac. We sat in the study, out of sight of the dead man.

You said, 'There's an Alpine about fifty yards along. Empty. I couldn't see any other company.'

I looked at your drained face. The brandy hadn't pushed the blood that far. I asked if you were all right, and you nodded your head briefly, which meant, not too much.

'Did he hurt you?' I said.

'I've forgotten.'

'He would have killed one of us, maybe both.'

'Why?'

'I don't think he was going to tell us why.'

You told me that I had to know. I said I knew as much as that guy knew now.

'What are you going to do with him?'

157

'What do you call morticians, undertakers?' I said. 'Well, we're going to undertake him.'

I went out and found the Alpine while you moved your Renault off the forecourt and opened the doors to the garage. Moresby hadn't owned a car. From the garage there was a rear door into the garden.

'Shouldn't we cover him in something?' you asked.

I said, 'We'll lock him in the trunk. It could be some time before anyone gets to open it. Wrapping him in a sheet will just make it look like we were ashamed of what we were doing.'

'Won't they be able to trace the car?'

'It's got to be hired, under a false name. A man doing this kind of job doesn't leave calling cards. He accepts that if he winds up dead, it might be difficult to organize the wake. Trade hazard.'

'What about us?' you asked.

'We never existed,' I said.

I had found a pair of gloves, Moresby's inevitably. I told you to keep your hands off the car, while I dragged the body out through the kitchen. For all the effect of dead weight he was still light. Moresby's garden was only overlooked by a crescent of white houses some distance away, too far away for anybody to catch an accidental glimpse of this moment of ghoulish pantomime.

You closed the door and switched on the light from one of the garage beams. There was a comfortable space for us to do what we had to. As I took the weight of the body, you kept the legs in line and folded them to collapse into the trunk of the car. I let the door down and turned the key.

'Feel better now?' I said.

'What are we going to do?' you asked.

'Park a car.'

'Where?'

I didn't answer. I just said, 'Let's go.' I opened the garage front and drove out into the road, while you followed in the Renault. I drove west, taking convenient junctions and bits of one-way systems till I came to a recreation ground somewhere past Wormwood Scrubs. I pulled in at a nondescript stretch of road along the side of the park and killed the engine. You were still with me, and as arranged coasted a hundred yards further on. I left the doors of the Alpine unlocked and took a walk. You had the motor running, and as soon as I let myself in beside you we were on the move again.

'Why here?' you said.

I shrugged. 'Cars come and go, people bring dogs or watch soccer or look for pick-ups. There's no parking restriction, so no police or wardens are going to check out the car just because it's standing there. I left it open, so with a bit of luck some budding auto thief will take it away. By the time he notices a smell from the trunk, it's his problem.'

You seemed cooler. Maybe it helped that you had to keep your eyes on a lot of traffic. You said, 'Why are you so important that somebody wanted to kill you?'

'Are you sure he did?' I asked. 'And, are you sure it was me?'

'He asked for you.'

'But it was you he was asking.'

You passed me a pack of cigarettes so I could light one for you to smoke as you drove. It started to rain, big heavy drops that flooded the windshield before the wipers could cut back at them. London became a dismal rain-swamped waste as we drove back to that tasteful mauso-leum where Patrick Moresby had lived and a nameless, faceless hit man had just died. We didn't talk any more that journey. We both knew that a lot of unspoken words were lying in wait for us back at the house. I shared your cigarette, although I didn't know what to do with the smoke once it was inside my head. I was trying to show that I cared about you more than ever, and at that moment I didn't have any words for it.

We cleared up the debris. I split the knife-blade from its wooden haft and used a screwdriver to splinter the haft into fragments of wood which I then threw into a garbage skip outside a house which somebody was renovating. I slid the blade into the back lawn and pushed it an inch under the turf and covered it. It didn't leave a mark. We put the bits of broken vase in a bag with the ordinary household trash.

I kept watching you. Once the shock wore off it would thaw the calm with it, and I knew you wouldn't let me tender you any comfort. It was very lonely where you were, and no good me saying that I understood. Eventually you started to cry, a terrible weeping that defeated me because I didn't know what it was for. I sat with you for as long as I could stand it, then I went upstairs. It looked callous, but I was too strung out myself to take your emotion on board, and I knew you didn't want to talk.

When you came into the bedroom you seemed to have calmed down. You said, 'How did that man know you were here, if it was you he wanted?'

'It was me,' I said.

'So how, then?'

'They could have been watching the house. Or maybe I was trailed here,' I said, but I didn't believe either of those things. I didn't tell you that a tap on Tessa Bateman's phone would have put them straight on to me, but that was how I read it.

I hadn't satisfied you first time out, so you asked again. 'Why did he want to kill you?'

'It's my guess,' I said, 'that he didn't want to kill me. He was just a very nasty guy who thought hurting people was fun. Don't feel bad about him.'

'He had a gun. What did he want you for?'

'Look,' I said, 'I came here to get to Moresby. Don't ask me for a reason. I said hi to him one day, the next day he's on a slab.' I wasn't sparing your feelings at this stage. I might have to depend on you, and I wanted you tough. 'After that, people keep trying to stomp me into the ground. I don't even care to go look at Piccadilly Circus, because somebody out there is gonna step out of the crowd and sandbag me. And I don't know why. You think I'm putting you on, but it's the truth.'

'How long do we have to stay here?' you asked.

'A lifetime,' I said. 'Give or take.'

You looked washed out. After a moment you left the room, and we never revisited this subject. By the evening we were getting slowly drunk and very depressed. You were stretched tight, and it wasn't just plunging a knife into somebody's back that was doing that to you. The rain thudded on the windows, and inside we were both climbing the walls.

'Where do you live when you're not staying here?' I asked.

'I have a flat,' you said, but reluctantly. I could understand why you might want to keep one place I didn't know about. I had never mentioned it, in return for the things you didn't ask me about.

'It might be better if you went there,' I said.

You asked what about me, but I didn't answer. I said,

161

'The day I came here you told me you were going to kill yourself. Why?'

'I wasn't serious.'

'The hell you weren't serious. Why kill yourself?'

'I don't want to discuss it.'

'Neither do I. But that's not going to stop me.'

'I just felt after Pat was murdered there wasn't any point any more.'

'Were you in love with him?'

You shook your head, but I didn't believe you. I asked how he felt about you. You wouldn't react.

I said, 'I've got to know some of these things.'

You looked steadily back at me, with those eyes like a wall-painting. Then you blinked, and when the blink passed you weren't looking at me any more. You got up and left the room. When you returned it was with two large ledger-type books. I had never really believed that you had them hidden there. Maybe you had been asking yourself whether you were dumb to trust me.

'Can I insist on one thing?' you said. I signalled agreement. 'When you've finished, we destroy them.' I concurred again.

'I'm going to bed now,' you said, and came to give me a very tired kiss. While I made coffee I heard the sound of the bath filling upstairs. I settled down with Moresby's diaries, and hoped that the caffeine would work fast. What I really wanted was to be up in that bathroom with you.

The first volume dated from the early seventies. There was a lot of personal stuff, much of it incoherent, some in the form of a code. A lot of people were referred to by initials. A 'D' cropped up amid the generally stiff, bitchy comments, which I assumed marked Delphine's last, sour passage over Moresby's life. I was past exploring all that now. Then there were many academic entries and magisterial comments on public events, now long forgotten, on which Moresby had fancied himself a judge. But mostly the notebooks reflected the usual diary-keeper's pastime of acting up to an image he had of himself. I sensed a man at great odds with himself, without any satisfactory human audience, a subtle, highly disciplined yet slightly unstable man attempting to break out and be spontaneous and honest in one area of his life, and it hadn't worked.

I sat up half the night, finally falling asleep where I was. I learned also why you had secreted the diaries. I couldn't decide whether your wish to obliterate them was from some obscure love of Moresby, or disillusionment with that revered man, or revenge for the things he had written about you. I could figure all three.

It was a horror-movie experience, as the night crept on, to encounter, from the inside of his own mind, someone else who had been obsessed with Susie Ellerman. By now I knew I wasn't going to be surprised by anything. The diaries began some time after her death, but the expressions of remorse and guilt only really started after he met you. It all came out obscure, because people like Moresby are at their most cryptic in intimate journals. It obviously wasn't the whole story, but all he chose to make clear to himself was that he had loved Susie, who hadn't responded to his charm and his power, which made him love her all the more. After her death he seemed to feel, mainly through his lust for her, that he had helped cause her death. I could only extrapolate this from random fragments in the journals, but already it had a gruesome familiarity.

Moresby enjoyed plotting emotional and sexual games, and he liked being the spectator of his own skilful manoeuvres, and the things he wrote about Susie, and for that matter you too, Judy, were no exception. I kept having to remind myself that she was dead when he was writing all this stuff, so I discounted half of it as post-mortem self-justification. When he wrote of Susie, the word 'maddening' was salient, and Moresby's thoughts seemed to turn to her in conjunction with feelings of his own aimlessness, of his life running down and the fear of giving way to despair. Adrift in middle age, he constantly returned to his relationship with Susie, to relive it, to find himself in it, to ask forgiveness for it. He was not specific about the sexual aspects, but sexually Moresby was an inconsistent self-revealer. He was one of those puritan sensualists whose passion is driven by disgust, and Susie seemed to be the only woman he had never had enough time to be repelled by.

The phrase 'green ice' occurred – 'she had eyes like green ice, and even now she is gone they still enslave me'. He wrote a lot like that, but for all the pretentiousness the diary had stab marks of pain all over it, mixed up with the heavier political material. A computer could have collected all those scraps and discovered a trend and capped it with a high-resolution graphic of Moresby's personal mandala, but all I had was the waning night-time and a brain that felt like the Chicago Bears had just worked out on it. I tried not to get involved with Moresby's suffering or both our recollections of Susie. I had other reasons for scanning these notebooks, and I could take the things about Susie without needing to push myself into death with her any more.

When you arrived in his life, applying for the post of research assistant, it seemed to provide a solution. He didn't pick you for your academic skills, and the fact that you didn't know about his relationship with Susie provoked a strange excitement in him and occasioned a lot of rambling, introspective entries. He also started to record a peculiar male-menopause fantasy to which the key seemed to be that he must never have physical contact with you. Mentally, however, he had a hell of a lot of contact with you, and it was all there in his scrupulous handwriting, along with notes on various women he was screwing over the years. It was no weirder than anybody else's sex life would be, written down, which is to say, pretty weird. But I knew why you hadn't enjoyed reading it. The whole thing was a man confessing to the world in order to keep the truth from himself. Every page reeked of it.

After hours inside the tormented mind of Patrick Moresby, I let the volume drop from my hand, and passed out. I awoke to the daylight washing through the fine, richly coloured curtains, and you moving about in the room. I tried to stretch the ache out of my body.

'I've made some coffee, and I'll run you a bath,' you said.

I said something grateful, but it emerged as a groan, and something creaked when I moved my neck. You came and sat in a bamboo chair while I soaked in two feet of water.

'In the end,' you said, 'he wasn't a very nice man.'

I said, 'Who is, if it's all written down?'

'Do you think that was all?'

'Enough,' I said. I could see how the references to yourself had blinded you to some of the other content.

'Enough for what?' you asked.

'I know who killed him,' I said. 'Now I know why they killed him.'

We both tensed at the sound of sprung metal and the

ensuing thwack inside the hall of the house. Our eyes met, and I made an attempt at a laugh, but it was getting less funny all the time. The paper was delivered like that every morning. You just stacked them in a corner, and we never opened them, but today, perhaps to defuse the moment of shock, I went and got them. The *Guardian* had a sub-headline on its front page: 'Professor Alleged Killed by Peace Movement'. It rehashed the career and murder of Moresby, indicating that suspicions now existed of a link between European peace and terrorist groups, which had produced a hit-list of targets drawn from their common enemy. The enemy in this case was naturally the US primarily, the armament faction generally. The article left it like that, vague and unburdened by fact, a good filler for the front page on a news-empty day. I passed it to you, and watched the disbelief grow in your face as you read it. You asked what I thought.

'A flier, somebody either keeping the story alive or trying to steer it away from the truth.'

'Do you believe it?'

'Not after last night. Have you ever felt a news headline was directed at you personally?'

'That's how you feel?'

'Yes.'

'What are you going to do?'

'Call a guy.' I dialled Simon Blakeway's number. He was still in, and when I announced myself he didn't sound the least bit surprised. He came on as if he couldn't quite remember the last time we had been together. The evening in Hampstead had disappeared into oblivion. That suited me for now.

'Simon, a couple of things. Do you have a number where I can reach Gerry Rettiger? And, I've got something important I'd like to show you. Can I come over right now?'

'It's tricky,' Blakeway said. 'I was just on my way out. I'll be away for a few days.'

'I'll delay you by an hour,' I said. Across the line the silence was heavy with reluctance. 'And on second thoughts,' I added, 'would it be possible for you to ask Gerry to be at your place as well?'

In the end Blakeway said OK, but he didn't mean it.

You drove me south of the river and left me to walk up Denmark Hill. The traffic was grinding its way into central London. Dregs of autumn mist lay in the courtyard of the block where Blakeway lived. Even the inside of his flat gave off a chill that ate into my clothes. Blakeway's high-domed bearded face looked earnest and clean, morally clean, with the look of people who have won through to some plateau of unshakeable certainty about the world. The world, at this moment, didn't include me.

'I can't hang around,' he said. 'I'm giving evidence at a public enquiry about a nuclear power station. I'll be gone a few days.'

'Did you call Gerry?' I asked.

'She's coming over. What was it about?'

'That party in Hampstead,' I said.

'Oh yeah.'

'You gather I left early?'

Blakeway had a good line in showing that things weren't important by not reacting to them. He gave me that obsidian stare. We had both loved the same woman, and I always found in his presence that I couldn't feel as hard toward him as I had programmed myself to be. He went on packing things into a canvas bag while I stood there.

'I noticed you'd gone. What happened?'

'Have you seen today's papers?'

'No, why?'

'They've got a new angle on Moresby. They reckon the peace people killed him.'

'The peace people,' Blakeway said derisively. 'Those well-known deviants with green faces and blood dripping from their fangs.'

'The story could be planted as a double bluff.'

'So could every other story.'

'You don't buy it?'

'I don't give a wank about the late Professor Moresby. Is this all you came about?'

Blakeway was careful not to convey too much disappointment, because that might have told me that he knew enough to have expected more.

'Who is that guy Rupertson?'

'Do your research somewhere else.' His voice rose in imperious irritation. 'Come on, man, I'm busy.'

From one of the photos I had cut the face of the man Cromer had identified. Identified, I reminded myself, in this same block of flats. I took it from my wallet and showed it to Blakeway. It was unlikely he would place the cut-out as a still from the party.

'You ever seen him?'

Blakeway shook his head, with just the right degree of indifference.

'I understand he lives round here.'

'So. One of thousands. Why should I remember if I saw him?'

'You don't know him?'

'No, but just for laughs tell me who he is. I want to know what I've missed.'

The ascetic righteousness of Blakeway's face gave way easily to a leering smugness which said that the game was as good as up, and he didn't have to pansy around with me any more. And now, at the end, he couldn't resist letting me see this. So I didn't see why I should go on fighting it either.

'I'll tell you who you are,' I said. 'Just a freebie from your neighbourhood intelligence man. You're a fink. Don't get me wrong – finks are important people. Society would break down if all the inmates observed the code of silence. But you fink on the peace movement. I don't know why, but you do. I don't care about it, except that you insult my intelligence by pretending to be something different.'

A moment of cold triumph hovered in the pupils of Blakeway's eyes. Telling me that, whatever I knew, I no longer counted for anything. He sneered and said, 'Go fuck yourself.'

Temper surged hotly inside me, like a haemorrhage inside my chest. I wanted to try him out physically, and I had just kicked off my self-control when the knock of a hard object against the wood came from the door.

I went straight across and opened it, ready for anything. Blakeway realized the experience he had just missed out on, and stood back, suddenly and openly scared. Gerry Rettiger stood there. My unexpected appearance gave me one moment of advantage, like the one I had gained when I saw her at the rendezvous an instant before she saw me. I still hadn't found a way of using these advantages.

'It's all right,' I said, 'I'm coming out. She looked past me into the flat, but I pulled the door shut on her line of vision. 'It's not a pretty sight in there,' I said.

Her look was unfriendly but respectful. 'What do you want?' she said.

'We have to talk,' I told her.

'About what?'

'Let's get out of here. Do you have a car?'

'Why the hell should I go anywhere with you?'

My left hand, without giving either of us any warning, grabbed the flesh of her shoulder and almost tore it from the bone. My other hand twisted her right arm up her back so that a breath of wind would have made it snap. I marched her along the landing. I guessed that she could handle combat to a degree, but I was the stronger and in less of a mood to frig about. We got down to the courtyard, past the art deco doors with brown paper stuck over the broken pane.

'All right, all right,' she said.

It was her dignity that hurt. I let go. Rettiger repossessed her body without grace.

'You sonofabitching bastard.'

'If there's one thing I hate,' I said, 'it's touching a woman in a place where she doesn't want to be touched. Nothing ever works after that. I'll know next time.'

We got in her car and drove out onto the main road, against the flow of traffic.

'Now what?' Rettiger said.

'Go where you like,' I said. 'We can talk in the car or we can get out, it makes no difference. But only you can remove this ache I have. It's called being fucked about and not knowing what's going on.'

'What should I know?' she said.

'If you want to play stupid, go ahead, but you'll ruffle me, and I'm already in no mood to be nice to you.'

She was over-revving her car in the low gears. I hoped it was a sign that she was rattled. Everything else about her spelled out confidence, and that rattled me.

'I don't think I'm the person you need,' she said.

'So who is?'

'That's your problem.'

'You were my contact. Or are you going to deny it?'

A slight twitch of her head and shoulders said that she wasn't, but that it didn't cut it any more.

I said, 'Is there any reason why you can't explain your grounds for aborting that meeting?'

'Yes, there is,' she said coolly. 'I don't trust you.'

'So what's your briefing on me now?' I asked.

'Simple. You're classified as a risk. I don't know how long they're going to let you run around like this.'

Through Rettiger's self-control I could sense a vein of professional rivalry about to be gratified by my wipe-out. 'What makes me a risk?' I asked.

'If I told you that, you'd be an even bigger risk, wouldn't you?'

'Listen,' I said, 'I was sent here to deal with Moresby. Somebody shot him before I could even talk to him. Then I was instructed to await a contact. The contact turned out to be you. But the problem was that by then we'd already met, in circumstances that compromised us both.'

'Wrong, buster. That compromised you.'

'OK,' I said. 'So you were supposed to be there. You're not undercover, or they wouldn't have used you to contact me. Your front is that you're working for the company but have slipped the leash. That's compatible with Blakeway being a fink, which is what he is, and you're running him. Just tell me why I don't blow you.'

'Who to?' Rettiger said, and she was together enough to make me feel that it really was a dumb question.

'The peace movement for a start.'

'No dice, sweetie, you're already tagged as CIA. I've blown you.'

Rettiger stopped by a stretch of parkland, the kind that outer London throws up in little clutches here and there. She got out and started walking like I wasn't there. I followed her. I realized it was a sore point, but I caught

171

hold of her shoulders and turned her to look at me.

'For one minute,' I said, 'stop disliking me and tell me what I should do.'

Rettiger was direct. 'Wait for them to pull you in.' She coldly disengaged herself from my grip. 'And work on your story.'

She walked on a bit further, down a path where the golden leaves blew fitfully along. I thought she was expecting me to make an exit. When she saw me still there she went on, 'You arrived at Blakeway's flat one night. I didn't know who you were. You weren't alone. The next time I met you, that first occasion had to make you suspect – don't you see that? Look, I don't want to speak down to you, but you are asking the questions with your feet. Since then, every time you crop up, I feel I'm in the presence of a rabid animal. Why did you beat up the man at the party?'

For once Rettiger sounded sympathetic, although she wasn't giving much away. I looked at her like a guilty schoolboy and said, 'I couldn't begin to explain.'

'As of now,' she said, 'I don't know you. I'll have to report on this meeting, naturally.'

'I don't like the word "rabid",' I said. 'Couldn't you use "temperamental" instead?'

Gerry Rettiger gave me a half-smile and said, 'Sorry, pal, you're too late.' She walked away again, and knew that this time I wouldn't go after her. I don't like being creamed by somebody else's decisiveness, but at that moment I had no choice. I came out on a hillside in the park overlooking miles of London sprawl, gasholders, tower blocks, acres of slate rooftops, flyovers, a railway yard – all a long way from anywhere I wanted to be.

* * *

Back at the house you were out. Because I didn't expect you to account for your every movement, this didn't worry me at first. You might be at your own flat, which I knew you went to from time to time, that part of your life which I hadn't intruded myself on. All the same I rang the number several times, but you weren't there.

Some hours passed, and my irritation grew. I had needed to talk something out with you when I got back, and I was annoyed that you weren't here, annoyed too at my dependence on you. I realized that I wanted you to break the logjam for me, tell me what to do. I was getting weary of toughing it out alone, and my head was full of B-movie images of you and me together in scenes of impossible simplicity. I realized that the situation had slipped out of my grip as casually but firmly as Gerry Rettiger's shoulders.

The phone interrupted this reverie. I guessed it was one of those sporadic calls we had been taking for Moresby, from people who hadn't heard the news, editors of overseas periodicals, wrong numbers, double-glazing salesmen, some of them genuine. Or it might be you. I picked the receiver up and said, 'Yes?'

The voice at the other end sounded as toneless and impatient as mine. 'Judy Ellerman?'

I said, 'What about her?'

'Is she at this number?'

'Did she tell you she would be?'

'Look, my name's Adams. *Guardian*.'

'You wrote the piece on Moresby today,' I said.

'Right. This Judy Ellerman called the paper earlier. She left this number. I phoned and made an appointment to see her. She's two hours late.'

'To see you about what?' I asked.

There was a pause, and I knew what was coming next.

173

'Do I know who you are?'

It was my turn to hesitate. Mentally I shook a dice, in a hurry. I only had one shot. If I needed Adams, I had to make him need me.

'Can I call you back in five minutes?' I said. 'Did Judy give you the name of anyone else, anyone she could trust?'

Adams said, 'No,' and sounded a mite too satisfied about it.

I didn't want to mention the diaries in case Judy hadn't told him about them. 'I'll get back to you,' I said, and hung up. There was no point in ceremony. Adams would be suspicious in any case because I was taking this time out. Whatever I said when I rang back, he had labelled phoney in advance. If I rang back.

I made a rapid survey of the house. The diaries were not where I had last seen them, on Moresby's study table, where I had – stupidly, on reflection – left them, or anywhere else. There was nothing else missing that I could see, no sign of your having left the house for more than a brief spell or under any duress. I was angry at this, and something in me wanted to plant my Nebraskan boot right across your pretty ass for getting involved in this farrago. Even when I reminded myself that only yesterday you put a knife into somebody's heart because of me, I still felt angry. I was glad you weren't here for me to bawl out, because I would have to sweat a lot to make you forgive me afterwards.

Deliberately, in the event you were using it for a hiding place, I had stayed out of the attic. Now I pushed up the trapdoor and eased the folding aluminium ladder down. There was a switch on a rafter, and the attic lit up from three neatly stationed bulbs. It was empty. Moresby hadn't been a hoarder. Immaculate runs of pvc cable were

174

stapled along the beams, channelled down under the bedding of fibreglass insulation. There was no sign of its having been disturbed. The valve on the cold tank dripped slowly. I went back down.

Either you took the diaries, or you stashed them where even I wouldn't find them. You intended to give the diaries to the press. This was originally a question, but I already believed it. Why, I didn't and don't know. Maybe you didn't want to take it any more. Or you want to shake off Moresby's ghost. You showed the notebooks to me, and perhaps this sheared away the compulsion to keep them secret from the rest of the world.

But even if I have a theoretical reason why you wanted to see Adams, I have no idea why you failed to keep the appointment. Or why you have not been in touch with me. One thing is for sure, Judy honey, you're not walking the streets in a state of indecision.

I rang Adams back as I said I would. My five minutes was precise. A female voice said he was on the line to someone else. I hung up. Suddenly there was nothing I wanted to tell him, and nothing he was going to tell me.

And because something is definitely over, and something totally different about to begin, I recorded this.

H. T. Kuunas – EURCOOPS

From W. J. Shealor

EYES ONLY

We in this Agency would hereby request you to take cognizance of the fact that Goolan has in a to-date reading of this evidence been observed to totally compromise the woman he used as confidante as well as the donor of sexual favours, to wit by placing on record her complicity in a killing. Judgment is still suspended as to whether Goolan's account was as upfront as he takes pains to induce. Notwithstanding these factors, the discredit accruing to Goolan via this latest recording we regard as critical prosecution-wise.

In the tranche of notes pursuant to this memorandum, Goolan reveals himself as an irrevocable renegade, a rogue elephant whose private hungers have now comprehensively displaced his operational duty in the area of real issues. We would not anticipate controversy in this sector.

Tranche 5

I'm back in the room, awaiting dinner. Boy, I'm hungry too, but I wish to Christ they'd just leave a dog-bowl outside the door so I could trough down without formality, and then sack out and forget this whole fucking shenanigan.

The outer annexe of Fernley's Shepherd Market office was a spectral maze of frosted glass, impossibly subtle shades of grey, and potted plants with in-bred dust-repellent, a cool and misty adumbration of the next world. The girl with purple lipstick had been replaced by one with astroturf-perfect orange hair, and fingernails painted with red, white and blue stripes. Underneath, it could have been the same girl, but if it was she didn't recognize me. Maybe I lacked the necessary visual impact.

I said, 'I have to see Mr Fernley.'

'Do you have an appointment?'

Her voice was bored and suggested low mental activity. I don't know why this surprised me. 'I think he would want to see me,' I said.

She gave me more speaking-clock voice. 'I'm afraid it's impossible without an appointment.'

'OK,' I said, 'can you tell me when is the earliest I can see him?'

'I'll have to check.'

'Please do that.'

'Could you call back?'

'I have to know now.'

I guessed that if Fernley was there, or one of his aides, they would have been gathering by now. But the only action was from behind an opaque partition where a xerox machine hummed contentedly as it printed and collated papers. The technicoloured receptionist started to say, 'I'm sorry – '

I interrupted. 'Honey, I have to know now.'

She sighed, through flaring nostrils, and muttered the word 'Tracy', and another girl materialized from the layers of pearled glass to watch over the reception area. I smiled at Tracy, but she looked stony and pretended to be absorbed in a shiny desk top with nothing on it but a blank VDU. Fernley had them well trained. The other girl came back on high heels that wobbled slightly and said, 'Mr Fernley won't be free for at least four days.'

I said, 'Honey, go right back in there and tell Mr Fernley that I want to see him now.'

'He's not in his office,' she said, like a trump card.

'I want to make an urgent appointment.'

'I'll take note of your name and the nature of your business, and when Mr Fernley's considered it we'll contact you.'

'Go get his appointment book.'

'I've already told you, he's – '

'Go get the book, honey.'

She hadn't liked me from the start. She liked me even less now that she looked at me over the barrel of an automatic pistol, a small neat job with the squat cosy menace of a Walther or a Makarov. One glimpse of the glossy black metal convinced her. Her face paled, and the orange hair began to look sickly. She tottered back to Fernley's room. I herded Tracy along and went after her, watching for give-away moments that would signal the triggering of an alarm. The place had to be creeping with them.

Orange-hair passed me the book. There were other rooms in this firm, but their high-quality veneered doors stayed shut. I could deal with anything that came out of them. I pointed into Fernley's room. 'Stay in there.' I closed the door on the girls, took the desk diary, and got the hell out of the building. I had left the pistol on the reception desk. It was a good realistic model, and I regretted that I didn't have some gunpowder caps to leave with it. A brisk walk took me to Berkeley Square. In Curzon Street a taxi drifted by and I spotted Fernley inside. He caught sight of me at the same moment and affected a friendly wave, but his meaty face lit up in a confused expression of real surprise and barely concealed anger. I still tied the visitor we had killed to Fernley, and I was sure JX himself had a lot of questions to ask me.

He started gesturing at the driver, and I anticipated his bulky emergence onto the street, dodging along a mews alley lined with sleek trattorias and effortlessly rich fine art shops. After a corner or two I had lost Fernley before he could even get me back in his sights again. I walked more slowly and riffled through the book as I went. Finally I tore out the pages for June 20-28 of that year, then I dumped the book so it would be clearly visible in a trash can. I ripped up the pages and disposed of them elsewhere. If the book itself found its way back to Fernley he might spend some time working on why I had such an interest in his life between those dates. The answer was, I didn't, but I found it very useful to know that Fernley was acquainted with a man called Rupertson. They had even met three days before – the day I first encountered Rupertson on that Hampstead terrace.

Wait for them to pull you in, Geraldine Rettiger had advised. But that wasn't really an instruction, it was a stalling device. The problem was, who would do the pulling? I had the feeling that when it started, my legs would be going in different directions. I went back to Kentish Town to move out. They had hit Moresby's house, and now Judy had disappeared, and I was in no mood for the rabid dog treatment, not without getting a few bites first.

In a small hotel of diverse customs and practices near Paddington, they had locked away a suitcase for me and accepted a sum of money to cover one month's caretaking. I was still well within the month as I went to reclaim it. The contents were of no great value, and anybody who had broken the lock in search of fair pickings would have found only a change of wardrobe. To the casual thief nothing else would have been obvious, particularly the false bottom inside which, packed tight in air-bubbled polythene to give no impression of movement or sound from within, a Colt automatic waited for me.

I travelled by subway. It was raining when I went underground, and raining harder when I surfaced at Kentish Town. Clouds like coalminer's phlegm hung over the city and punished the streets with rain that rebounded two feet in the air from the greasy tarmac. Darkness was coming down early. I hung about in the tube station hallway.

Another traveller, a passable-looking cultivated type also afraid to leave the dry, turned back from the mouth of the subway, specifically to me.

'Far to go?' he said.

I smiled ruefully. 'Some way.'

'Want a lift?'

When they came at me, this would be the way. I answered, 'No, thanks.'

He pointed across the street. 'That's my car over there.' He seemed eager for me to believe him. I ran through the possibilities. He didn't seem like a gay pick-up artist. He might be an honourable Christian gentleman, but that was already too much to take on trust. Then he might be a lot of other things I didn't want to find out about.

'It's all right,' I said. 'I'll wait it out.'

'This could last for hours, you know,' he said.

He was a touch insistent, and I expected a briefing on London weather at this time of year. I said, 'Thanks all the same.'

He seemed mildly offended, and insisted, 'You're not in any jeopardy, you know.'

'I never said I was, friend.'

'You're damn well insinuating – '

It if was a ploy, it was clever. If he was genuine, I could see his point. If he went on any further, I would have to loosen his teeth.

'I respect your generosity,' I said. 'You have to respect my right to decline.'

He looked huffy, almost hurt. I had made him feel foolish, and that put him out. 'It was meant in the sincerest way,' he said.

'Sure,' I said. 'Thanks.'

He pulled his collar up and went out into the rain. Across the street he got into the car he had indicated and pulled away. I knew it was all my imagination, but there were so many shadows dancing in my mind that I couldn't shrug it off. The day you had no imagination in this game, you were dead.

The storm growled distantly over the hills of London and the rain bit down hard. I walked through it. There was no point running. I would save the running for when I might need it. I had a spare key, and got into Moresby's house and put a gas fire on for my clothes to dry. I changed into a new set and checked out the gun. I preferred an arm with a barrel shorter than the Colt's five inches. It weighed over a kilo, and I could do without that too. I rehearsed the movements: it was well broken in by Uncle Sam and they had greased it so it worked effortlessly as an organism. I broke the profound silence of Moresby's study with the clicking of the automatic as I got the feel of the springing and the safety as I brought down invisible intruders in the doorway.

Finally I loaded the seven shells. My cache had thirty-five rounds. I never knew who had costed the ballistics of my mission, but I figured that after seven shots either I had lucked out or I didn't want to be around anyway. I hid the other four sets under the fibreglass in Moresby's attic.

When the phone rang I supposed it might be the reporter, Adams, calling to ask why he hadn't heard from me again. Or somebody who wanted to know if I was at the house. I took up the receiver but didn't answer. The voicing of the very faint 'Hello?' that came down the line conveyed fear.

'Judy?' I said.

'John, is that you?' She was almost breathing the words rather than speaking them.

'Where are you?' I said.

'I can't talk long. Listen – ' She speeded up, once she knew it was me. 'I'm being held. I found this phone, but I can't stay long. There's a code on the phone – write it down.'

She gave me a six-digit number. 'Do you know where you are?' I said.

184

'No, I don't even know which way we came out of London. It's very flat around here, that's all I – '

'Did you see anything from the window?'

'Only fields, a ruined house, and some sort of canal.' She sounded badly scared. 'Find me, for God's sake.'

I took a breath. 'Judy,' I said, 'it's going to be hard, but this is where I pull out. It's all getting too deep. I already have my ticket back to the States. Otherwise somebody's going to kill me.'

The feeling of betrayal at the other end was so potent and bitter I could embrace it. The silence was equally eloquent.

'Don't expect me,' I said. 'I'm sorry. Goodbye.'

Lightning struck somewhere near by, and the thunder-crash was instant and devastating, sending a tremor through every window in the house. Then the storm wheeled away again. Moresby's desk lamp flickered for a second while I combed through the book of telephone codes.

There were thirty pages, and it took me nine of them to tie the number Judy had given me to an exchange listed as Dillbourn. That was not necessarily the village she had called from. I searched Moresby's library. He had been a reference book man, and a comprehensive motoring atlas located Dillbourn somewhere in eastern England, north of Cambridge. Only one village of that name was listed, and the terrain fitted with the flatland and drainage dykes which Judy had suggested to me.

I fought it, but I couldn't shake off the awareness that she had suggested it all too damn well. The phone she claimed to have discovered was too convenient, and the person who had written the local exchange number on it could not have been more helpful. The only advantage I had scraped for myself – and it was hypothetical – was that Judy, or the people monitoring the call, would not know for sure to expect me. That was some advantage.

Days ago she had given me the spare key to her car. It made life easier at this moment. I loaded everything into the Renault and said goodbye to Moresby's house forever. It was so sad to discard so brusquely something that had marked so many important scenes in my life, but at that point I didn't have the right emotional coinage for too much sorrow. The Renault had a trombone gear-shift which I found tricky, and I kept sounding the horn by mistake, but I was a million miles nearer Judy already.

I threaded across to the origin of the M11 and headed out of London in the direction of Cambridge. I could pick up a local map in the area of Dillbourn once I was there. On the way I cursed a lot because I had only taken the exchange code, whereas if I had asked Judy for the house number I could trace it exactly. Or, if she had told me: because there was a doubt prickling in my mind about the nature of this set-up. A set-up it undoubtedly was.

It would be easy to pretend that, as I drove out into the rainswept, flat darkness of eastern England, I knew what was coming, and that was why I drove with a certain desperation. I wanted to see Judy again, but almost certainly not in the circumstances that awaited us both. Apart from that, my eagerness was just a matter of having so many things to get away from. I called it a day at Ely. Through a miserable night the cathedral, floodlit, drifted above the town like a vision, and I knew how the architect seven hundred years before had first seen it in his mind. I checked into a hotel, and the next morning I bought a map.

Imagine an area of flat country which was under the sea until centuries of reclamation and an elaborate drainage system rescued it, with few trees and nothing you could call a hill. Translate it to a map and you get what I was looking at, a white page of flat terrain devoid of contour strips and covered with a grid of fine blue lines indicating dykes that fed into the massive drains that threw the flood water right back in the sea's teeth. It looked a hell of a place. From the hotel I got the telephone company and found out what villages were on the Dillbourn exchange. On the map I drew a circle to encompass the villages in question, which gave me a few square miles of desolate fenland, dotted with isolated farms and crossed by only one major road. Everything on that map was labelled 'fen' or 'drain', and designated by a network of spidery lines.

The idea I had formed proved accurate enough when I drove into the area I had circled. What I hadn't predicted was the feeling of exposure. The roads were raised, and you could sense the oceans of water still out there somewhere, swelling themselves up to return and retake these plains someday. Efficiently cut dykes lacerated the landscape, there was no clear horizon in this world where the fields just went on, and I felt more conspicuous than I ever wanted to be in my life. Nebraska is also a wide open space, but the resemblance ended there, and I didn't feel at home.

I had sliced into the fabric of the passenger seat and fixed the automatic inside with insulating tape. The district I had pinpointed was easy to patrol – the more so since I had no idea what I was looking for. Judy had mentioned a ruined house and a canal, but the ruined house was no clue; it could be anything. All the same, I was looking out for ruined houses. I had nothing else to go on.

But in the middle of a great flat expanse of nothing, a landscape bare of hedges or trees, I was developing an acute feeling of claustrophobia. I knew I would have to wait for dark, even as I drove down a lane which for once I couldn't see the end of. It led to one of the villages within the circle. There was no dyke running parallel to the road, and the road itself was not merely a plane surface tapering infinitely into the distance. Past some scrubby undergrowth, even the ghost of a hedgerow, the land buckled slightly and the lane twisted. Maybe it led into a finger of country which the North Sea floods had never quite closed over. It was the most seductive thing I had seen all day.

Before I followed the turn in the road that brought me in sight of the Army personnel, I had one more thought. The idea had not really struck me till then. They would have planned for Judy to give me the telephone number entire, and from that to trace the precise location. So if they were expecting me at all, they would have planned for me to be zeroing in on the exact house she thought she was calling from. I toyed with the idea that in not giving me the total information, Judy was sending me a message.

One thing was not speculation. The two Army men were waiting for somebody, and they were not about to stand and watch as I halted and reversed the hell back out of there. Even at a hundred yards, everything in their demeanour said they were not about to do that.

They wore mottled combat jackets and green berets. I didn't fancy an argument with marines of whatever nationality. One of them, the heavy moustached one, had a sub-machine gun strapped behind his shoulder. They looked patient, friendly even, like nothing surprised them less than me turning up there. I programmed myself to behave as the idiot tourist bemused by the timeless muddle of English country lanes. Right from the start I knew it didn't work. Their jeep was blocking the road. As I slowed down, they took a step toward me.

'Sorry,' I called, 'is that MOD property? I seem to have gone wrong somewhere.'

The older marine, a middle-aged man with the lean, well-scrubbed youthfulness that way of life gives them, asked me in a manner that was deferential but positively not servile, 'Where were you headed for, sir?'

I had my answer predesigned for just such a situation. 'I wanted to get to Newmarket without going through Ely.'

The moustache with the gun made a tour of the car's outside. The other marine noticed the map on the passenger seat and asked to see it.

'Perhaps we can show you where you are.'

'It's all right,' I said, 'I'll just back down here and – '

But the game wasn't even worth playing. As I handed the map over, the marine said, 'Mr Goolan, is it?'

The circle I had drawn couldn't incriminate me more than my own name at that moment.

'If it's not a stupid question – ' I said.

He didn't open the map. He just passed it back to me. Perhaps they were giving me a chance to reach for a gun. Moustache was beyond my field of vision, and I guessed his fingers were stroking the SMG in anticipation.

'It would be a stupid question, sir.'

'OK,' I said, 'what do I do?'

'Just leave the car, sir, if you wouldn't mind.'

I got out slowly, keeping my hands visible. The moustache went over to the jeep, always watching me, and made a muttered call on a field telephone. I looked at the older marine. His grey eyes and chiselled leathery features told me with friendly tolerance not to bother asking anything.

189

The sky was fractured by a brace of planes, F-111 bombers that snaked low over the flat terrain and were gone, pursued only by the sound of the rending air. I knew their provenance. They were US Air Force planes from what the roadsigns only posted as 'RAF Lakenheath'. But at Lakenheath the sole RAF personnel was a single liaison officer who dealt with complaints about the rolling thunderous noise of the endless take-offs by the flights of bombers stationed there. The base itself housed five thousand USAF personnel on two thousand acres of British soil, an arsenal aimed at the heart of the Soviet Union. Britain was a small country, and since 1950 it had been a whole lot smaller.

I asked where I was. The marine said, 'There'll be a car here for you shortly.' But I knew exactly where I was, I thought. Along this road lay the house with the telephone number which Judy had been looking at when she called me. I was chewing this over when a large Rover saloon bounced down the lane towards us. The driver didn't believe in methodical braking.

'Thanks, lieutenant, I'll take over now.'

'Very good, sir.'

The two marines took up a respectful distance, and the newcomer approached me. He had the well-bred anonymity I knew so well as the mark of a certain group of public employees.

'Mr Goolan? My name is Legion.' He paused. 'No cracks. I dislike cracks.' He had Fernley written all over him, even to the extent of James Xavier's slightly drawling speech mannerism.

'If you'd get in the car, please. Back seat.'

'I have a few things – ' I said, motioning to the Renault. Legion shook his head, as if he already knew what I meant. If he was one of Fernley's boys, the marines had

190

handed over to him, and the marines were for real, so that made Legion official and told me a little more about Fernley too.

In the back of the Rover there was something else. I didn't look at him too closely. In that sadistically pleasant British way he said, 'Sorry about this,' and handcuffed me. Then, as the car vibrated into action, he put a blindfold on me.

All along I had thought I would make it to that village at the end of the track. But the jeep didn't move, and the Rover turned about and took a course back where it had come from. The driver took it very fast, and I soon gave up trying to calculate mileage or directions. The driver was a smoker, I guessed pipe rather than cigarettes, and the one next to me wore some French-type stuff under his arms which even this early in the day was getting sour. I felt safer while the car was moving, but I held myself tense for any movement to my right which would suggest a pistol being drawn and aimed at my head. If I concentrated hard enough, I assured myself, I would know where the pistol was.

It was maybe half an hour before we stopped. As the time passed I knew they were not going to kill me. They didn't need to drive that far. Eventually I heard gravel under the tyres, and the car rocked to a halt. The man in back fed me out with the cuffs and the blindfold still on. I was guided up some steps and into a house.

By now I had realized that the number which Judy had seen on the phone was put there for the occasion. She could have been ringing from the place they had brought me to now, or from anywhere. They had suckered me in, knowing I had no choice but go along.

They took me to a room and freed me. Although the light in the room was poor, as my eyes were exposed my hands went up to shield them. When I took them away again it was to see Fernley, meatily genial, standing in front of me, legs planted firmly apart. His voice boomed off the wood panelling around the walls.

'Johnny! Baby!'

He didn't sound paternal, but then he didn't wish to embarrass.

We psyched our way through the wordless beginnings of lunch, just the two of us alone with the scraping of the cutlery against the china. I wasn't hungry, but I ate to keep my sense of balance, apart from which you never knew when you might get the chance to eat again. I felt Fernley's eyes playing over me across the length of the polished table. I didn't know if he wanted to irritate me, but he succeeded. I decided that my silence gave him too open a field in which to enjoy the scam he had pulled on me.

'OK,' I said, 'so you ripped me off. So what?'

Fernley beamed, his big ugly face lapping it up, as if he had broken me into speaking.

'We all have to give sometime, Johnny,' he said. He always had that cryptic, confidential way of talking, as if to say intelligent men got straight down to the subtext without garbageing around.

I stared at him with all the cool I had. 'I wouldn't give you the time of day.'

His coarse, thick hand, every finger like a bratwurst, swept my scruple aside. A man who thrived on needle, Fernley. 'Johnny, let's stick to business. Eat a good lunch, then a spot of business, like a good chap, eh?'

'What business are you in, X?' I said.

'OK, Johnny, I won't prat about with you. By now you

gather that I'm legit with HMG. In our freedom-loving democracies the state is on the wane, and governments like people who can go out and generate their own income. They like me, Johnny. I give them everything they need, and boy, do I know what they need.'

'The need to bring me all the way out here?'

'The Brits like to get away from it all. You know how it is – weekend in the country, that kind of thing. You Yanks go for a walk in the woods, we find that the odd muddy field helps us make the tough decisions. Shades of Agincourt and Waterloo and all that rubbish.'

'You never really left, then?' I said.

'You never really leave, Johnny.'

'Just tell me one thing,' I said. 'Who's the enemy on this one?'

Fernley had just stuffed his mouth with a hash of cold meat, mayonnaise potato and lettuce, but it didn't stop him answering.

'Good boys and bad boys is always a tricky one, you know that. If you could go out there and just label the bad guys, hang a card round their necks, it would all be easy – take them away and bump them off, no more problem. But what if some of them were really good guys, and some doing the bumping off were in truth naughty chaps in disguise? Chaos, my friend, a jolly poor show. But that's how it would be. So that's why people like you and me are able to ply our skills.'

'Thanks,' I said. 'Is this it? After you've rehabilitated me, do I get shipped back to the big city to start a new life as a useful citizen?'

'You're almost there, Johnny,' Fernley said, 'almost there. Relax a little, finish your lunch, we'll go for a little drive.'

* * *

193

'You see those fields, Johnny?'

I looked out of the Rover. It was the same car I had been handcuffed in, but now I sat freely in the front passenger seat. I stared out and hoped the fields I saw were the ones Fernley meant. We had coasted along country roads through a more undulating landscape, no longer the fens. Here there were hedges and woods and hills, and something Fernley wanted me to look at. After the warm-up over lunch, we were both shaping up. In spite of his avuncular style, I knew that really Fernley was thirsting to ream my ass.

I had my own gambits to make. 'Sorry about your appointment book,' I said.

Fernley was careful not to show rankle. 'Small potatoes, Johnny. All in a day's work.'

'It's in a trash can in Berkeley Square if you still want it.'

The birthmark on his temple was like a Rorschach blob, and right now it conjured up to me the condition Fernley would really like to see me in. But he was under orders too. He didn't have all this pull on his own.

'You always were a humorous one, Johnny,' he said.

'Did you know,' I said, 'that the one thing that never changes across the whole of a person's life is their sense of humour?'

'You're a good operative, Johnny,' he said. 'In the garage of politics you're a good little grease monkey.'

He pronounced 'garage' the American way. And when big men like him used the word 'little', they weren't being friendly.

'What about a guy who came to call on me, with a gun in his clothing?' I said. 'Would he be anything to do with you?'

'All in good time, Johnny.'

194

'He went on a trip. If you want his forwarding address, let me know.'

Fernley said, 'Are you a country lover, Johnny?'

'Depends which country.'

'That's what we were wondering, Johnny.'

He pulled the Rover in and stopped, half on a grass bank, half on the road. He jabbed a large finger at the view. In a hedge along the road, where a track branched off, there was a painted wooden sign, the paint blistered and the wood part-rotted. It said Ugly Farm, and it sure looked it. But Fernley was staring past the sign, and his eyes had a rhapsodic mania in them.

'Somewhere out there, right at this moment, they're building the underground bunkers and the missile silos. This little old island scared the shit out of the world plenty of times before, and she's not finished yet. A green and pleasant land, Johnny. Bristling with dragon's teeth, and that's the way we like it.'

I yawned. 'You British must be out of your fucking minds.'

'Do I hear you right, Johnny?' Fernley said. 'Are you not a US government employee? Is this the voice of the US government I hear?'

'Listen, pal,' I said. 'Uncle Sam likes a good deal. If the guy he's trading with is an idiot, that's not his problem.'

Fernley drilled me with a gaze. 'And where do you stand in all this, Johnny?'

I said, 'If the British want to hardball with the big guys, there's a price to pay. Militarily you've handed your country to the USA – you know it, I know it. It's not my problem.'

'So why the evasive attitude?' Fernley asked. 'Why not give us Brits more credit for paying our dues?'

'In the cause of what?' I said. 'World peace?'

'That's it, Johnny.'

I laughed through my nostrils. 'Who are you kidding, Fernley? Britain moves towards a war economy because people like you want to go on feeling powerful. Don't get me wrong – I don't care, it's your business. But you know the US will never go to war to save Britain. The Soviets could wipe you out for breakfast and as far as we're concerned the good news is that it's weakened them for when the real thing starts. And the British government can jump up out of the ground like gophers, but you and I both know what they'll find.'

'You disappoint me, Johnny.'

'I guess.'

'We can't leave it there, of course. With you disappointing me.'

'I had that figured too.'

'The importance of the UK at the present time,' Fernley intoned, 'is that if we go, Europe goes.'

He waited, but I didn't reply. He wound the window down to let some air in. Somewhere above us another flight of bombers screamed through the banks of low cloud.

'I'm talking cruise,' he went on. 'You know exactly what I'm getting at, but I'll spell it out for you. A lot of elements in this country would love to stop any further developments of the British security system. Halt it right now, and then dismantle it. Weapons systems are like a business, they're either expanding or dying. It's not in their nature to stabilize. Now these elements, if they all come together at the critical time, could spark off a Europe-wide resistance, coordinated and no doubt funded by our enemies, and we could have one hell of a time beating that. Whereas if Britain goes cruise, the rest of

Europe will follow without a murmur. And in no time they'll have forgotten the day when they didn't have cruise. They'll live with it and love it, and they'll be well softened up for the next stage in the escalation. This is the battle we're fighting, Johnny. And we have to destabilize our enemies before they can get their arses organized. We have to keep the bastards walking on jelly.'

'Thanks for the drive,' I said. 'I have a feeling we're not through yet.'

'You came in at a tricky point, Johnny. There's always a good reason why things happen, if you search deep enough. You're still a very valuable member of the team.'

'Great,' I said.

Fernley said, 'I tell you that just in case you'd lost some self-esteem over all this. Plus we want you to know that we're decent, patriotic people. Your kind of people, Johnny.'

He switched on the ignition, and the Rover's engine roared agreement. I watched the Ugly Farm sign as we passed it, and wondered if this place realized that its time had come.

I didn't let Fernley work on me, and I didn't try to work on him. I knew by now that he wasn't the king-pin. He was there to tenderize me, not to do the eating. They showed me to my room. I realized that my presence in this country house was of the type that meant I had to have my own room. But the windows and doors were left unlocked. They knew I would get the message. The room had a washbasin and some toilet things, a bed and a chair and not much else. The chest of drawers was empty save for a pale blue pamphlet called *Cruise Missiles: A Vital Part of the West's Life Insurance*. I thought it was a spoof, because life insurance only paid off after the owner was

197

dead, but I read it and it was no spoof. I guessed they had put it there for me. It was a change from half a lifetime of Gideon Bibles.

Across the landing a small toilet cubicle had been left conspicuously open. I made a visit there, and before I got back to this benign cell I heard a footfall at the end of the landing. Around the corner came the ponderous figure and white-maned head of the man I knew only as Rupertson. He turned up a little half-spiral stair and I watched as he grew from a torso to his full height. He wore a tweed jacket with elbow patches and a spotted handkerchief drooping from the breast pocket. He kept his eye on me with steely precision as he approached. His Hush Puppies squeaked on the polished oak floorboards.

I didn't have any idea what I was waiting for, but it seemed the most natural thing in the world when he clasped my arm and smiled confidentially, saying, 'My dear Mr Goolan, do come and join me.'

A minute later we were in his study, among the cases of butterflies and stuffed fish, and he had already invited me to ask him anything, anything at all, and he would do his level best to answer. I took a drink before the dream faded. It was usually bad news for things to be this easy.

'OK,' I said, 'for starters, why was a guy called Philip Devoil taping microfilm of American bases for somebody to pick up from phone box drops?' I figured if Rupertson could bounce that one back at me, he could accommodate them all.

In his studied, sing-song drawl he said, 'I think you know the reason for that.' He stressed the word 'know', in a mild reproach.

'I'd love to hear it from you,' I said.

'Very well. The gentleman you refer to places film for us in British intelligence, some of it cooked up, some

198

authentic. Why, you ask. Well, as you're aware, planting disinformation is one thing, tracing the people who pass on the good stuff is something else altogether. We play at both tables, of course.'

He beamed. His eyes were round and fishlike, but strangely peaceful and wise. 'Next?'

'Devoil works for Fernley?'

'You surely know that, or you wouldn't be asking.'

'Various people have pursued me or wanted to give me a hard time since I came here – '

'Mr Fernley's employees. Not always the cleverest of people. However – What you want to know is why you attracted so much aggro.' He made it sound very English.

'Astonish me,' I said.

'We had word that you were here possibly to abduct the late Patrick Moresby, and we had our own plans for dealing with the good Professor. You were not part of them. You also, I understand, fouled up with your own people. That was unfortunate, but we often deserve our misfortunes, don't you agree – sometimes manufacture them, even?'

He sipped his scotch and didn't care if I agreed. I refused to ask about Judy, because it would be like fixing the electrodes on myself and placing Rupertson's hand on the switch.

'Simon Blakeway?' I asked.

Rupertson gave a slight raise of the eyebrows and said, 'You realize, I'm sure, that the peace movement, so called, incorporates a range of people not all of whose interests are either peace, in the normal sense of the word, or indeed the security of this country. For that reason we have a number of people who have thought deeply on this matter, strategically located in that movement to serve as, let's say, filters. National security has a great deal in common with the water supply, if you think about it.'

'Blakeway,' I said, 'is a frustrated romantic, probably defeated in peace movement power games, a sneak from university days who's still rattling on people who regard him as a friend.'

'He is one of us,' Rupertson said genially.

'He might be on our side,' I said, 'but he's not one of me.'

'As you wish.'

'Why is Geraldine Rettiger involved with him?'

'She passes on chickenfeed to some of the politically more ambitious peace people. Blakeway is her passport, her ID. And she is his super-ego – I'm sorry, a poor Freudian joke for which I apologize unreservedly.'

'That party at your place in Hampstead?'

'Just a party.'

'Why the photographer?'

Rupertson's manner was almost camp as he answered, 'Oh, parties are more fun if one takes a few snaps. We were interested in you. We're satisfied now, and it's a measure of my personal confidence that you're here. You must realize that Mr Fernley's agency has no official contact, and none of any kind with the CIA. They were briefed to conduct a routine surveillance on you, which was intensified by your suspect behaviour. But we feel comfortable with you now, and we're all back in bed together.'

'So I'm up to date,' I said. 'Then what?'

'You'll be my guest for dinner. Yes? There's someone who's dying to meet you.'

Call it instinct, or a psychomotor defect, or plain stupidity, but I couldn't face this room any more. Rupertson escorted me back upstairs. It was a rambling house, and clearly only got up to look as if people actually lived in it. No other secret service in the world could be so well off for ancient buildings, so loaded with dry rot. Rupertson suggested I might need to rest for an hour before dinner. He didn't lock the door or chain me to the bed, but I took the point. Two minutes later I quietly closed the door behind me and went walkabout. I was interested in any detail that might strengthen my hand at our next meeting. I also wanted to find out if they were holding Judy there.

I made it to the top floor. One of the boards creaked. There was a musty smell up there, as if it wasn't heated much in the winter. All the doors I tried were locked. From a small window I saw over a corner of the grounds, where an old man was tending a bonfire. The smoke was drifting towards the house, and as I looked he turned his eyes in my direction. I quickly drew back. The corridor was bare except for flyblown prints of Victorian legal figures arranged in precise rank along one wall. I moved along to a corner, round it and down a half-flight of stairs, then turned another corner – and it was here that I was seen.

I stopped, and something inside me froze and became very still. The man I was staring at was the materialization of a nightmare. He was bald, neatly and assertively bald, and his sideburns were carefully, squarely trimmed, forming a matching set with his moustache. His eyes slanted at the sides and had a malignant sparkle. His ears were prominent and pointed at the top. I knew every detail of that face, and I had known that eventually I would have to measure up to it. Its owner watched me with the same air of finality. I braced myself for the first flicker of movement from his hand. He was ten yards away, and the corner was a yard behind me. I stared at the face which

Cromer had identified as Moresby's killer. His eyes refused to leave mine, and I knew that he knew everything that I did.

His hand went to his pocket. I moved sideways in a powerful, lashing, crazy action that took me in a monkey-like ballet round the turn in the corridor. I couldn't breathe until I was sure that bullet had missed me. But the crack I waited for didn't come. I staggered upright, shelving my confusion, and ran back to where there was an alcove that would shelter me. I got out of sight as the footsteps came after me.

He wore soft-soled shoes, but the emptiness of the corridor magnified the slightest sound. Generations of discreet adulteries had made the musty walls sensitive. I stood in the window recess and didn't even think, because in that place thought would have been audible. He had a microsecond to see me before I hit him.

I got my left arm round his neck, with my right arm tightening it back, like a shackle on his throat. At the same time I pulled him downwards so that my knee could grind his lumbar vertebrae. He groaned and struggled. It was not a difficult hold to counteract, so I expected him to come back at me. He looked strong, but I had the edge in terms of shock – more than enough, it seemed, because he went down like a giant kitten. He wedged one hand between my arm and his throat, but that was only because I let him, and I only let him because he didn't seem to have any fight in him. I allowed for the bluff, for the moment of relaxation in which I would suddenly find myself on my back with his knee in my groin and his fingers in my eye-sockets.

But it wasn't going to happen. I pulled myself back from the edge and released him before I killed him. I frisked him first, but he had no gun. I leaned against the wall while he dragged himself up and collapsed on the window seat. The breath spat out of him.

'My God, was that necessary?' Apart from what I had just done to his larynx, he had a gently spoken voice which didn't gel with his evil features.

'The best policy pays up before the accident,' I said.

'You must be mad. What did you think I was going to do?'

'What were you going to do?'

'I was on some business for Mr Rupertson.'

I remembered the way Jake Cromer had shaken and sweated over the photograph of this man. 'Who the fucking hell are you?' I said.

His voice was soft, plaintive, verging on the apologetic. 'My name's Moon. I'm a duty officer.'

'Do your duties include assassination?'

'I don't understand you,' he said.

'Moresby,' I said.

'You think I killed him?' A spasm of well-bred outrage distorted those of Moon's features which had returned to normal.

'Didn't you?'

'Certainly not.'

'But you were there.'

'I was on lookout. My God, I don't kill people. What do you think I am?'

I kept my hands behind my back. My fingers were drumming on the wall.

'An apartment block on Denmark Hill,' I said. 'Does the name Simon Blakeway mean anything to you?'

Moon was busy readjusting his tie. He said, 'I don't have to tell you anything.' He looked at me. He knew that before he could summon help I could take out on him some more of the tricks life was playing me.

I spoke to him very quietly. 'You were doing something in the same building Blakeway lives in. I can see by looking at you that you don't live there. So what was it?'

'We were working in the flat above,' Moon said.

'Wiring?'

'Yes.'

'Did Blakeway know you were bugging his flat?' I said. While Moon was thinking about his answer I said, 'Of course he knew, he was the bloody quizmaster.'

I paused while my pulse rate came down below a hundred and my brain left off hammering the inside of my skull. 'Is there a girl being held in this place?' I asked.

Moon said he didn't know. I couldn't prove he was lying. I had no further desire to beat him against the wall.

'Who killed Moresby?' I said.

Before Moon could dodge the question we both heard Rupertson's aristocratic drawl resounding towards us. Moon gratefully dusted himself down, and I knew I would never get an answer.

H. T. Kuunas – EURCOOPS

From W. J. Shealor

EYES ONLY

As you point out, in this recording Goolan is addressing himself directly to the above writer. Since for normal procedural security reasons not one word of this tape is admissible evidence-wise, I have therefore no further comment.

Tape 6

This one's for you, Shealor, you smooth bastard. My recollection of that meal doesn't run to the food or drink or who served it, or what security clearance I estimated they had to have. Once I saw good ol' Wayne Shealor in there I didn't think about anything else.

Your greeting was businesslike but warm, as if you had something to make up to me. You looked the same as when I last saw you, the same bushy hair that you can almost see growing, the steel-rimmed glasses and the orthodontic smile. The clasp of your hand left mine a helpless jelly, and your voice filled the room without trying. The same old Wayne.

'John, buddy, long time, long time.'

Rupertson beamed at us in the background. 'You know Mr Shealor, of course.'

'How are things, Wayne?' I said.

Your full-lipped grin told me that from your point of view things were fine, and from mine – well, you'd be letting me know. 'We'll talk over dinner,' you said. And that was it.

Rupertson had the whole thing staged, except for our casual clothes, or maybe he always ate like that. Over the brandy and cigars, which you and I both smoked just to humour him, Rupertson said, 'Apart from the obvious charm of the occasion, Mr Goolan, we are met here to discuss your mission in this country.'

'Since I came here,' I said, meaning to England, 'life

has got complicated. I don't know what I'm doing any more.'

Rupertson breathed smoke into his brandy glass and watched it drift over the tawny liquid, then said with bland generosity, 'This is why Mr Shealor has been brought in. We hoped it would clear things up your end.'

'Always nice to see a friendly face,' I said.

You said, 'We just wanted to make it simple again, John.'

'Sure, I appreciate it.'

I thought about Judy, but it was the same as all the other times I thought about her – a frozen image that I was afraid to thaw. I knew you were both waiting for me to speak her name, and you had everything planned from that moment on. I didn't ask about her, because it would hurt too much. Most likely you had not reckoned on that possibility. You thought I was being tough.

'It's still the same assignment, John,' you said. 'The same pay-off at the end.'

'It doesn't feel the same,' I said.

You asked me if I wanted out. I said, 'No, but only because I know how far out "out" can be.'

Rupertson's face, below the fleece of white hair, was flushed and well-fed. He seemed to be enjoying all this hugely. 'That sounds like a good line to end on,' he said. But you had got less mellow. Across the table a beady-eyed sharpness glowered back at me.

'Listen, buddy,' you said, 'two things, right, and get this straight. First, our British friends had their own emergency programme relating to Patrick Moresby, and they had to go overdrive on that one for reasons which have been made clear to you. They had no time to warn us, and all we could do was put you on the back burner. Then you turn up in a place where you should never have been, where everybody is suspect and has to be checked out. You didn't know the operation we were running there, and you walked right into it.'

I tried to remember why I had ever gone to Simon Blakeway's flat. My obsession with Susie Ellerman had got lost in time somewhere, like the ache people are supposed to feel in limbs that have been amputated.

'The guy that brought you there,' you continued, flicking your middle finger at me like a switchblade to signify a new point in the analysis, the way a whole clique of you do at Langley all the time, 'we had this guy looked at and frankly, he's a person that's never going to come out clean. His own mother would have to think carefully about showing on the street with him.' Your monkishly razored blue jaw flexed as you prepared another lunge. 'So you knew him ten years ago. Surely to Christ that's the best reason for avoiding a person?'

I knew that you were just clearing your chest because the doctor had told you to cough, Wayne, so pardon me if I didn't get too excited. 'I'm no good at apologizing,' I said.

'Who needs it?' you said. 'From now on, just play ball.'

Rupertson had a dozy smile on his face, and seemed eager to usher us out. You got rid of me first. As I was leaving the room he laid his hand on my arm and said, 'My dear John, the business we have the honour to be in may be called Intelligence, but that doesn't mean we have to be too intelligent.'

He was a little drunk, and it wasn't snappy enough, but he laughed at it himself. I would have laughed too, but I could tell how many times he had said it before. You just don't laugh at epitaphs, somehow.

* * *

I should have felt good, but I felt like shit. I had been seduced into your parlour, and by all the standards the politicians, philosophers and agony aunts invoke, it was a sewer. You very smartly reminded me that I had never done anything I hadn't chosen to do, and you were right. I had fucked up enough people in the past and expected them to take it, but I hadn't acquired a taste for being fucked up myself, especially when you wanted me to feel warm and grateful about it.

What ate me worst was the way I had resisted all temptation to mention Judy. I had sweated that one out, in the belief that I was saving something of myself that the stench couldn't pervade. And by a fine irony the only result of it was that I knew I would never trust her again. Because I didn't trust her – that was really why I kept quiet, and I had just confirmed it. I had betrayed both of us worse by saying nothing.

I had also shown you that I was a man who could detach himself easily from his deepest feelings, act as if they weren't there. In other words, I had demonstrated that I was exactly the schizo you were telling me I was. Call it totalitarianism or just good management, but once they know you better than you know yourself, you're not human any more. You had gotten me to feel that without once ceasing to be sweet to me, and that was really clever, too goddamn clever by a long shot.

At one point in the conversation you made an interesting reference, Wayne, as part of your program for softening me up. 'They were lice,' you said. Rupertson had left us alone for a minute.

'Maybe,' I said.

'Lice, John,' you repeated. 'Better off dead. The world was a cleaner place without them.'

210

'There's half the human race you can say that about,' I said.

You're not an easy man to budge, Wayne. 'Somebody has to make the judgments,' you said. 'This old world never was a come-as-you-are party.'

'Death makes them like all the others,' I said. I thought, death humanizes everybody, whatever scum they've been before. I didn't go so far as to say this to you.

'You feel like an assassin?' you asked me.

'That's about it,' I said.

'You accepted this assignment.'

'It felt different back in the States.'

'Reagan's cut public spending. It's not like the old days. We can't send shrinks out on missions now. You have to make it on your own.

'How many have you killed, Wayne?' I asked.

'Three. And one of them, I put the gun to his head and blew him away, and believe me, it's worse than you read about, because words can't convey the body heat and the smell. It's the smell you never forget. The rest washes away. That's something you've never done, John.'

You were soft-pedalling me, because the second man I killed was about to kill you, and half did. I didn't think about it. I shot a man who was about to rip you to death after kicking half the life out of you. It was easy to do, a relief and a mercy, and my only concern at that moment was saving you. You survived and did well, but I guess you didn't do well by nursing sentimental attachments to people just because they saved your life once.

You remember that dead guy, Wayne? An American, working for the other side, who could have been useful to us except that he wanted to go out the hard way. Maybe you don't remember him anymore. It was in Iceland, and

I was thirty, and my pubic hair and the hair on my chest had as yet no grey in it.

The other man I killed, it was in anger. I did it with my bare hands, and he would have killed me if I hadn't. That guy was the first, one of those virginities that you lose in the half-scared but fascinated appetite for whatever comes next. It's only later that the knowledge becomes sickening, deadly. Obscenity is just the exaggeration of a common defect, and a dead body is obscene because it exaggerates the death present in every one of us.

Calling them lice didn't help, Wayne. Calling them traitors made it harder, and telling myself it was just a job made it worst of all.

So they drove me back to Ladbroke Grove. As soon as I got in I dialled Judy's number – her own, not Moresby's place. When the receiver was lifted, I was already sweating in anticipation. She was there, as if knowing I would call. The bait had worked, and they had released her, but at the back of my mind heavy odds said she had never even left London, and I was in no doubt now that somewhere along the road they had gained Judy's complicity. I tried not to care how they had done it. Suddenly I wished I had a pet name for her, something that would declare that we were still the same people we had been before. But all I said was 'Hi.' She must have thought me a jerk. I sure felt it.

In this penultimate notebook, as we in this Agency will proffer as our finalized adjudication, Operative Goolan reveals beyond further query his ambivalence towards his mission and his determination to smear the authority which ultimately he was contracted to serve. His account, let it be said, is partial in the extreme, and we would state forcefully at this time that no one has been found to lend it corroboration.

Tranche 6

Under the night the river's oily swell tore the reflected lights apart and churned them up. A heavy wind shook the air, with a suggestion of squall that gave the Thames Embankment a sudden maritime feel. It had left off raining, but everywhere patches of yellow light spattered the wet streets, rippled by the cars that swirled by in the darkness. South of the river somebody was setting off early fireworks. As we stopped to watch, a shower of green glitter hit the sky, then disappeared, and after it a Roman candle shot up, bright red and enduring. It hung there for a long time then glided diagonally down, like a signal flare or a warning. It was a warming, pleasing sight, out there over the murky glow of the city, but by the time it finally went out we still hadn't found a way to say things.

I had my arm round Judy, but the raincoats we were wearing sealed us from the kind of physical closeness that might have broken through where words had no power. She lit a cigarette, and I shared it. The smell was good on the raw riverside air, better than the taste of it.

I had already said it once, but I said it again: 'They didn't hurt you?'

'No.'

'They were using you to get me.'

'They seem to have succeeded.'

She was cool and fastidious, and very remote from me, although we were both being very polite about it.

'If you blame me, I understand,' I said.

215

'For what?'

'Look,' I said, 'if you tell me everything that happened, maybe I can fill in some details, and it might become clear – '

'What everything? Nothing happened.'

'You've really no idea where they took you?'

'I told you, it was somewhere in the country. They must have wanted me to call you, because they gave me so much opportunity to do it.'

'What reasons did they give for holding you?'

'No reasons.'

'Did they identify themselves?'

'People like that don't have to identify themselves. Do they?'

'Don't they?'

'Have you ever identified yourself? What do I really know about you?'

'What did they tell you about me?'

'Nothing.'

She turned her head away as we walked. The wing of hair fell across her forehead and added to the shadow over her face. I was beginning to realize why she had insisted we meet in a public place after dark. I had never walked far with Judy before, and I was surprised at how fast she walked. It seemed like her normal pace, not hurried, but it deflected a lot of the tension. Our steps made solid tattoos on the Hungerford footbridge, and the other side of the criss-cross girders a train dragged itself into Charing Cross station. The irritation of being made to appear stupid was seeping into my voice in spite of anything I could do.

'What do we do now?' I asked.

'What do you want to do?'

We had only kissed once when we met, and it had been

216

a false moment. I slowed right down now, so she had to clip her stride or leave me altogether. She turned and I watched her face in the light from the terrace of the Festival Hall. It was as pale and beautiful as the moon on a frosty night, and as communicative.

'I guess you're going to say we can't get back to where we were before all this happened,' I said. 'For Christ's sake, it's only three days. What's happened to us since then?'

Judy seemed more vulnerable now, and the feeling showed. 'Well, what's happened to you?' she said, her voice strained.

She knew before I spoke that I was going to lie to her. It was only a matter of how deep the lie cut. 'I'm the same guy I was before,' I said.

'Why did they want you so badly? And when they'd got you, why did they let you go again?'

'Do you know who *they* are?' I said.

'Of course I bloody well know.'

'OK, tell me who they are.'

Her face expressed a vaguely theatrical distraction. 'I don't want to say it. And I don't want to say who you are either.'

She walked away. I could have let her go and ended it at that moment, with the rainy air misting the lights of London's South Bank and the river groaning behind me. Something told me not to go after her, but it didn't tell me why. I was desperate for reasons, and I ran after her. There was no point being proud, because nobody would see it. On this street, I felt, for once nobody was watching. I walked alongside her, just to let her know I was there and wanted her.

'Honey, this is insane,' I said. 'Can we go somewhere for a drink?'

'Don't call me honey,' she said, then, 'All right.'

We went into the next pub we came to. It was full of smoke and the smell of fresh bitter from the bar and stale bitter from people's mouths. In one corner somebody was pounding on an off-key piano. I made myself heard through a wall of South London accents and finally squeezed over to a side of the bar where Judy sat crouched on a stool, looking miserable and unforgiving.

'We have a choice of three comfortable bedrooms,' I said, 'and we're sitting here.'

I only quote that because it was the smartest thing I said that whole goddamn evening. Judy sipped her scotch. She wouldn't meet my eye more than momentarily.

'For men sex is just a carpet to sweep things under,' she said. She lit a cigarette. The bar was drowning in smoke – smoke that made my eyes crawl around in their sockets.

'I never argue with women about sex,' I said. 'They hold all the cards.'

She asked, 'When are you going back to the States?'

'It could be a long time.'

'Or not.'

'Why is it a problem?' I said.

'What happens to us then?'

'We can work something out,' I said unconvincingly. 'People conquer the Atlantic all the time.'

'But you don't have any control over that. Do you?'

'Sure I do. More than most people.'

'Can we get out of London?'

'In a week or so, no problem.'

'Why not now?'

'Now?'

'Tonight. First we get out of this fuckawful place, then go away somewhere.'

'Why the hurry?'

218

'I want to hurry. Why not?'

'There's something I have to – '

'That's right, you've got something to do. A little business to take care of. I don't have to know about it, right?'

I made a reassuring gesture with my hands that satisfied neither of us. 'You know I can't tell you everything,' I said.

'But you want a relationship. You don't want to pay a price for the kind of life you lead. You want a woman like a TV dinner.'

I was starting to resent the punishment I was taking. 'A week ago you thanked me for saving your life,' I said.

'You might have extended it,' Judy said. 'You didn't save it.'

I recalled that she had been Moresby's research assistant for two years. It wasn't surprising she was a verbal butcher when she needed to be. I recognized the clothes she was wearing inside her unbuttoned raincoat, and the familiarity hurt. It pained me even more to think about the body I would recognize beneath the clothes, and I was almost glad she was giving me such a hard time. It forced me not to look at her in that way.

We were near the end of our drinks. The noise of people insistently having fun had got intolerable. We quit the pub and returned to the bleakly lit concrete walkways of the river's south side. I felt the helplessness of a teenager going through this failure of communication, except that I had something the average teenager doesn't have – tiredness, a brittleness of emotional bones, the fear that the next break won't mend.

Judy stopped, and stared out at the lights sparkling on the water. Clouds flew across the sky, rippling the moon. 'The world's run by people like you,' she said.

'You're telling me,' I said.

'At least, the bastards who run it can only do what they do because of people like you. You run your public activities like your private life – only tell half the story, pretend certain things don't happen, make things OK by giving them a different name, bend reality all the time to cover up the fact that the same people are getting ripped off who always got ripped off.'

'You spent too many years listening to Moresby,' I said.

It was a cheap shot, product of a weak moment. Since I had been with Judy this time, the image of Moresby and her long association with him had repeatedly forced itself between us. The look she gave me was knowing and laced with rejection. I told myself I hadn't blown anything, she had planned this from the start.

'What did those sons of bitches put in your head?' I asked her.

I wished I hadn't given Rupertson such an easy ride on the subject of Judy and me. While I was busy toughing it out, they were pissing their pants in silent laughter. I was getting mad about it – too late maybe, but real mad.

'They didn't need to tell me much, did they? Thinking about it. I knew all I needed to know.'

'So what changed you?'

'I just saw what life with you was going to be like,' Judy said. She could see that all the emotion in me had turned to ice. 'Look,' she said, 'it was a nice interval, it helped both of us over a difficult time. Let's remember it like that.'

I was afraid she might offer me a token kiss. But she was very self-possessed, and didn't come close.

'One piece of advice,' I said. 'Don't go near Moresby's house again.'

'I already moved out.'

'Fine,' I said. 'Let's leave the goodbye.'

She turned away, and rather than watch her go I walked off in the opposite direction.

I dropped the taxi a few streets away and went on foot. It was that section of St John's Wood that lies back and thinks of England while enjoying the sweaty embrace of Kilburn – decrepit and awaiting conversion behind puny front gardens and rows of lime trees. In the dark, papery yellow leaves blew along the wet pavements and plastered themselves against any stationary target. I knew the district – I had lived there briefly ten years ago. In those days the girls used to photograph each other on the Abbey Road crossing, and everybody had a good time, oh yeah.

My clothes were damp and my soul felt like something in a laboratory jar. They had just given me the address and the time and the brotherly advice not to foul up again. As soon as I saw the street I knew what the place was – a safe house, an accommodation address, rented for six months then decommissioned regardless of use. The usual thing. They were not too bad inside, these places, because it might be a potential Russian defector they had to entertain there, and they wouldn't want the decor to repel. Tonight they had me, and I fancied that hospitality wasn't in the package.

I rang as instructed, three short touches on the button marked Crombie, a pause, then another four. There were cars along both sides of the street, so I hadn't tried to check them out, but obviously one of them had checked me, because while I waited for a reaction to my signal the iron gate opened and someone came up the path behind me. It was Gerry Rettiger. I behaved as if we had never met before.

She did the same, unlocking the house door and silently leading me up a clean but bare staircase which showed no sign of daily human traffic. On the second floor she turned the key in a heavy brown door and we ushered ourselves into the living room of a furnished apartment in which the lamp was already on. The room contained no evidence of occupancy, of style or taste or use. The whole place was nondescript but eerie at the same time, customized to leave no trace on the memory.

Rettiger took off her soft wool coat and dropped it over a chair-back. She didn't even carry a handbag. I wondered if, after our last encounter, she had a little something hidden away in her clothes, but I didn't push the thought.

Our meetings had been brief, and I didn't kid myself that there was anything like a relationship between us, but it must have been a reflex chauvinism which made me demand to be taken seriously by this self-possessed, attractive woman who settled her skirt demurely as she crossed her legs and began the briefing for which I had come there. But she spoke as if we had never met, would never meet again, and I was just some two-bit hit man they had scooped off the sidewalk in Marseilles or Benghazi. I didn't like it, but she knew I couldn't do a goddamn thing about it.

'The last phase,' she said, 'is down to you. Once you're in the Barbican, you make the schedule. Just keep to the mainframe program. You want to go over any detail again?'

I said no.

'Then that's it,' Rettiger said. She gave me that lucid but depersonalized stare, waiting for me to move first.

'Fine,' I said. I was about to get up when she grabbed

222

her coat. I tensed at the suddenness, betraying how rattled I was. But all Rettiger did was pull a handkerchief out in time to smother a sneeze. For a moment that mask of hers flexed and revealed an uncool humanity. She kept the handkerchief over her face until a second sneeze erupted, one that shook her frame and made her eyes water.

'*Gesundheit,*' I said.

She tried to recover fast, but I knew that for days she would hate herself for the professional dereliction represented by that sneeze. I stood up. Still dabbing with the kleenex, Rettiger got up too.

'You don't have to see me out,' I said.

'I'll be at the meeting,' she said, 'but I only activate in the event of a malfunction. Naturally we don't know each other.'

I grunted assent. She was pretty, in a flawless, controlled way that created distance. Good looks could intimidate as well as attract. I don't know what it exposed about me, but if she had been plainer I wouldn't have been half as scared of her.

'Don't screw up,' she said. She couldn't resist it.

'Listen, doll,' I said, 'they'll pull you back anyway, when this is all over, won't they? Maybe you dug the pit yourself.'

'Meaning what?'

I shrugged. 'If I know all about you, any question mark that hangs over me hangs over you, right? So if I go down, you can't be long. It suited you to pull the rug from under me – '

'What makes you think I did that?'

'Come on,' I said.

'You like easy conclusions, that's part of your problem.'

'It goes with the job.'

223

'On the other hand,' Rettiger said with grim sadism, 'if they ship me back, I guess I'll have to blame it on your little sortie over here.'

'How long did it take you to work Blakeway up?' I said. 'You've got quite a guy there.'

As when I had spoken of him before, I noticed a self-conscious hostility flicker in Rettiger's eyes.

'Do you screw him?' I said. 'Is that the hold?'

Instantly, I knew it was, although she would never admit it. Her eyes were flecks of pure hate.

'One day,' she said, 'I'll have a desk. You just better pray that your name doesn't land on it.'

But I was already half out the door. A nauseous swell had started to heave in my stomach, and I clattered down the staircase to get outside. I didn't care about the virginal linoleum, but I wasn't going to let Rettiger see me with my head between my legs.

I made it to the street, and from a kneeling position on the curb I threw up noisily into a grating. I didn't see or hear any movement from the house behind me. When I got up and walked away my body felt hard and light again. A lot had come out of me with the vomit. All the stuff was back in place and working.

The first thing I did after I let myself into the house in Kentish Town was to go to the kitchen to wash the stench of vomit from the back of my nose. As far as I knew, I was alone there. But as I lifted my head from the jet of water and reached for a towel, a voice behind me said, 'What are you doing here?'

I didn't look round. I towelled my face and said, 'Hello, Professor.'

'I don't get it,' I had said, but it wasn't true. I got it instantly, in all its gruesome, seedy logic. It made all the sense of the grin on a skull, but I got it all right. I was just holding out for as much detail as they were prepared to give me.

'Moresby is a man dominated by guilt,' Rupertson said, in the laid-back public-school drawl that made everything sound like a discussion of cricket.

'There are two dangerous types of men – ' Wayne Shealor said, 'really dangerous – those who have no sense of guilt whatsoever, and those who have cornered the market in it. Moresby is one of the latter.'

'How does that make him dangerous to us?' I said.

'Shealor speared a green cocktail olive with a stick, gazed at it for a moment, then opened his mouth and chewed it up. 'The Greens,' he said.

'Right,' I said.

Rupertson took over, as our man on the spot. 'Here in Europe,' he intoned, 'as you know, Mr Goolan, we are sitting on a powder keg. Many groups of people who a few years ago ignored or despised each other are now on the verge of uniting in a movement that we can generally characterize as anti-nuclear and anti-American.'

He relit his cigar, and I nodded. I was only there to nod, anyway.

'We are not talking about armed insurrection. Far more seriously, we are talking about a climate of opinion. Here in Europe there is always that old dragon, liberty, threatening to reawake. On a worst-case analysis it could mean not only the rejection of cruise missiles, but as a direct result the dismantling of the entire American presence in this country. In an impoverished island like Britain the costs of defence are high. And let's be frank, we have a military economy, but we have to maintain it by stealth. Joe Public is happy with his hamburgers and video cassettes. He doesn't want, and we certainly don't want, the burden of decision to be forced on him. The British, you see, are an obtuse race. The battle of ideas rages unobserved way above their heads. We have to win that battle without alerting them to its true nature. Otherwise a candle will be lit which, to quote somebody or other, will not be put out in our lifetime.'

Wayne Shealor burped silently, and I stifled a yawn. Rupertson was obviously one of those people who talk to themselves in mirrors.

'The Dutch and Belgians,' he went on, 'are just waiting to be pushed. As for the Germans, our Germans that is, they have finally realized that the price of our defence of their territory is that it will be the major battlefield of the next war, whether conventional or nuclear. They may find this a less than persuasive reason for a continued US presence, once the British give a lead.'

'Those Green bastards,' Shealor chipped in.

I noted with irony the way politics had hijacked the words for colours. Yellow and black were full of threat, reds were everything we hated, and now green was eating away at us like verbal cancer. The blues were OK, but then they were entertainment, even if they were created by blacks who were also often reds and might well have been greens too, if anybody had ever bothered to ask them.

'You were telling me about Moresby,' I said.

'Quite,' Rupertson said. 'Well, the extreme Left always has its spokesmen. They are usually embittered, discredited figures. The patriotic press generally takes care of them. Often they are marginal people whose sense of their own integrity depends on them remaining marginal. They don't want to take on the responsibility for people's lives, they don't want to corrupt their principles. The role of outcast and martyr is often precisely what they're seeking. Our problem comes from a bit nearer home.'

I must have looked less than excited, because Shealor zapped another olive and gave me the switchblade-finger routine.

'The asshole of it for the Brits is, they all went to public school, which in their cockamamey language means private school, and they all got a bad dose of not letting the side down and playing the game and all that crap. Propaganda-wise they're right, but for all the wrong damn reasons.'

'Thanks,' I said. 'It's all becoming very clear.'

'It's when our own people turn against us,' Rupertson said. 'Oh, we've had the odd retired field-marshal express doubts about some aspect of our nuclear defence policy, but all within the rules. Mountbatten even did that, for God's sake – nothing wrong with it, elder statesman and all that – '

'There was a rumour that not only the IRA wanted him dead,' I remarked. Two pairs of raised eyebrows told me not to introduce irrelevancies.

'As you know,' Rupertson continued, 'Patrick Moresby for many years has been one of our most outspoken and articulate supporters, a scourge of the peace movement, the ecologists, the make-up-with-the-Russians rabble. And all from a position of academic impartiality. If a man like that were to go over the wire, the weight he would carry would do us great harm – '

'Plus,' Shealor said, 'Moresby has picked up a lot of information over the years. Christ knows what he could do with it.'

'Why should he?' I asked.

'We're not interested in *why*,' Shealor said, 'only in *if*.'

'I thought that had been taken care of,' I said.

'Not quite in the way you thought of,' Rupertson said. 'You gather by now that Moresby is still alive.'

'I had kind of worked that out. What do you want me to do now?'

'That's easy,' Wayne Shealor said, crunching up another olive. 'We want you to kill him.'

I stared at Shealor and laughed. I disliked the way he was so gung-ho about it. My gaze stuck to him like a leech, and after a minute he had the grace to start looking shifty.

'Sorry I'm amused,' I said, 'but this has been going on for some time.'

Rupertson chipped in, to give Shealor the space to plump himself up again. 'The details changed along the way, but the ultimate aim remains. Moresby has to be removed. We would, however, like him to be useful to us first. All we have to do is persuade him that his guilt on many other matters can be expiated by doing the right thing now.'

'And me?' I asked.

Shealor said, 'You remember that clip of training film, they still use it on the course, the guy being taken into the execution shed, and all along another guy goes with him, reassuring him – it's all right, they're not going to kill you, they're just going to tie your hands and ask you a few questions, they won't kill you. And the first guy is docile because this is what he wants to hear. So then they tie him up and blow his head off.'

'I remember,' I said.

'You're the sweet talker,' Shealor said.

I recalled Judy. She was already getting more distant in my mind, blurred by the filthy tide that was running in on me now. I wondered when they had got to her. The question how they had enlisted her was easier to dispose of. If she hadn't already surmised for herself that Moresby was not dead, they would have enlightened her with a package that would guarantee, in return for a little work on her part, his survival, perhaps even a generous future. I could only hazard what they would have to tell her about me for all that to fit together; but whatever it was, I knew they had told her. As I looked at the faces of Shealor, pumped up and manic with go-for-it tunnel vision, and Rupertson, pink and suave in the complacency of power, I wondered where Judy was and what truth I would ever find again in her eyes.

I dried my face and took a good look at Patrick Moresby. The angle of light on his face exaggerated the haggard pallor which men always have after a prolonged debriefing. His eyes, once deep brown and full of lively menace, had the haunted vacancy of someone whose life had been swept away before him and left him stranded.

'I guess you didn't expect me,' I said.

'Not tonight, and not like this,' Moresby said.

'They didn't tell you I had a key?'

'No.'

The cast of his face was sad rather than grave. There was none of the old irony or potency. Things were falling into place in his mind, laboriously, so you could hear the clicks.

'You've been here before,' he observed.

I said, 'That's right.' I wasn't about to apologize. It hadn't been a tea party. His personal feelings didn't interest me.

'I suppose you know everything?'

'I know why they disappeared you, if that's what you mean. And why they've resurrected you.'

He had trouble meeting my eye. There was a glimmer of hate there, but it was more for himself than for me.

'Shall we go and sit down?' he said.

'You don't have to be a good host,' I told him.

'No,' he said sourly. 'You evidently know your way around.'

I hadn't meant it as a rebuff, but I didn't argue. Moresby led me into his study. I looked at the bookshelves, the pieces of pottery, the lamp in the corner, the green leather armchair, with a grateful pain of recognition. I felt that in an obscure way it all belonged to me more than to him, and maybe he was beginning to divine that as well. The last time but one I had been there was with Judy. I also wondered how much Moresby had picked up of that. The last time I was there I was doing target practice with the Colt.

We sat down. I declined his offer of a drink. The need for stimulants, even for sleep, had bled its way out of my system. Moresby had displaced everything. He shredded some Royal Yacht tobacco between the palms of his hands and tamped it into a yellowed meerschaum pipe. The haze of smoke around him added to the impression of someone still returning from the dead. He undid the top button under his bow-tie. He was still in daytime clothes, but his jacket had been replaced by a fine cashmere sweater of the sort academics wear on Sundays. He watched me with care and a degree of impotent malice.

'What do I know about you?' he said.

I said, 'They told you I was sent here to kill you. You of course realize that was just to panic you. The fake murder threw me, but its real purpose was to put pressure on you. You became a dead man. They wanted to break you down, and they made a damn good start. It worked too. I read your diaries.'

'Where are they?' Moresby said, his detachment cracking ever so slightly.

'You had an assistant, called Judy Ellerman.'

'You met her? Yes, yes, of course you did.'

'I guess she knows where your diaries are. And the things I never saw.'

'What things?'

'The lists of contacts and networks you've been building up over the years. The reason people are so keen to mess around with you.'

'I've no idea what you're talking about.'

'The great Professor Moresby,' I said. 'The champion of freedom, in reality still the head prefect, writing down all the naughty boys on the punishment sheet. Full of contempt for people intellectually inferior to himself, resenting it when they reject his leadership – '

Moresby held a match to his pipe. Through the smoke he said, 'You make your contempt for me more than clear.'

'That's not all,' I said. 'The great Professor then has a change of heart. The friend of NATO becomes a Little Englander. The persecutor of the peace movement himself becomes a man of peace. Now, there's an international conference on the agenda, at which the Professor is going to be the surprise package, the fortune cookie. The Professor has a lot of stuff to blow. The Professor has always cleverly avoided signing the Act. Certain people don't like what the Professor has in mind, so they take him out of circulation and persuade him back onto the team. In other words, Professor, once they've got you by the balls, they tell you where to piss.'

Moresby said, 'I see, Mr Goolan, that a year of my seminars did nothing to deepen your awareness of complex political issues.'

Once an academic, always an academic. It hit the right note, because it helped me to hate him. But he had his back against the wall, and they had got him badly scared. It didn't cost me to let him put me down. Take away his bow-tie and his pipe, and he didn't have much dignity left.

'Let's get it straight,' I said. 'I've got nothing against you. In fact, for once we're on the same side, we have a common interest. So what say we keep out of each other's hair? My job is to look after you, get you through this conference, and then we're home. You get your pay-off and I'm on the next flight back to the US.'

I watched his lined, sensitive face, and noticed something retreat in his eyes. I said, 'Are you OK for this conference. Because remember, I'm only there as your bodyguard. You've got to cut the mustard yourself, and once you get up there and blow the peace movement apart, you're on your own. I'm only your tame muscle.'

Moresby's face was like a woodcarving of someone who had died a long, noble, but agonizing death. 'I shall be ready,' he said.

'Fine,' I said. 'Now, the car they brought you here in –'

'In the garage.'

'The keys?'

'I have them.'

'OK. Pack anything you need. You've got ten minutes. Then say goodbye to this house.'

It was raining again as I pulled the car into the long yellow-lit tunnel that carves its way into the earth beneath this city-within-a-city called the Barbican. Moresby rode with his head close to the window so he could see better through the reflections in the glass. He didn't know where he was going, whereas me, I had trodden every necessary step only hours ago, before I went to meet Geraldine.

On the way here I said, 'Nobody else can tell me this, and I'd just like to know. Why did you – ?'

But that moment I had to hit the brake and swerve to miss a bowler-hatted jaywalker struggling across Holborn as the wind ripped at his umbrella. As we drove on Moresby took up the point anyway. It must have been on his mind a lot.

'Contrary to what you may think, or have been told, I wasn't being paid by anybody. Your friends were afraid that I'd become a tool of the KGB.'

He gave a brief 'Ha!' of superior laughter, then continued, 'Apart from bribery and blackmail, you people can't see why a man should do anything, but in the history of ideas these moments are well known – the final revelation, the falling of the scales from the eyes. In this particular case, I realized that the coming of cruise missiles, their deployment over the British countryside, would be a watershed. To oppose that, one had to stand against the whole NATO strategy. If that meant exposing much of its dirtier side, so be it. I was in constant touch with many academics and scientists throughout Europe, many of whom will be at the conference – '

His articulation was clear, but his rambling voice projected a troubled personality within. He was for sure not the Pat Moresby of ten years ago. I didn't want to look at myself too closely either, but I knew that sympathy was going to be bad for business, so I restrained any impulse to get inside him. I figured his real motive, back of it all, was vanity, but I knew I would never get to the total truth, and I doubted if Moresby himself ever had.

'How did they claw you back?' I asked. But he didn't have to answer. I could imagine the mixture of inducements and threats, the appeals to his vanity. Stalin had found the intellectuals the easiest people to eliminate, because if they were fixed right they would just stand up and proclaim their own guilt. Not much had changed in fifty years.

'They gave me several choices,' he said, then became petulant. 'Oh, don't misunderstand me, Mr Goolan, I haven't changed. Years of dialectic, of striving for a conclusion, are not shrugged off as lightly as that. I'm going along with the plan your colleagues have imposed on me because I feel that in this way I can best protect certain people and even an ideal, the belief in objective truth – '

'And yourself,' I said.

'Either I pay a price,' Moresby snapped, 'or a great many other people do. What they require is my public humiliation, and a knife-thrust to the heart of the peace movement. For that they will reward me and spare others.' He shrugged. 'I betray my country rather than my friends, you see.'

The car bumped over a stretch of road repairs, and the pipe which hung from Moresby's jaw rapped against the window. He wasn't convincing me, but I didn't let him know.

'Why should they trust you?' I said. 'How do they know you won't get up on that platform, with all the TV cameras there, and blow everything?'

'I'm sure they'll have someone in the audience to deal with me if I don't play along.' He sucked a matchflame down into the bowl of his pipe. 'It could even be you, Mr Goolan.'

We pulled into the Barbican. It was like entering the Forbidden City. It seemed a good moment to terminate the conversation.

* * *

234

From the third floor of our building we looked out onto acres of other apartment blocks, dominated by two towers some forty floors high in which a few lights still dangled through the blackness of the small hours. Stretched out below, half visible in the subdued public lighting that remained on, was a kind of piazza and an expanse of dark water shaking the reflections over its skin. I let the curtains go, and we turned back into the safe house that would be home for the next couple of days. My resident's card gave the name McQuarrie. It sounded like an in-house joke, the sort that someone somewhere would be either fired or promoted for.

I asked Moresby, 'Can I get you anything?' He shook his head and sank back into his armchair with the style that only intellectual high-fliers can. He began to clean out his pipe with an elaborate multi-purpose tool. I found a glass ashtray and put it beside him. After raising a cloud of smoke between himself and the world, he pulled a letter from his jacket.

'This was waiting for me when I arrived at the house.'

There was no envelope. It read:

Dear Pat,
    Take care. We will get back together again one day. Lots of love,

Judy.

I read it without emotion and handed it back. 'What about it?' I said.

'You met Judy Ellerman?' he said.

'Sure.' I knew my defensiveness showed, and couldn't do a damn thing about it.

'You also mentioned that you had seen some of my notebooks.'

I asked, 'How do you know it was only some?'

'Believe me, Mr Goolan, I know.'

'Who has the others?'

'That's not your concern.'

I was tired. I knew he didn't mean to irritate me, but that's what he was doing.

'Just say what you've got to say, Professor. It's nearly three in the morning. Don't give me a lot of shit.'

'Do you know where Judy is now?'

I flicked a fingernail at the letter. 'Is this all the contact you've had with her since – '

'Yes.'

'She really thought you'd been killed,' I told him.

'There was no way I could communicate with her.'

'So how come she knows you're alive now? Or do you think this letter was a piece of female intuition?'

Moresby sank further into the armchair and the cocoon of smoke. I could see he had already put these questions to himself. 'I wondered if you had any idea,' he said.

'Listen, Professor,' I said, 'I've got so many ideas you could paper the walls with them. How did Judy come your way in the first place?'

'She answered an advertisement. She was one of, I think, two dozen.'

'Why did you pick her?'

'She was well qualified.'

'You mean she had a sister called Susie.'

Moresby's face grew anguished again. A tic started up in his right cheek. 'Do we have to go through this?' he asked. Like the true masochist, he was fighting shy of the pain he was determined to feel.

'I knew Susie,' I said. 'All those years ago.'

'Really?' he said. He was mildly surprised.

'I want to know about her death.'

He waved his pipe languidly. 'What can I tell you?'

236

'Come on, Professor. I've read your bloody diaries. What was all the guilt about? Why did you appoint Judy? Why did you write all the weird stuff about Judy?'

A red wave swept across my brain, and by now I was across the room. I smacked Moresby's pipe out of his hand and grabbed his lapels and pounded him into that goddamn armchair.

'What did you do to Susie, you bastard?'

In front of me I saw a broken, frightened human being, cringing from my anger, made ugly and pitiful by violence. I let go. There were tears in my eyes, and I turned away. From the window all that brick and concrete outside was shiny with wet, bleak and pitiless. When I could face Moresby I turned back again.

'I'm sorry,' I said. 'I guess I need sleep. That means you have to go to bed too.'

'Wait,' Moresby said. His voice was hollow. He was fifty-five, but he looked ten years older, suddenly aged by self-disgust and fear. I retrieved his pipe and gave it back to him. The meerschaum had chipped. It had been like hitting a child's toy away, and I felt bad about it. I sat down and massaged my face with the palms of my hands.

'You gave evidence at the inquest,' I said. 'The verdict was accidental death by inhalation of vomit. Why do you feel so goddamn guilty about it?'

Moresby's voice was flat, bleached of feeling by the fact that he had made this confession to himself a thousand times. 'I lied,' he said. 'I lied at the inquest when I said there was no cause for it to be regarded as suicide.' He shrugged, with that phoney humility which had been so characteristic of him. 'My authority was accepted.'

'And the truth?' I said.

'The truth was that Susie was pregnant. The autopsy found that, of course. It was regarded as incidental.'

I hadn't known this at the time – too stunned, too reluctant to know anything when she died. I recalled Imogen's tantalizing discovery of the inquest record. There were at least three reasons why she had withheld this detail from me, and they were all sad reasons.

'You were the father?' I asked Moresby.

Hollowly he echoed, 'I was the father, and I had told her that in no circumstances would I acknowledge the child, nor was I interested in any further relationship with her, whether the child was got rid of or not. I offered to pay for an abortion, and a holiday to recover from it.' He cleared his throat, but the constriction in his flesh was not so easy to shift, and his voice remained hoarse. 'Susie had also discovered that she was on a political blacklist at the University. I had tried to warn her about the company she was keeping, but by then there was little I could do. It was out of my hands.'

'By when?'

'The later stages of our relationship.' He paused and stared sadly at his pipe. 'You must understand the power of a man in my position at that time. After 1968, Western governments were running very scared of their vast student populations, and those of us in touch with that movement wielded great influence. The other factor was the enormous sexual release of those years. It's difficult to recapture now. Can you believe that I was forty before I had sex with any woman other than my wife? And suddenly London was seething with sexually active, available young women. I soon made up for years of dreary monogamy.'

I thought of Delphine, even the way she was now, and I couldn't imagine that it had been dreary; but as with the other women Moresby and I had in common, I felt we had just experienced totally disparate parts of them. The

238

knowledge gave me neither any fellow feeling for him, nor tension in the presence of a rival, and I was glad that isolation in his ego restricted his perceptions about me. At this new note in his disclosures, Moresby met my eye for a moment, checked himself out, and visibly decided to go on.

'I had a weakness,' he said, 'a need not only to fall in love, but to have women fall in love with me. That was the ultimate sensation. Because in sex itself it's the woman who has the real power, not the man. All the macho cultures in the world are protests against the sexual power of women. There were times when I hated, literally hated, all those randy young women I was screwing, hated their delectable, insatiable cunts that could devour me, and drain me and leave me puny and ridiculous. I needed love because I wanted power, and you only truly experience power by abusing it. Marx was right – individuals act out their respective social systems in their private relationships.'

'And Susie was in love with you?' I said.

'Yes. I think she was looking for a refuge. She didn't see the rocks below the surface.'

I thought what a crappy, shallow metaphor it was, and it reminded me that Moresby had once been a naval officer. Even knowing what he had just been through didn't help me like him.

'What about Judy?' I said.

With an air of pedantic masochism, Moresby said, 'For two years I have loved Judy and refused to let her fall in love with me. It seemed like a way of expiating what I did to Susie.'

'You're a strange man, Professor,' I said, but he just stared back emptily at me. He wasn't interested in what I thought.

239

My hand rasped the stubble on my face. My tongue scoured the inside of my mouth, and when I massaged my cranial bone it felt like someone else's head in there.

'From here on,' I said, 'you know the rules. You're locked in here, and the only way you can go is through the window. Anybody gets to you has to get past me first. We hole up here tomorrow, the media release goes out tomorrow evening, and the following day you hit it at the conference. Immediately after that we come back here for the handover. You know, and I don't know, what deal they've lined up for you after that, because at that point my assignment ends.' I coughed. 'Are you together on the details?'

Moresby nodded. Purist to the end, he said, 'It is already tomorrow.'

'You have to meet with someone,' I said. 'In the afternoon. You need some sleep now. Do what you have to do, and hit the sack.'

Ten in the morning had come and gone before I took another look out at the strange self-enclosed world of the Barbican. The weather had lifted, and a warm autumnal light caressed this surreal, concrete Lego landscape. In the sunshine it had the abstract lightness of fantasy, like a science-fiction city risen from the waves or left exposed by retreating seas. Down on the terraces in front of the Barbican Centre people were sitting at white tables drinking coffee and watching the fountains. I estimated six hundred windows, minimum, in the Shakespeare Tower, which loured down on us from across the piazza. I wondered how many people jumped to their deaths in this East London Atlantis. My eye traced the drop from our window to the brick-paved thoroughfare forty feet below.

There was no sound from Moresby's room. I unlocked the door to find the Professor already dressed, propped up by a pillow, calmly smoking. I went to the kitchen to make some coffee.

Somehow there was no more to say, since it was all by the book from here on out. During the briefing, Rupertson had stressed the leverage I possessed through being Moresby's ex-student, and they wanted me to use that to psych him up for the conference. But there was too much they didn't understand, and I hadn't enlightened them. Their requirements assumed that about everybody.

Moresby took a long bath. Although they had stocked the flat with groceries, neither of us ate anything.

'You OK?' I asked him.

He answered my question by ignoring it and said, 'When do we have to go down?'

'An hour before the meet. Remember the drill, and don't look at me. If anything worries you, get up and walk into the Centre, turn right in the foyer and go upstairs to the first rack of payphones. Ring the number I give you, this will answer at a different rack, and then tell me what the problem is. After that, go to the men's toilet on the next landing up, and if there's any hassle I'll take care of it at that point. Otherwise you stay out on the terrace, in full view, and leave the ulcers to me. As far as the world knows, you're still a dead man.'

Moresby, dispassionate, almost disdainful, asked, 'Who am I meeting?'

'You don't know, I don't know. They put through a tip-off call to some peace movement figure, maybe someone you already know, stating the rendezvous. It's only a hint, your name wasn't mentioned, and if you're not happy out there, blow the whole scene immediately.'

'And if it's someone I don't know? Do they approach me?'

'Right. You confirm the identification, you refer the contact to the early edition of the London papers, which will be primed at the correct time, and you tell him to alert the relevant conference people only after the news hits the street. They will then be expecting you to strut your anti-NATO stuff for them. You discuss anything that needs discussing, so there are no hang-ups about tomorrow. Then you walk with the contact through the Centre, following the signs for Barbican subway station. This takes you along a lot of deserted corridors where I can pick up any unwanted company. The contact may have a car, in which case he'll leave you. Whether he does or not, you go to the station. If the contact stays with you, go to the platform with him, let him take the first train, and after it's gone you return to street level and go along Beech Street, Whitecross Street, Silk Street, and in through the residents' entrance which I'm about to show you. Can you repeat this?'

The pipe still clamped in his teeth, Moresby said, 'Don't treat me like an imbecile. Go on.'

'If the contact leaves you, go down to the trains on your own. Keep away from the track, stay right by the wall. Let two trains go, then come back. You won't see me, but I'll be there. Got it?'

'Perfectly,' Moresby said.

'There's a hat and a raincoat in your room,' I said. 'Wear them. Let's go.'

Half an hour later I stood in the terrace foyer of the Barbican Centre watching Moresby as he sat out on the brick-paved lakeside area. There were not too many people now, and against the old church which they had left standing amid the space-age complex the trees wore

242

muted greens, browns and golds. Along the rectangular lake the water-jets still buffeted the air with inverted cones of spray. Moresby had got a sandwich roll. Maybe he didn't trust the stuff in the flat. He was holding the sandwich out, and the sparrows who grifted that terrace were queueing to fly at his hand for a peck of the bread. Occasionally one would perch briefly on his hand to hack off a bigger chunk. A few red leaves blew along the brick pavements. It would soon be time to bring in the tables for good.

I didn't know who would be making the rendezvous, but I knew more about him than Moresby did. That was why I didn't get a surprise when I saw Simon Blakeway's long angular figure moving slowly across the waterside terrace, the pale bearded face cautiously scanning the area for Moresby with all the little signs of not knowing who he was there to meet. But he knew him all right, and when Blakeway and I had discussed the late Professor, he was just being cute with me. He zeroed in and pulled a chair alongside Moresby, but made no overt approach as he sat down. All he did was open his parka and gaze at the water for a minute.

There was no sign of a minder, but then Blakeway didn't need one. He didn't need any introductions either. I could see now what had happened all along the line. Blakeway had snowed Moresby from the start. He had been the shadowy contact Moresby had come to depend on, the reassuring voice in the dark alley. Right now Moresby was telling Blakeway of his readiness to blow God knows what secrets of the CIA infiltration of the peace movement, the contingency plans for the cruise installations, and all the other stuff he knew because he had been a part of it. I saw Blakeway nodding and gesturing sympathetically. All I could see of Moresby was his back, hidden by the corduroy hat and the pale raincoat with the nylon-fur collar. He was telling Blakeway all that, and planning to do the opposite. And while Blakeway was appearing to suck it all in, he knew what Moresby was really going to do better than Moresby did himself. I wished I could laugh about it.

The meeting was short, about eight minutes. Maybe the maintenance people were doing some work, or it was the end of the season, but suddenly the sprinklers on the lake shut off. The place became instantly flat, deathly. Moresby and Blakeway got up and walked over to the Centre. I knew which way they would go and positioned myself accordingly. It was a big, soft interior, dark and many-faceted, the kind of place you walk through in dreams. We went through our paces, three men who had all loved a girl called Susie Ellerman, who was long since dead. It was a hell of a club to belong to.

Our cardinal observation on this final set of evidential notes is that had Goolan not been stalled at the airport, they would in all plausibility not have been written. This we believe indicates a constructive admission that Goolan's account has a manipulative rather than a verificatory substance. In other words, Goolan was creating what he cognized as an insurance for himself in the event that his plans malfunctioned. This Agency will continue to predicate that this fact disvalidates any claim to ascertainable truth in the sequent pages.

Tranche 7

Fog has grounded everything. I came out here at day-break, only to find the darkness yielding to a silvery gloom that has thickened to a twenty-yard visibility and pinned everything to the earth. I hadn't intended to write any more of this. Last night somehow made it all obsolete. But now I have no place to go, waiting on the fog to clear, and it seems I have no choice but to write it.

The streets of Islington streamed with people, all walking unhurriedly to the same destination. We drove around, just checking the place out, as the conference built up to its start. An eerie religious feel hung over the district, seeing so many people there at once, mellow in the dusty sunlight, making their way with a calm purpose that you don't often see on city streets.

The Bradlaugh Hall was a recently constructed conference centre, next to a multi-storey car park and not easy to distinguish from it. Moresby and I knew when we had to arrive, which level to drive up to, which communicating door to use into the hall. When we drove in, another car would pull out from that level to give us parking space. For now we were just checking it out and trying not to go stir-crazy.

We headed back to the Barbican. Moresby obsessively read the articles about himself which by now had made the national papers. I had bought him a wide selection. The story was the same in each – rumours of terrorist kidnapping, possible involvement of KGB proxies, the

East Germans, the Bulgarians. The IRA had been thought worth a mention since Moresby had always been a good friend of Ulster. None of it made any real sense. The papers said that the Professor was in hiding and a full statement would be issued later. They weren't kidding.

One paper was drumming up business with the headline 'Anti-Green Prof Cheats Left-Wing Death Squad'. Moresby jabbed the mouthpiece of his pipe at it. 'Look at this trash.'

I was driving, but I glanced down. 'That's fame, Professor,' I said. 'Sew up the film rights now.' He wasn't amused.

It was going to be a long day. It would be a lifetime, that day. Moresby's unscheduled entry at the conference was late afternoon. In our Barbican fastness he got some paper and sat at the table with it spread out in front of him. I asked if it was notes for the speech. He answered brusquely, 'I don't need notes for that.'

He kept toying with his gold pen, then putting it down again. He fiddled endlessly with his pipe and matches and the reaming tool he used. If his hands told anything about what was going on inside him, it didn't look good.

'I want to write to Judy,' he said.

'Fine,' I said, 'but it has to pass me first.'

He looked round with outrage in his deep-set brown eyes. 'It's none of your bloody business.'

'Off limits, Professor,' I said. 'Up to the conference, not a word leaves your hand without I approve it. You can write Judy all you want, but if I think it raises a security problem my orders are to tear it up and send it down the tubes.'

Moresby didn't like this, but it hadn't been designed for him to like. He sat and stared at the sheets of blank paper for hours. He seemed to be familiar with the activity. Maybe it comforted him. We didn't talk about the conference, or anything else. Moresby opened yet another of the small flat tins of Dunhill tobacco, of which he had an apparently unlimited supply in his hand luggage. He changed pipes too, carefully cleaning out the meerschaum and propping it up to dry. The new pipe was a straight-stemmed briar, which changed his whole appearance, making him look cooler and sharper at the edges, more businesslike. His pipe got him through the day, and I realized how easy it must have been to destabilize a man like that. I could see now the first thing Wayne Shealor had done when they got their hands on Moresby, the juicy grin as they confiscated the pipe and dripped white spirit on the tobacco.

Eventually it was time to leave. Moresby wore the fur-collared raincoat and corduroy hat. I wore a quilted nylon jacket with two fluorescent strips down front and back, a white woollen hat, denims and marine boots. My feet were within half a size of Moresby's. They had been really pleased with that detail.

Bradlaugh Hall was one of those whorish multi-function buildings which echo to 'Rule Britannia' one day and the Red Flag the next and only pause to count the take. This weekend it housed a European conference on the advent of cruise missiles to the NATO countries front-lining it with the Russians. It was a prestige show, with a scattering of German philosophers and Dutch physicists. However, it was anticipated there would be language problems, and a lot of the time would be taken with speeches from the floor – those interminable sessions of democracy in which everybody wants to talk and nobody to listen. As an event it needed electrifying. Moresby didn't look charismatic as we quit the Barbican, but his face had all the doomed tenseness of a man whose hour was waiting for him just along the line.

We drove through the dark levels of the car park building to our appointed place. I flashed the beams twice and waited, and after a moment a car pulled out of the tightly packed ranks and followed the yellow arrows exitwards. I heeled into the space. A minute later we were at the mouth of a brightly lit concrete corridor that gave into the hall complex.

'This is where I fade,' I said. 'Just go by the drill or I can't help you. Don't fuck up.'

There were No Smoking logos all over the place. Moresby got his pipe belching, shook the match out, and tossed it into an overflowing garbage receptacle that hung from the wall. The nonchalance in the way he threw the match said that he was shaping up. I let him go. Simon Blakeway would be meeting him in there, and it was better if we didn't coincide.

I went into the hall by the front entrance. A girl thrust a broadsheet at me, and I pretended to read it while I headed for the action. I had clean-shaven, and they had equipped me with plain-lens photochromatic glasses. I was reasonably well hidden. On my left chest I wore a big round badge that said 'Yankee Nukes Out', and several layers of clothing below that my Colt automatic kept getting erections.

The main hall was preceded by an anteroom where stalls were selling protest literature and a creche where the kids who hadn't been stuck in the playpen were fighting over a video game. There must have been a thousand seats in the hall itself, but even so people were standing. I eased my way in, towards the back. I didn't want any attention. The current speaker was a white-haired lady with an upper-class English accent, talking about pacifism with a fervour that didn't seem to have gripped her audience. The people on the platform manifested all the usual conference faces: boredom, blankness, resignation.

The speaker wound up, and the audience started flexing stiff muscles and breathing deep again. There was relief in the applause, then large numbers of people got up and converged on the various exits. The hall was clammy from all that body heat. I kept to one side, and saw Simon Blakeway go up on the platform and speak to the chairman in a whispered, conspiratorial dialogue. I didn't want to be the only one watching them, so I let myself be carried along with the crowd. People were jostling for toilets or fresh air or plastic cups of coffee. Although it was steamy in there I had to keep everything on, including the hat, to imprint a firm image on anybody who might wish to recall me later.

I nearly laughed when I caught sight of Jake Cromer in the crowd, although on reflection it was the kind of place he would be. He moved through the pack of bodies with that same scathing arrogance on his face and the grim loneliness oozing through every crack in his seedy façade. He had got the part to perfection, and he was saddled with it for life. I guessed he was there to steal something, ideas at the very least, and I thought how cute it was that he should be in at the death, Moresby-wise. By Cromer's standards it was going to be a good day.

In another part of the crowd I saw Gerry Rettiger. I had known that she would be here, but I thought, why not, it was her show more than anybody's. I was straightened out on all that now. She was birdlike and watchful, and while she was not an easy person to summarize from appearance, she still looked ordinary enough not to make anybody wonder. There were so many things she could have been that you would never have suspected the one she was. An epitaph on a whole generation. I tossed around the question of how many more of this audience were intelligence personnel, provocation agents, or just plain finks. For one moment, before I could drift away into the crowd, Rettiger looked straight through me. I guess I did the same to her. It felt like another exchange of blows in an unconcluded combat.

The conference came slowly back to order, and I got a hollow, taut sensation in my gut. There had clearly been an urgent meeting during the recess. A woman now occupied the chair, and in a voice whose hoarseness was partly nervous excitement, she announced that they had a special guest speaker. The final speakers on the programme, both eminent men, had agreed to limit themselves to ten minutes each to accommodate this revision.

The audience fell into a hush of anticipation. Moresby's name had not been disclosed. A sudden outbreak of spontaneous muttering rippled through the hall. The next two speakers were tolerated, but the wait was a killer. A doctor talked about the unworkable medical scenario after a nuclear attack, and the last speech was an emotion-rouser from someone whose rhetoric was a colourful upbeat that didn't quite make it in this new situation. Both speakers were given a token question period, but nobody in the hall wanted to ask questions.

Simon Blakeway appeared on the platform again. He looked gaunt, almost noble, with that stiff beard and high forehead. For a moment I wished I knew less about him.

'Friends,' he said.

He didn't need to project his voice. The audience were still, as at a moment of execution. If he had whispered they would have lip-read him.

252

'We've all heard about Patrick Moresby in the last few days. In the past he hasn't exactly been a supporter of this movement. But recent events have changed his view of things. He wanted specially to come here today to nail his colours to the mast of the anti-nuclear weapons cause.'

A wave of applause rolled through the crowd. The TV people had been primed, and both main British channels were there, together with some European cameramen. At Blakeway's words they all scuttled forward to get better angles for their shots.

Blakeway glanced sideways and took a step back. I wondered what was in his mind as he announced, 'Professor Patrick Moresby.'

They were a restrained audience, but the handclapping went wild once they saw him. The media coverage of the Moresby case had wound them up, and a lot of emotion was crackling in the air as Moresby took his place at the centre of the rostrum. He was a seasoned lecturer. I had sat in the LSE theatres and seen him play with audiences, sock them around, massage their egos, make them love him. But this time there was a difference; it was as if he had a cross on his shoulders, and every step up there cost him.

He carried no notes. His hands, those sensitive, mobile hands, roamed through his coat pockets in a search for talismans. His voice was choked and he found it hard to get going. The audience also picked up on his strain, and froze in unbreathing tension. One of those timeless instants gaped through the hall, and momentarily I thought he was going to blow it, to blow it from fear or ineptitude. Life the last few weeks had not trained Moresby well for this spot on the international stage. His bushy hair was haloed by an overhead light as he tried to put together some formal preliminary words, steeling himself for the rest.

I felt for him. I sure didn't like him, but it was too complex to say I hated him either. I knew what he had to do, and what I had to do. I was only there because of him, and that fact bound me to him. I kept myself focused just one minute ahead, no more. It worked better that way. Moresby stiffened his back, and his voice rose. I could see that in his mind the right cogs had locked into place and he was ready to go.

'I have been called an enemy of the peace movement,' he began. 'I am certainly an enemy of terrorists, spies, infiltrators, and dupes of the Soviet Union. I equally detest romantics, dreamers, the long-haired cavaliers of this ideological civil war which is being fought out on British soil.'

The expectant silence was getting embarrassed already. Up on the platform people looked at each other uneasily. A spooky chill swept through the hall as the blood went cold in a thousand bodies.

'You all thought I was going to blow the whistle on the Americans. But this country has worse enemies than the Americans, and many of these enemies are in this room. I know that some of your motives are decent and patriotic. I also know that many of you are confused and have been manipulated by people whose true loyalties you do not know, some of whom I can see before me in this hall now. Your so-called peace movement is so penetrated by laundered KGB money on the one hand, and government double agents on the other, that I wonder if there is one genuine unilateral disarmer among you. I have here a list of people from both this country and Europe whose true function is to inform on the peace movement while ostensibly supporting it.' He handed a paper to the chairman. 'Documentary evidence for this list will be made available later.'

His voice had an icy resonance. Whatever changes he had been through lately, this was in a way the culmination of Moresby's life-work. The people on the platform craned round the sheet of paper. All the names on it were smears, but they would never be clean again. The documentary evidence he referred to had been carefully assembled by his controllers, and would be the kind that can never be disproven. It would wreck the peace movement with the public. I was suddenly glad I was leaving England the next day.

'An attempt has been made to silence me. I don't wish to speak about this now. But you, all of you, are going to have to accept the inevitable link between the peace movement and international terrorism. You are a shopfront for these people, and you deceive yourselves – '

The noise was growing in the hall, an ugly wounded crescendo. Moresby broke off his address. People were getting mad and protesting, jumping to their feet and flailing their arms. But there were also many hundreds who sat stunned, unhappy and suddenly filled with doubt. I guess these were the silent majority, and although his performance was shaky, Moresby had got to them. In my opinion sending him to this conference had been a lousy idea, but it was working incredibly. Moresby would have been the star of the conference, the great convert, the new leader, and now all they had was a weasel, spitting their beliefs back in their faces.

It was out of hand within minutes. People were yelling at one another, at their anonymous neighbours, needing a target for their anguish. It had always been obvious that Moresby would never get to the red meat of his speech. The harm was done, and it was already on a countdown as to how long he could last up there. He had started to react like an angry professor, trying to shout down a mob of loudmouths who called themselves students. Conditioning would hardly let him do otherwise. We had to lift him out of there before it got physical. The whole place had gone apeshit.

Simon Blakeway had leapt up. He stood shaking his fist at Moresby, yelling in his face. I wondered if Moresby really knew about Blakeway. Members of the audience were screaming at each other so that nobody could hear anything any more. Across the hall two guys were punching each other out. The boys with the cameras were eating it alive.

Then Moresby flipped. I spotted it first, but Blakeway saw it too, and he was nearer. All of a sudden Moresby had put his hands over his face. Then he started waving his arms in the air as if forcing his way through a cloud of heavy smoke. A lot of the audience saw something wrong and quietened down. Moresby grabbed the microphone from the lectern and started shouting into it, his voice a husky roar.

'No, no, no, no – '

I moved for the exit.

'I want to tell the truth – the truth – '

Famous last words, Professor. Blakeway had him, but Moresby was out of control and some people were pelting him with cartons and cans. I had less time than planned, but I didn't need much. My last view of Moresby was of him shielding his head as he was dragged from the hall. I just hoped nobody got between him and Blakeway, because if things went wrong, this was when they would do it.

I walked out fast through the street entrance, then ran past the automatic barrier and up through the levels of the car park. My instructions were to go in for Moresby, to reach back into the hall complex as far as was necessary to pull him out. By going this way I missed the crowds. If Moresby followed his rules, we should meet up where we had split two hours previously.

I still didn't trust Simon Blakeway. Never trust a man with a front to maintain. I went in at speed, my right hand poised over the underarm Colt. Along the glaringly lit walkway between the two buildings I could hear the uproar from inside the hall. Moresby hadn't shown. The door he should have come through stood shut ahead of me. A cleaner was emptying the garbage can off the wall into a plastic sack.

A cleaner might wear new coveralls from time to time, but he doesn't have the careful neckshave I noticed below the baseline of this one's checkered cap as he leaned his head away from me. He was black, and that was a clever touch, but everything in the stance of his body said he was a dude. When he reached for the broom he was a mite too eager; he lacked the reluctance, he didn't hate that broom.

'You,' I said, 'out of here. Don't argue, man, just go, fast.'

He spun at me and swung the broom so it caught my rib cage. I grabbed the shaft, but as I heaved at it the black guy pushed back. I took the head of the broom in my gut as the concrete wall stepped forward to whap me from behind. Then the door opened. Moresby was alone. I waited for the black to admit one moment of distraction, but his eyes were only for me. I reasoned quickly. If he was there to kill, I would be dead already, since he had all the drops. I jerked my head at Moresby.

'Let's go, Professor.'

He came past as I circled with the black. This was a

delaying job. Somebody wanted to separate us.

I shouted, 'Moresby, stay there.'

I reached inside my jacket. The black stared at the Colt and suddenly looked very frightened. His whole body tried not to twitch. Even his lips were scared to move. 'No, please, man,' he breathed.

I wanted to know who he was, what outfit he worked for. He was going to tell me, too. I flicked the safety on the Colt. At that range, in that confined space, his body would have plastered every square inch of concrete wall.

If Blakeway was holding back the tide in the Bradlaugh complex, it sounded like he was failing. A lot of people were about to come through that door. I pushed the black around and hit him with the flat of the Colt right across his dandy neckshave. He went down with a groan that might have been relief. He knew at least this way he would wake up. I clenched Moresby's arm, and we hit Level G of the car park.

'Let's go,' I said.

'The car – ' Moresby protested, adjusting his hat and looking round as I forced him to run.

'Forget it,' I said. They would have it staked out, or wired to blow up, or fitted with a bleep tracer. That car was an *à la carte* disaster area.

We followed the downward ramps. Somewhere in the darkly shining ranks of stationary cars a headbeam lit up, and the car rolled along the yellow arrows after us. I pulled Moresby behind a concrete pillar, my hand nestling the automatic under my armpit. But the car, a Ford with a dented fender, went by us, rocking on the corner.

'OK,' I said, 'run.'

At the out barrier we caught up with the Ford as the driver was struggling to insert his ticket without dislocating his arm. I sniffed at the idea of hijacking the Ford, but dismissed it. We passed the barrier and disappeared into the streets.

'What about the car?' Moresby demanded. He was desperate to stick to the rules. They were now the only security he had.

I didn't mention what had happened to him at the end back there. 'Skip it,' I said. 'Just look out for a public toilet!'

Moresby looked unhappy, and I wasn't surprised. He was rehashing what he had done in the conference hall. He was also worrying what I was going to do with him. But it was too bad – his private agony wasn't on anybody's agenda any more, and I had to keep prodding him to move faster. The direction of the Barbican was easy, the distance less than a mile. We could afford to mess with the route and stay lost for a while. At intervals one of the Barbican towers, an irregular honeycomb of square lights chewed at by the darkness, fingered the night sky.

The toilet we found was a Victorian relic, discreetly underground. Moresby went down, and when he had not returned after a minute that signalled for me to descend too. It was a formerly opulent place, with Victorian tiles and marble urinals, but it reeked of vintage piss and cracked sewers leaching into the London substratum. The floor had been splashed with a fearsome disinfectant. We took adjacent cubicles and bolted the doors. I stood on the toilet bowl to watch the entrance as we traded clothes over the partition. Then I flushed the can and left, and Moresby followed me.

We headed for the Barbican. Moresby kept surveying the streets, as if to test out the glasses he was now wearing.

'I once lived around here,' he said. 'When I was a student, just after the war, when it was all bomb sites. I was here during the war too. I remember the sky burning around St Paul's.'

'Save the nostalgia,' I told him. 'You might get to see it again.'

The apartment was clear, but all the same I went in with the user-friendly Colt aimed two-handed and ready to blow a human-shaped hole through the wall. Only silence and darkness, and the gleaming threads of light round the residential sections of the Barbican, met my gun barrel. Down at the Centre the evening people were arriving for the concerts and movies and drama presentations. I stood out on the access deck and watched as Moresby emerged from the shadows and crossed the lakeside terrace. He looked as incongruous in my clothes as I did in the fur-collared raincoat and corduroy hat. He made it to the apartment without incident, and we settled in for the necessary wait.

The hours began to pass, very slowly, weighed down by the fact that we ignored each other. Finally I was able to look at my watch, for the hundredth time, and say, 'OK, this is it. Let's go.'

Moresby had that abstracted, helpless look which the very important get when they have surrendered their lives to someone else's safekeeping.

'Now?' he said. He breathed a leisurely stream of smoke from his mouth, and had to take my silence for an answer.

'Remember,' I said, before we left the apartment for the last time, 'keep to the shadows. If there's any heat intended for you, I'll draw it. Don't even react if someone calls your name.'

I still didn't know what they had told Moresby, but he clearly had it all laid out in his mind. He expected to be spirited away and looked after by Her Majesty's Government. He had tried to cross the wire, and in return for letting them change his mind he thought they would reward him. I remembered his lecture on Machiavelli, and how easy it all sounded from a university platform.

Meanwhile, he had done what they wanted. He was only a part of a much bigger operation that neither of us knew much about, and they still wanted him dead because he represented a threat and they could hang the killing on the peace movement. The media would be fed leaks to indicate a revenge assassination, and the headlines would say, 'Professor who put his country first murdered by peace terrorists.'

The smartest sequence in the whole game-plan was what they had done to me. All I wanted was to get out of this intact. I knew I could kill Moresby with one blow of the hand, given the motivation. I didn't care whether we were on the same side of the fence or not, it wasn't about that any more. As we prepared to leave the apartment, I knew I could find it in myself to kill him. I would peak at the right moment, and I had my own plans laid for after that.

'I'm ready,' Moresby said. I questioned his air of relaxation, and wondered if he was running a scam of his own. But it seemed for real. 'They said I should leave all my effects here and they'd be collected.'

'Surely,' I said. Effects – I liked that. In the end it was his arrogance that had destroyed him – the arrogance of the man who controlled everything via words and ideas, the things that didn't bite back. I couldn't find a redeeming feature in the guy, and that made things easier.

'There shouldn't be any snags,' he said. Right to the end he was going to act as if he was in control. Self-importance, and maybe a subcutaneous layer of fear, wouldn't let him do anything else. It made him a patsy for what was about to happen to him. The exchange of clothes, the cryptic movements, were just a diversion, a device to keep him pacified. He hadn't guessed it.

'No snags,' I said, and we left.

All the indoor public spaces of the airport are now crammed with delayed travellers and their luggage. A message has just come over the p.a. system asking Mr John Goolan to report to some desk or other. I think this is a try-on. They can't know for sure that I'm here. At the same time, there aren't many other places I'd be right now. Moresby's effects, as he called them, didn't include his passport, and his passport didn't contain his photograph after I had finished with it. They presumably checked the airport computers for a flight booked in my name, and I gambled on them not hunting for the name Moresby. Clouds of fog are pressing against the windows and obliterating all visibility outside. People have bottle-necked into here to the point of chaos. It doesn't mean that whoever's looking for me won't find me, but I figure my best chance at this moment is to sit and wait it out.

Moresby and I took the stairs rather than the elevator. Outside, it was raining again. The culture consumers were packed into the Centre, and the open spaces were rain-swept and deserted. A cold, malign glare came off the brick terraces, and rain like birdshot puckered the surface of the lake.

'Stay in there,' I said, and Moresby faded into the shadows.

For credibility, I even had one of his pipes. It stank of tobacco tar, black and acrid, as I hooked it into my teeth. Across the terrace, beside an entrance to another residential block, there was a winding concrete stair, a poorly lit melancholy place whose sole function was to take residents to their car ports below street level. I walked quickly over to assess it, and followed it down. It also gave out to the Silk Street exit from the Barbican itself. I came back, having seen nobody. Moresby believed I would be handing him over in the below-ground car park.

The rain was savage now, hammering the acres of concrete, beating the discreet floodlight back and seeming to extinguish it. From where I came back out in the rain Moresby could see me. He started walking. I should have made him run, but I knew what was coming, and I didn't want to rook him of that extra minute. Then a cry came out of the rain-beaten night, from the dark area across the lake.

'John!' The wind shredded the word in mid-air. Moresby stopped and turned sideways, peering out into the dark screen of the rain. He hadn't reacted to the name, but to the voice. It was Judy Ellerman's voice. She was calling me, but once Moresby realized it was Judy he couldn't move.

'No – o!' I shouted. My cry was broken up and scattered by the rain. I yelled again. 'Moresby!'

But he had seen her. On the other side of the lake, where a few lights fractured the rain and picked out the old church, Judy stepped forward from the low overhang of a building. Moresby knew it was Judy, and raised his hand to her. We were blown so finally that I didn't even have time to get angry about it. Moresby lunged forward. For a moment I thought he was wading through the lake to get to her. But through the howl of the rain I had heard a rifle crack.

It must have been a chest shot. Moresby plunged forward like somebody eager to get into the water. He lay instantly still in the rain-spattered lake, a dark hump with two fluorescent strips down its back.

I started running. They had hit Moresby, but it was meant to be me. Judy had suckered the man she thought was me, got him to stall in the open long enough for a rifle shot from a balcony somewhere up there in the night. They wanted Moresby. That was why they were taking me out. I put it all together as I ran.

My job was done, and I should have gone for the fastest exit from the Barbican and not messed with this thing any further. But I ran round the end of the lake to where my name had been called. Judy was still there. She knew already; the truth had reached her before I got there. She didn't need to cry, the rain was doing it all for her. Somewhere along the way I had lost the hat and pipe. The rain plastered hair over my forehead. Judy looked at me with horror, and backed away instinctively at the Colt in my hand as I approached.

'Why?' I said.

'I just wanted to save Pat. That's all I wanted.'

'Even if it meant killing me?'

She nodded.

'Who was it?' I said.

Judy said nothing. Her white, rain-streaked face was more like Susie's than ever.

'Fernley?' I asked.

She didn't have to answer. I stared at her long and hard. It must have seemed like hate and bitterness to her. Maybe she thought I was winding myself up to shoot her. She didn't care. I felt so sad that she didn't care.

'I love you,' I said.

It was like saying it to someone who had died. In a way that's what it was. I got a grip of myself, because what I had done was suicide. Somebody was still up there with a rifle, had heard my voice by now, and was nursing the trigger for a second shot.

'Where is he?' I said.

I had never decided if Judy had been Fernley's girl in the end, or for how long. I didn't want to know now. At my question she turned her face to the brick steps that led up to a residential block. I muttered thanks and took off.

The concrete balconies were stacked in dark, inhospitable layers which in places had collected standing water from the storm. The rifleman might be three or four floors up. Then again, he might be on his way down, or waiting for me. He might have access to an apartment, or be leaving by a central staircase. I used what cover the unadorned concrete walkways allowed me. I knew I should have left it right there. But I was mad, because they had only killed Moresby in the belief that it was me they were gunning down, and something in my gut, some biological outrage, refused to let me walk away from such a trivial extinction. They wanted Moresby because in Fernley's world he was still valuable, and to get him they had iced the man they thought was me. I couldn't let that go. No way, old chap.

I came to a stretch of communal balcony on the second floor. The darkness and the rain had given me grace, and the gunman wasn't ready. He was on his way down, relaxed at a successful kill. When he saw the raincoat with the fur collar it confirmed that I was Moresby. Then I advanced into a penumbra of light, and he glimpsed my face and the Colt which I drew from the dry shelter of Moresby's coat.

'Hello, Johnny baby.'

I sniffed the rain away from the end of my nose and bared my teeth at James Xavier Fernley. I guess this job had been too important for him to put out to hire. As soon as he identified me, he shook the cover away from

265

the sporting rifle which he carried as casually as a fishing rod on one arm. On that narrow balcony I made a target he didn't even have to take a bead on, and his beefy face smiled contemptuously as he slammed the bolt and swung the barrel up.

I wonder now if for a split second the thought had really hit him, that he had shot Moresby down out there. He had killed me once already in cold blood, and now, gun to gun, he faced me again. Maybe the good fieldman in him knew that he didn't deserve to make it this time. I brought the Colt up double-handed, and two bullets cut Fernley down before he could hit the rifle trigger. He sprawled back, his big rubber boots kicking the air.

I went up to where he lay. Blood pumped out of his body, thickening the oily wetness of his clothing. His small piglike eyes glimmered up at me from between puffy lids. His lips were curled in a sneer of futility and approaching death.

'He was mine, Johnny.'

I had to listen hard. The voice was guttural, slurred. I wondered why he bothered to talk, but he seemed to need to justify something to me.

'He was worth a hundred grand to me.'

Well, there were always markets, and there were markets for people like Moresby and the things they knew. I didn't care who the final buyer might be, only that Fernley had set Judy up in a deal that would have left me lying dead out there. The rain screamed in under the awning of the balcony, and I didn't like any of it. So that Moresby might live, Judy had seduced me into Fernley's gunsight, and he had shot down the man he thought was me while Judy stood and watched.

Fernley was a complex man, and once he had his fingers on something he never let it go. What else had he offered her? During the seconds it took me to reflect on all this he was still alive, at the end of a long painful thread that a friend would have snapped for him.

'So long, X,' I said.

Nobody had come out. People didn't inhabit silence any more, they walled themselves in with sound – the TV, the audio set. A gunshot out in the night went unheard or merged with the battering of the rain on a thousand curtained windows. I turned away and walked back down the way I had come.

The open spaces of the Barbican were a clinical no-man's-land. The rain came down without mercy. Moresby's body lay out there in the water, dark and formless, a little lower now. I returned to where Judy had stood. I wanted to say goodbye, but everywhere I walked, by the church, in the shadows, against the shattered lake, there was nobody to say goodbye to. Except Moresby, and I guess Judy had already said all the farewells he needed.

I allowed myself to believe that the trail had come to an end with Fernley. The big man himself had been laying for me, and I couldn't see anybody else coming down the pike. I confronted the question of how he had known where to be, but I didn't like either of the answers. We could have been followed there, Moresby and I. The black at the Bradlaugh Hall was without doubt an employee, probably one in a chain. Even if they were all meatheads, I only had the one pair of eyes. In fact the Barbican bolt-hole could have been staked out since we arrived, if Fernley had access to the same sources that had directed me there. Or Simon Blakeway could have been into that particular pie, and maybe I was less smart than I thought that day on the terrace. But I was away, and it didn't matter now.

I returned to the apartment, briefly, for a change of clothes and to pick up some useful documents. I followed the covered way to the underground station and headed for a West End hotel where I had booked a room the previous day. Early in the morning I came out here.

And that's it, Judy. I guess I was writing this for you all along, but I had to simulate otherwise, or I couldn't have done it. I have an envelope and stamps in my hand luggage, and if I can't find a convenient mailbox, I can always slip this small parcel to a reliable-looking stranger and ask them to help me out.

I don't anticipate too much leisure for this myself. There were no more calls over the P.A. system, and I thought maybe I was clear. The fog has not thinned, and the airport halls are barely traversable now, but in spite of that someone got to me. It was the guy called Moon, the one I nearly strangled at that place in the country, the john whose face gave Cromer nightmares. He was smoother this time, feeling he had the upper hand, just another smooth Englishman, squeaky with that glib reassurance they once fooled the world with, and are now using to fool themselves. I let him fool me, because I had no real choice. He told me there was a private flight waiting for me, arranged by 'your people', he said. It would be leaving as soon as the fog broke. He indicated the door I should go through to bypass the normal system, and suggested now. I told him I was through hurrying. He suggested five minutes, tops. I said I couldn't wait to be back in the USA. Moon said good, and picked his way back through the sullen mass of people.

So this is it, Judy. I don't blame you for last night, and I love you for a lot else. If they intercept this, maybe my feelings will come to you another way.

Now, I don't know. They're watching me from some-where in here, and they're offering me a walk in the fog. I don't have to take it.

So long, baby, see you.

H. T. Kuunas – EURCOOPS

To W. J. Shealor

EYES ONLY

Noting your assurance that all other personnel deemed to be potentially of danger to us in the matter of Patrick J. Moresby have been neutralized, we register that after Goolan's disappearance from London Airport we are in a zero-information posture vis-à-vis *his current whereabouts. However we concur with your verbally expressed proposition that Operative John Goolan be as of now classified as a defector. It follows from this that Field Intelligence should be alerted to terminate with extreme prejudice in the event of Goolan's relocation. Such people can rarely hide for long.*